GRIM TALES
OF THE
BROTHERS KOLLIN

Pay UP (and enjoy)

Enjoy it

Thanks for staying Grim — Dani w

GRIM TALES
OF THE
BROTHERS KOLLIN

WINNERS OF THE PROMETHEUS AWARD
DANI KOLLIN AND EYTAN KOLLIN

WordFire Press
Colorado Springs, Colorado

ISBN: 978-1-61475-466-4

Cover design by Janet McDonald

and Dani Kollin, www.danikollin.com

Art Director Kevin J. Anderson

Cover artwork images by Adobe Stock

Book Design by RuneWright, LLC
www.RuneWright.com

Published by
WordFire Press, an imprint of
WordFire, Inc.
PO Box 1840
Monument CO 80132

Kevin J. Anderson & Rebecca Moesta, Publishers

WordFire Press Trade Paperback Edition October 2016
Printed in the USA
wordfirepress.com

THE GENERAL VERDICT

Washington vs. Napoleon

"The Anglo-American War got off to a very strong start and in truth should have been a revolution. We came so close in the summer of 1776 and even wrote the oft-touted, yet wholly unrealized Declaration of Rights. You see, even though it said we had the right to rebel, we never actually followed through. How in the name of Providence could we have managed that?!"

—Ben Franklin's comments on the war
September 17th, 1785

The General stood on the deck of the large ship, breathing in the thick Atlantic air. The sails billowed gently in the warm summer wind, and a cacophonous gaggle of seagulls flew above, leading the large seafaring vessel out of the harbor. It was a cargo ship that had been converted into a slave ship and then converted once again into its current configuration as a troop transport. The last alteration had been structurally easy but emotionally draining. Removing the stench of human suffering had been rough going, and the bloodstained floor had needed to be completely refinished. The General had ordered it not because his men had a problem with the sight of blood but rather because he believed that the blood spilled had been senseless.

"I'm old," he murmured to no one in particular, "and must be careful with my health."

A young aide, standing by his side, looked up, hoping to be given an order or at least a word.

"Sir?"

General Washington looked over at the young man with fatherly kindness. He would have been, Washington saw, about the age of Washington's grandson, if he'd had one.

"Just something mother tells me," he said referring to his wife, "when I take in the air." He looked back out to sea.

"But General, sir," answered the too-anxious-to-please aide, "you're the youngest old man I've ever seen. I mean, it's not that you're old—well, you are—but ..."

The corners of Washington's lips curled slightly upwards. He watched as the young aide attempted to back out gracefully. *Hamilton wouldn't have stumbled over his words*, thought Washington. *He would've spoken with elegance or shut up*. But Alexander Hamilton was a full colonel and with his men on one of the many ships now transporting the continental reserves to the mother country.

"You can ride and shoot better than most men half your age," continued the aide, slight desperation evident in his voice, "I ... I hope I do half as well—God grant that I grow to be as old ..." The boy's face suddenly turned a new shade of red. "... er ... to live as long as you, sir."

Washington mulled the boy's mangled compliment. Indeed, he thought to himself, it was a bit of a miracle that when most of his childhood friends were either dead or crippled with age, he could still ride, shoot a gun with some measure of accuracy, and, of course, manage to command an army. The fire in his voice was still evident, as was the determination in his eyes—both of which he depended on to inspire as well as to shame. But he also knew the truth: that he *was* old; that the cold bit deeper, the body reacted slower, and the weariness of his years seemed to follow him everywhere. He also knew that he had to be careful lest any minor illness, once so easily cast off in youth, kill him now. Yet his age had not deterred a lifelong conviction that he'd been born to greatness. It had, though, made him painfully aware of just how far short he'd fallen. To preserve any chance of fulfilling his destiny, he must approach it with both vigilance and care. Long past were the days in which he could count on unbridled passion and fury to sweep him, like so many others, into the annals of history. He was an old man in a young man's game and knew that this voyage was a last chance for the yearned-for prominence that had so far eluded him. By any other measure, George Washington had arrived, had achieved that which most men could only dream of—by any other measure other than his. And so, it was how the *almost great* General George Washington found himself sailing with a pitiful few thousand men to the aid of a former enemy in her war against the French. He'd chosen his spot on the deck, turned his back on the New World and set his sights on the Old, wondering what possible future lay beyond a distant horizon veiled by the unending sea.

"Well, Lieutenant," answered Washington, turning around and taking hold of the rail, "young or old, General or private, Martha would strongly disapprove if I were to not dress appropriately for our little romps on the deck." Then, "You're from New Jersey, are you not, lad?"

"I'm an American, General!" answered the boy, beaming.

Washington chuckled. "I'm sure you are, son. But where-abouts?"

"New Jersey," the boy answered firmly, as if the name's mere summoning bestowed higher rank.

"And why," asked Washington, "are you here?"

"Why ..." sputtered the boy, "you, General." He seemed genuinely surprised. "My father served with you at Brandywine when you defeated the British ... right after Saratoga. The way he talked about you, sir ... well, I knew I had to join."

Washington nodded his head solemnly, noticing the way the boy was staring at him ... *through* him. Always that look—as if he were somehow an apparition and not the living, breathing man that he was. It used to unnerve him, but eventually he grew to accept it. If God had seen fit to bestow such an invaluable trait on him then, who was he to argue? It suited him well as the leader of an army, and that was that.

3

Washington narrowed his brow. "Brandywine, you say?"

The aide nodded vigorously.

"Well, boy, it wasn't me who defeated the British at Brandywine."

"Sir?" asked the boy, face blanketed in confusion.

The General turned around and once more faced the sea. He placed both hands firmly on the railing and inhaled the thick salt air. His answer was almost inaudible against his labored breath and the sound of water splashing against the bulkhead.

"It was Lafayette."

Washington's jaw grew rigid and his knuckles whitened as he gripped the rail ever more tightly, trying to suppress the worst type of memory—one tinged with regret. Lafayette, perhaps one of the greatest friends of the civil war and the closest confidante of a man who had few, was dead. Washington blamed himself. Hadn't it, after all, been Washington's attempt at liberty that had inspired Lafayette's? His encouragement that had rallied his friend and friend's mighty nation to throw off the yoke of monarchical oppression? Who could have foreseen that that revolution would implode so spectacularly, that those in power would turn on the very people who'd sacrificed all to give it to them?

Of course Washington had tried to help. First with letters of support for his friend to the newly emplaced revolutionary government. When that went nowhere, he'd resorted to bribery, offering to take Lafayette off French hands so as "not to make a martyr of him." It was a thin play, and all who'd seen the offer knew it, but at the time it was all the General had left. "And besides," responded an ambassador of the new regime, "we like our martyrs. It is the French way."

Washington often wondered if perhaps his insistent campaign to free his friend had in fact achieved the opposite. After all, the help of a British General, however reluctantly he bore the title, did not carry well in revolutionary France. And so, under the cover of darkness and with the help of a network of sympathizers, the General had played his last card—the successful smuggling of Lafayette's youngest son out of the country. It had been dangerous and risky, but Washington had been insistent. "It was," he'd remanded at the time of the plan's inception, "the least we could do for so noble and brave a man as Lafayette." That son was now the aide to Benedict Arnold and like his father before him, he had the fire of revolution in his belly—only his called for the decimation of the country that had at once robbed him of a father while inadvertently placing him in the hands of another. The child, who Lafayette had named George in his friend's honor, had become Washington's son in spirit if not in name and showed the same blind devotion to him that he currently showed to the destruction of the country of his birth.

Perhaps because of his youth, or the simple fact that he hadn't wanted to relinquish his raison d'être for having signed up, the aide ignored Washington's turned back.

"But," he continued, "you commanded the army, held it together through the retreat across New Jersey, chose the leaders, led the attack at Trenton ..."

Washington listened as the aide de camp retold a tale that almost had the signature of mythology. Legends, he realized, that would be critical to a young *almost* nation in search of an identity. He put an end to it quickly.

"The past," intoned Washington, still staring out to sea, "is all well and good, but 'tis the future that concerns me now. We are a small army of barely 10,000 sailing to duty in a country not truly our own. One storm or a few French ships of the line could end us before we ever see land." He once again turned to face the boy. "War is never certain," he continued, exhaling deeply. "Best to concentrate on tomorrow."

With that, the young aide seemed to stand erect as a smile formed on his lips. "We'll be fine, General Washington."

"Really, lad?" The General answered with a raised eyebrow. "And what makes you so certain?"

"Why, you, sir." Then, "Will you be needing me any further?"

Washington shook his head as the aide darted off. The old General turned once more to the sea. Not that anyone could hear it, but he sighed heavily as thoughts of lost possibilities invaded his sanctuary.

* * *

Dani Kollin & Eytan Kollin

February 3rd, 1799

To his Excellency General Washington and the representatives of the 9th Continental Congress

From General Cornwallis, Commander of the Armed forces of his Britannic majesty George III

Sir,

Due to a small landing of French forces in Ireland and the subsequent uprising of the local population, the main part of the British army in Great Britain has been sent to that miserable Island. This has left the forces protecting our homes less than adequate. You are urgently requested to present yourself and your men at Plymouth, England. Rest assured your forces will not be expected to fight in Ireland. They will be stationed in England or Wales itself, allowing for the maximum number of English regiments to pacify the Irish. Still, while in the defense of England, you will be paid and ranked as members of his majesty's army. God speed, sir. God save the King.

Your obedient servant,

Charles Cornwallis

—Considered one of
the five most pivotal letters ever written.
From *A study in the importance of
correspondence on history*
Emily Caulfield
New York City: Empire Press, 1967

* * *

As incredible as it seems today, it must be remembered that the only reason the American reserve, a standing army of roughly 10,000 men, was even in existence was to ensure American liberty against renewed British Parliamentary interference after the Anglo-American War of 1775–1779. It

6

was, in fact, a wholly American army commanded by General George Washington and paid for by the Americans themselves. It was also an army that had won an independent war against Spanish-held Florida. Despite the French incursion and subsequent Irish uprising, the British were not all that eager to have 10,000 fully trained American combat veterans in their midst. For their part, the Americans, too, had little interest in defending a country thousands of miles from home. Plus, the Americans had fled their mother country for numerous reasons; all of which were still fresh in their memories despite the intervening years. It was during those years of de facto independence that the Colonial Army had become the unifying factor in all local politics. It protected against Indian incursions (while assimilating other Indian tribes), conquered Florida and, more importantly, kept the British at bay. So given that both sides had no reason to trust or help one another other, how is it that history as we know it came about? The answer is, by the abject determination of two men: General Charles Cornwallis, who would meet his demise in the defense of London, and General George Washington, who would take up his charge. The former made sure that Parliament backed the order, and the latter ensured that it would be accepted.

—From *Cornwallis & Washington: Partners in Empire*
Martha Hernandez
Union City Press, 1967

* * *

June 7th, 1799

Benedict Arnold's head was slightly askance; his brow furrowed. "Cornwallis is dead?"

Of all the men at the table—Hamilton, Green, Lee, and Washington—Benedict was the only one to have served with the man in India, a fact that did not make him popular with many politicians in the colonies but that made him invaluable to George Washington.

Until that moment, Washington had been happy to be on land, safe in Plymouth harbor with, miracle of miracles, all his ships in and almost all his command fit for service. Contrary to his fears, the people of Plymouth were very kind and gracious to their "American Cousins" and had gone out of their way to make them all welcome. Washington was given the mayor's house to use as his headquarters, and when the General offered to pay, the offer had been declined. Finally, when Washington explained that it was American law and custom that soldiers could not be quartered in private homes without consent and pay, the incredulous mayor accepted a nominal fee of one schilling.

Once things had become reasonably settled, Washington called a meeting of his commanders. No sooner had it gotten started than it was interrupted by a young messenger bursting through the door.

"Urgent dispatch, sir!" he cried, keeling over slightly and holding on to his knees. He took a few deep breaths, righted himself, and pulled the document from inside a leather sack that had been stuffed into his shirt. An aide took the document from the young man's hand and handed it over to General Washington. The messenger, having delivered the goods, allowed his face to crack a proud smile.

"Well done, lad," Washington said, bowing his head slowly and accepting the trifolded paper held together by a black wax seal. The letter had been addressed to:

George Washington
General of the
Continental Reserves

It was stamped in black ink, "LONDON, July. FREE." The young boy was quickly escorted out the door as Washington removed the wax seal and read the contents. Then he read them again. Slowly. When he'd finished, Washington handed the note to Hamilton, who first looked to his friend's eyes. Washington pursed his lips slightly. Hamilton nodded, read it, and passed it along. The last was Benedict Arnold. He shook his head, folded the paper, and pushed it across the table's surface towards Washington.

"Gentlemen," began Washington, now running his forefinger gently across the broken wax seal, "It would appear that in the three weeks it took us to get here, Great Britain has been invaded and is on the verge of collapse. It would also appear that a very young General by the name of Napoleon Bonaparte has attempted a very dangerous gamble. He invaded England with 40,000 men, getting them here under cover of a storm. In the past three weeks, he has fought numerous engagements and three major battles, all over southern England. He's never in one place very long and has been raiding the countryside for all the supplies he needs."

"And what of the invasion of Ireland?"

"A diversion, Colonel Green."

"But Cornwallis?" muttered Light-horse Henry Lee.

"The one bright spot in this whole disaster."

"How so?"

"Bonaparte only made an exploratory advance toward London. It was small enough that Cornwallis' cavalry unit—which barely managed to get there in time—was able to beat off the advance."

"With the help of the townspeople," added Hamilton.

"Yes," agreed Washington. "This once." He then looked up and turned his head slowly in order to meet the eyes of every man in the room. "If Napoleon persists with this advance, gentlemen, London *will* fall; Bonaparte will have succeeded in taking the capitol."

Washington's commanders sat mute. They may have hated London, and some at the table would've been more than happy to have nothing to do with her ever again. But the thought of her being conquered was too much to grasp. It was, in many ways, their ancestral home. The city of Tudors, Plantagenet, Shakespeare, and Sir Isaac Newton was as much a part of the Colonies as Philadelphia, Boston, New York, and Charleston.

"But how?" asked Hamilton.

Washington looked to Arnold, who tipped his head towards his superior officer in deference. "Speed and daring, sir; speed and daring. Think of it as a cavalry raid using infantry. This Napoleon fellow is attacking the British before they can concentrate their forces. The Frenchie's not concentrating on any major city or waiting around for an army to concentrate on him. As such, he has the British confused and uncertain."

Lee's upturned mouth betrayed his amusement. "Clearly, suh, they're not the only ones."

"Indeed," answered Benedict. "If Bonaparte can take London—even if only for a day—the political ramifications will be incalculable."

Lee's face twitched briefly as he looked towards Washington. "I'll suppose there's a plan."

"Of sorts," answered Washington. "We've been ordered to march to London as quickly as possible."

"And just when we were all starting to get comfortable," Hamilton added.

Benedict laughed. "What's her name?"

"If we dump everything," said Lee, ignoring his peers' friendly banter, "exceptin' what we need to fight with, of course, why, I reckon we can be in London in two days."

Before anyone could respond, the unmistakable sounds of fast-approaching hooves could be heard.

"Best to wait," said Washington as the commanders turned their attention towards the door. Moments later, the second messenger of the day sauntered in As it had been with the first, this one was also filthy from the journey, but by virtue of his age—he was a good eight to ten years older—his manner was far more formal. The messenger scanned the room; spotted Washington, then strode up and saluted.

"General." The messenger had not only surprised the war council with the squawk in his voice but had clearly surprised himself as well.

Washington indicated to his aide to bring the man a drink.

The messenger gratefully accepted, took a large swig, and exhaled. "General," he now repeated more clearly, "I have the pleasure to request that the newly promoted Major Wellesley and a troop of cavalry be allowed to join the protection of your camp."

Washington's lips turned upwards. "Permission is granted, of course. What unit does the major have the honor of commanding?"

"The remnants of the 3rd Fusiliers."

"Remnants?"

"With many from scattered units all over southern England, sir."

Nathaniel Green, no slouch in the military tactics department, had finally had enough. "What in God's name is going on here? How can one man do this to an entire country—and in three weeks, no less?"

"Colonel Green, if you please," answered Washington, purposely lowering his voice and therefore the tenor of the room, "it is *exactly* what we did to the British during the war; hit and run and never let the enemy concentrate." Washington then turned to the messenger. "No offense, sir."

The messenger bowed politely. "None taken, General."

"Don't you mean we'd never let them concentrate," repeated Benedict with a toothy grin, "until we were ready to win?"

"Good point," admitted Nathaniel, "though I liked it better when it was we who were applying the tactic."

"Napoleon seems to be having as much luck with it as we did," continued Washington. "He's not a magician; just a very good general who happens to be thinking while his opponents are not. We, too, need to start thinking, or we may as well go home."

Washington turned to the messenger in front of him. "Sir, if the major could meet me here, we will see to getting him a bath and proper food as well as what aid we can provide for his command." Washington paused, a glimmer of curiosity in his eyes. "You said 'recently promoted'?"

"A group of nobles were rounded up from their estates ..." the messenger's eyes narrowed as he steeled himself, "... and guillotined; the major's brother and our commanding officer were among them."

"What crimes were they accused of?" asked Benedict.

"None, sir," answered the messenger in a voice that left no doubt as to the ignominy of the act. "Unless you count being born to nobility a crime worthy of death." The messenger then bowed his head politely to the group. "Good day, sirs."

"Good day," answered the group as one.

"Gentleman," said Washington, getting to his feet. The sound of chairs pushing against the wooden floors filled the room as all the commanders arose. "We will be leaving sooner than expected. Have the army ready to march in six hours." Washington moved to the map wall and began to study them with the eye of the surveyor.

"Off to London, then," suggested Hamilton.

Washington's crooked smile never made it to his eyes. "No."

"Then where the devil to?" demanded Light-horse.

Washington continued to stare intently at the large map, methodically tapping his forefinger to his chin.

"I don't know."

* * *

The meeting between the first and third future chancellors has been commented upon, reenacted, and used as the subject of countless paintings. Maybe it was the contrast of the two men—most obviously, one was old and one was young. There was Washington, about to fight his last battle, and Wellesley, beginning a glorious path to many. Their relationship was typical of the type curried by Washington. Having no sons of his own, the General seemed to attract men of incredible talent in search of a mentor and, as often as not, a father figure. Among the General's acolytes: Hamilton, Lafayette the junior, and Bushrod Washington, later called Duke of Vernon. It should, therefore, not be surprising that this great man of history would himself be called "Father of the Empire." Yet Wellesley was his greatest protégé, clearly influenced by the Napoleon outing and his proximity to Washington. Sadly, history did not record what was said at their very first meeting. As both men were strong-willed individuals who were known to disdain flowery public discourse, it can only be surmised that their first words were straight and to the point.

—*Washington: An Intimate Portrait*
Martha Brody
University of Pennsylvania Press, 1987

* * *

"I should kill you where you stand," shouted Wellesley, "you cowardly bastard!"

At least, thought Washington, the bedraggled and mud-covered English nobleman had the good grace to wait until they were alone to make himself heard. And Washington fervently prayed that they'd gone unheard. English noblemen were not the most popular figures in American circles. There were even some he knew who surely would have applauded the French for the recent killing of the nobles. Had Washington's men heard what had just been said, Washington would've had a difficult time keeping this brash Englishman safe from the American army, let alone keeping him safe from the French one.

"Actually," replied Washington, "I am the product of my father's second union, but I can be reasonably assured that the marriage ceremony took place—unless, of course, the two hundred or so witnesses to the event conspired to keep me in the dark." On Wellesley's wide eyes and open mouth, Washington indicated a nearby chair. "Won't you have a seat, Major?"

Wellesley, however, demurred. "Are you, sir, or are you not abandoning London to destruction by that villain?"

Washington once again extended his hand to the nearby chair and in a peremptory voice said, "Major ... if you please."

Wellesley, mouth sealed tight, sat in as dignified a manner as one covered in dirt and mud could.

Washington bowed slightly. "Major, you're correct. I will not march to the aid of London." Washington quickly held up his hand to stifle the protest that had already started, "Because I believe that London is in no immediate danger."

"I suppose, then," scoffed Wellesley, "that every unit of the army has dropped what it is doing and along with most of the able-bodied men in southern England is heading toward London because that city has been deemed perfectly safe?"

"No, Major, they're heading towards London because that, I suspect, is exactly what Napoleon *wants* them to do."

Wellesley opened his mouth to protest but stopped.

"Cheeky bastard," Wellesley finally said, mouth twisted into a half smile. "The past three weeks have been about this—attacks in all the different places; us never being able to pin him down and make him fight. Then the attack on London out of the blue and a second one threatened; we've run right where he wants us."

Washington nodded. "I fear, Major, that the beheadings of the nobles, your brother among them, has something to do with that."

"Your meaning, sir?"

"This Napoleon does not strike me as a radical, and I doubt

he cares one fig about who someone's ancestors were. I have followed his career since Italy, and he's never done anything like this—till now, that is. It is inconsistent that he should suddenly start playing the role of Robespierre."

"You think he did it to confuse or frighten us?"

"More, Major. He did it to cloud the judgment of all the nobles in England, from the King down to every third son of an Earl. All feel threatened and all want revenge and protection. So ..."

"So all," continued Wellesley, "are heading towards London to save the King, who refuses to leave the city!"

"Exactly. But why cause that much ill will for what has been, till now, nothing more than a glorified raid?"

Wellesley's eyes suddenly lit up. "Raid, you say? Hardly. The monster has been burning and looting England, man!"

"But don't you see, Major? With never enough men to hold any ground. This is nothing more than an attempt to rub your nose in the mud of war. Oh, I will grant that it is a spectacularly successful raid, but only a raid. Till now."

"I do not clear with your meaning, General."

"He wants to conquer England."

Wellesley laughed out loud. "With only thirty thousand exhausted effectives?"

Washington nodded and then indicated the large map on the wall. Wellesley got up and walked towards it. All of Napoleon's strikes and advances had been marked. Wellesley slowly traced his finger from London southwards toward the coast and eventually came to the same city, and then conclusion, that Washington had. He turned around and stared, dumbstruck, at the man he'd only moments before been cursing. "My God, he's planning to take Portsmouth!"

"And he's going to damn well succeed," answered Washington. "I'll bet you gold coins to cow pies that whatever garrisons the port cities had have now been reduced to gun crews while the rest are off to ..."

"... London," finished Wellesley in a whisper.

"London," agreed Washington. "And your Admiral Nelson is still in the Mediterranean. Even if he's been made aware of

Napoleon's recent forays, he'd have to make the fleet ready *and* beat out the storms."

"Quite possibly the Spanish as well," quipped Wellesley, now fully on board

"It would be the prudent move," agreed Washington. "So, given all the known facts, I do not expect Admiral Nelson for at least another week or two—more likely three till the Channel is truly secure. Meanwhile, if Napoleon does capture a first-class port, the French fleet will have a secure point to start shipping men and supplies through on anything that can float. If he gets another 100,000 men in England, possibly as little as 70,000, you'll probably be joining me in the Colonies—assuming any of us survive, that is."

Wellesley continued to stare at the large map with the same focused energy Washington had a few hours prior. "But how can you be sure?" he asked. "This"—Wellesley turned around to face Washington while his hand continued to point back towards the map—"is all speculation. You're gambling the safety of London— and possibly all of England—on a hunch, on the belief that you've somehow got into the mind of a man you've never met, much less fought. And if I'm reading you correctly, good sir, you would propose to send the most experienced, best-armed soldiers in Southern England marching *away* from London on this sup-position."

Washington tipped his head slowly while keeping his eye level on Wellesley.

The major's dirt-smeared brow folded into smooth, neat lines. "What if you're wrong?"

"Major, this is war—a war in which, I'm at pains to remind you, we are outnumbered and outgunned. You may not be familiar with such a scenario, but I can assure you we are. In a situation such as this, you must replace your missing numbers and arms."

"With what? Lads barely able to hold a pistol?"

"No, Major—with daring, luck, and," Washington paused as a half smile twitched his face, "speculation. Napoleon's army is marching south towards Portsmouth. I know it, and, I suspect, so do you. The only question now is will you be a party to my 'wild' suppositions?"

Wellesley looked at Washington, then briefly back towards the map. When he turned around, he nodded his acquiescence. "Heaven help us."

"Indeed," agreed Washington, "but it's your cavalry whose help I could really use at the moment. Can they accompany us?"

"The horses are exhausted and the men not much better. However, if we walk the horses and have the men ride in the wagons ..." Wellesley paused, bringing his forefinger and thumb to chin. "Yes, General. Yes, I believe they can."

* * *

"I were only a boy. Lord, I could not have been more than twelve. Of course I wanted to fight with all the men who went off to London. But they all said I was too small. Then the Americans came. They marched with pride. They had a fife and drum in the front with the old colonial flag. Every country had its own flag before the Imperial Parliament approved the good old red, white, blue, and green we have now. But my, it was pretty. I can see it now, a flag of red and white stripes with a field of blue in the upper left. Thirteen stars in a circle protecting the old Union Jack. Then came the man himself—Washington. So tall, and on the horse he looked like a giant. The Duke of Wellington and Arnold were by his side. Of course, he weren't the Duke of Wellington at that time. Then comes all those men marching on by. But the General and his staff, they pulls to the side, and Lord if they don't beckon to me."

—My Life in the Army
Sergeant-Major William Williams, 1798–1858

* * *

"The General wants to see you, lad."

The young boy, no more than ten years of age, stared blankly at the young aide de camp addressing him.

"I said," repeated the aide de camp, "the *General* requests your presence."

"I clear your meaning," answered the boy, "it's just that, well ... where are you from?"

"New Jersey," answered the aide—clearly not for the first time—leading the boy by the elbow.

"I wasn't aware there was a new one."

The aide de camp smiled politely, and the boy seemed ready to ask another question when the aide suddenly stiffened up, indicating men approaching on horseback.

Together, the two made their way through rows of marching men until they were finally standing next to Washington's horse.

"... just saying that damn, your lads can march, General," said Wellesley. "Hard to believe that less than twenty-four hours ago they were on ship."

"You forget, Major, that this is an American army and America is a very big place. One of the things our army is very good at is marching."

"Forgive my impertinence, sir, but let us both pray they show equal skill and perseverance at fighting."

"Let's, indeed."

Washington then looked down and saw the boys keeping pace with his horse. "Is this he?" Washington asked the aide.

The aide nodded.

"What's your name, son?"

"William Williams, sir," squeaked the boy.

"William Williams," repeated Washington as his mouth drew up into a half smile. "Do you know the land around this village?"

"Oh, yes, sir! I know every road, path, nook, and knoll, sir."

Washington took the boy's measure. "I need a guide for the next ten miles." He then leaned down from the horse so that his face was a little closer to that of the child. "Are you up to the job?"

"Yes, General!"

"Good lad." Washington righted himself once more and then looked towards his aide de camp. "Mr. Bergen."

"Yes, General."

"This boy is to ride on your horse."

"Of course, General."

"Have the lad take us by the quickest route to Portsmouth. If Wellesley's cavalry spot any of Napoleon's troops, we are to use another way. We must avoid detection as long as possible."

"Yes, General." Mr. Bergen led the boy by the arm, only this time towards his horse.

Wellesley watched the two youths walk away and then turned towards Washington. "Is it really wise to trust the fate of our entire army, possibly even our country, to those boys barely fit to be drummers?"

Washington watched as the young Williams was hoisted up and onto his saddle. "During the war," Washington finally answered, "we had the advantage in that most of the time we knew the land, while the damned redcoa …"

Wellesley's eyes narrowed.

Washington cleared his throat. "While the *regular* army did not. Most times, the ones who knew the land best were the boys. I'm hoping that children are the same on both sides of the pond."

The major nodded and smiled. "Risk and luck, eh, General?"

"Risk and luck, Major."

* * *

I have been writing about Napoleon's outing for most of my adult life and in fact wrote my doctoral thesis on this very subject. I am considered by many to be the foremost expert in the Empire on the subject. I know every unit, every officer, and even most of the men in the Colonial detachments as well as Wellesley's cavalry. I have walked the route that their glorious army took and have helped countless documentarians recreate the Battle of Portsmouth. Therefore, please allow me to state unequivocally that there is no evidence to support the existence of the supposed "Napoleon letter." It does not now, nor, the evidence bears out, has it ever existed.

—Interview with Prof. Michael Thofton.
London Daily Post
April 17, 1989
Arts & Letters Section

* * *

"Letter for you, sir."

Benedict Arnold waited for the tent flap to be drawn down. It was a warm June night and most of the soldiers were asleep outside, and nothing short of Napoleon's army charging the camp itself would've disturbed them.

After two days of marching and coming within twenty miles of Portsmouth, the Americans had found Napoleon; or, to be more precise, Napoleon had found them. The English scouts had reported on an already entrenched twenty thousand–man French army near the city. To the English and Americans' great vexation, there were even more French troops pouring in. Washington wisely called a halt to all movement while there were still a few hours of sunlight. Both the American/English and French armies seemed content to wait for morning rather than risk a night engagement. And though most of Washington's army was now blissfully in Morpheus's embrace, as per usual, they'd kept their shoes on and guns at the ready.

"Ah, Colonel Arnold," said Washington, looking up from a stack of maps. "The men have the campfires going?"

"Yes, General," answered Benedict, pulling up a stool in front of Washington's table.

"Enjoying your new rank, *Colonel?*" asked Washington with a slight twinkle in his eye.

Benedict, who'd been a general in the American army since 1775, had been forced to accept a demotion when the colonial troops had been incorporated into the British army—but only for the duration of the current campaign. Still, it rankled, which was why Washington couldn't help himself.

"Typical British insolence, General. Though there does seem to be a little less of that now."

Washington nodded. "You mentioned a letter."

Benedict reached into his coat pocket and slowly withdrew it. When Washington saw the seal, he gave pause. Benedict extended the letter across the pile of maps. Washington took it, made quick work of the seal, and began to read.

> *To my friend and brother in liberty, the great George Washington,*

From his most humble servant, Napoleon Bonaparte of France:

Greetings and good health. I offer my congratulations. You are clearly cleverer than these shopkeepers who fancy themselves generals. I knew that it had to be you when my scouts told me a column was marching straight for the city—a city I myself had determined to take many weeks ago. Part of me would be honored to do battle with a warrior of great renown. History would record our battle for all time. But, my friend, it would hardly be an equal contest. You are out-numbered three to one by the finest soldiers in Europe. I am sure that your troops are more than adequate for the needs of fighting Indians and Spaniards. But even if the numbers were with you, I must point out that I have talent for winning in difficult situations that surpasses even your well-deserved reputation. I mean no disrespect; I only wish to clarify the situation honestly so you will consider my offer without false perceptions.

My dear General Washington, why are you here? You should be in your country, the United Colonies of America, which should of right be the United States of America. If ever a country earned freedom, it is yours. Soon it will come to you as a divine gift. God meant for America to be free, and it will be as soon as England is conquered. Make no mistake; I will conquer this accursed island, and then America will break away as naturally as a lion cub fending for itself upon the death of its mother. When that happens, your new country will need you and your army to help guide it to its proper place in the world: the second of many new republics to do away with the old monarchies of the past. What good will it do your people to fight a battle you cannot win for a decrepit nation that attempted to subvert your liberties by force and only by your force was ultimately stopped?

My dear General Washington, I beseech thee: go home. There will be no battle tonight, and if you leave in the morning, I will do nothing to hinder you. Your ships await you at Plymouth. The British forces are waiting in London for an attack that I'm sure you're well aware I never planned to make. What is left of the British fleet is in the English Channel. All you now need do to secure your nation's freedom is refuse to fight another nation's battle. It is just like the British to use American lives in a hopeless cause. Don't be fooled, General. Go home, my friend, to the just country only you can make.

Your most obedient servant,

N.

Washington put down the letter and heaved a large sigh. He lifted his head, and his probing eyes were met by Benedict's look of concern.

"Where did you get this, Benedict?"

"As my desire is American independence, General, I have made contact with certain gentlemen who would desire the same."

"I see," was all Washington said to Arnold as he picked up the letter once more. "Call the others." This time, Washington did not look his friend in the eyes.

* * *

The five men huddled around the trestle table in the tent. The space was very cramped, but no one seemed to mind being ears to elbow with his neighbor. They all slowly read the letter and then passed it on from one to another in stunned silence. By the time the letter had gone through all the men—Lee, Hamilton, Green, Arnold, and then back to Washington—the disquiet in the command tent was total. Hamilton cleared his throat to speak but then lapsed back into an uncharacteristic silence.

"It's what we always wanted, isn't it?" asked Nathaniel Green.

"Then, suh," added Lee, "why do I feel like I need a bath?"

"American Liberty is at stake here, gentlemen," added Benedict. "Something we have gotten into the mud for in the past. For the first time, we can be free of the British. Think of it: no more parliamentary commissions or King's agents or a British navy as wont to seize our ships as to protect them. No more waiting for the King to approve our choice of governors—that we elected as free men!" Benedict paused for a moment, slowly turning his head in order to meet everyone's eyes. He tried to stand, but due to the confines of the tent was only able to hover over the table. "Finally, good sirs, our own flag, our own laws, and by God, our own nation! We can be free! This is an historic opportunity," he finished, sitting down. "I strongly suggest we act on it."

"But at what price?" asked Hamilton in a voice that was as quiet as Benedict's was loud. No one in the room mistook Hamilton's lack of resonance for lack of resolve.

"We'll be called cowards," warned Green, "but they've been calling us that since Lexington and Concord …"

"… when we blew them to bits from behind the beautiful stone fences of New England," added Lee, slapping his palm down on the table. A spate of laughter worked through the room with the exception of Washington, though even he managed to twitch a brief smile. The men quieted down as the looks of surprise from only a moment before were soon replaced by something altogether different—a politician's calculating gaze. A decision of such magnitude could not be commanded, Washington knew, but rather would need to be put to a vote. Benedict, with the slight bow of his head, seemed ready to do just that when a small voice wormed its way in from the outside.

"General Washington, sir?"

All heads turned towards the squeak emanating from the entrance.

"Come in, young Williams," said Washington, eyes radiating a grandfatherly warmth. The boy poked his head in first, then slipped in. He tried to salute and take off his cap at the same time but only managed to knock his cap off in the process. He finally did succeed in the salute—after a fashion.

"Permission to report, General," said the boy.

"Permission granted, Mr. Williams."

"Sir, I've got seven boys here and one girl, but she knows the way to Portsmouth as good as the rest, I reckon, even if she is a girl—and you did say to get the best."

Washington smiled at the lad's apology, nodding for him to continue.

"Also," Williams said, "she knows how to ride 'n has a horse all her own, so I thought she should go with the Major, sir."

Washington nodded once more. "You've done well, Mr. Williams. So well, in fact, that I'm putting you in charge of the scouts."

William's eyes lit up, and he now stood more stiffly, soldier-like.

"My aide," continued Washington, "will see to it that you have whatever supplies you need. Make sure your scouts are well fed and that you have blankets."

The boy nodded vigorously.

"They should also rest now, if they can." The General indicated over to his aide. "Lieutenant Bergen will get you what you need for your men,"—Washington allowed a half smile—"and girl."

"Yes, sir," exclaimed the boy, prancing out of the tent like a child who'd just won an entire barrel of rock candy. The men all heard him running off, excitedly shouting orders towards his new "command."

Once more the mood shifted as an awkward silence made its awful presence felt. The letter, which had earlier commanded so much attention, now stood untouched—unlooked-at, even—accusing. Benedict surrendered the vote to the moment. Like Washington, he'd need full and unstinting support, which now seemed to fade away, tethered to the distant echo of William's footsteps.

"Alexander," asked Washington.

Hamilton brought his troubled eyes up towards his commanding officer.

Washington eyed him coolly. "You asked a question before."

Hamilton nodded.

"Will you please repeat it?"

Hamilton looked nervously from one face to another, to the men who were his friends, his compatriots, his family. He was met with a round of blank stares.

"What is the price of our freedom?" repeated Hamilton. This time, though, the words were lifeless. Even Hamilton's studied passion had succumbed to the pervading silence.

Washington nodded with his entire torso. "Indeed, Alexander, everyone. What would it really cost us?"

The rhetorical nature of the question kept all mouths firmly shut.

"It would cost us *nothing*, gentlemen."

The gathered warriors' eyes darted back and forth, speaking with a sort of nervous energy that their mouths dared not utter—was Washington really going to take Napoleon up on his offer to abandon the mother country, to put aside his heretofore stentorian code of honor, to abandon the boy officer he'd only just recently promoted?

"We could pick up and leave right now," continued Washington, "and really, who would blame us? Certainly not the British; they're well versed in such skullduggery."

Tepid laughter momentarily filled the tent—sweet release from the rising tension.

"Oh, they may hate us for such treachery, but even they would understand. So who, dare I ask, is going to go out there and tell young Mr. Williams that we are leaving?" Washington looked pointedly at the gathered war council, but of them, only Benedict held his gaze. *You would at that, Mr. Arnold*, thought Washington.

"You see, gentlemen," continued Washington, "when we had to take *our* freedom, that we could do. To wrest it away from Britain on the field of battle—again, that we could do. But we had *our* chance, gentlemen,"—Washington's eyes suddenly narrowed—"had it and did not take it. It pains me to this very day, this very *hour*, that that was the course of action we chose to take. I wish that we'd declared our independence along with our rights, that we'd sundered the rotting umbilical cord that once sustained us. But we did not! We remained a part of the British Empire, however tenuous and fragile that connection may be. And now,"—Washington's eyes regarded the letter—"this. A chance to truly be free. But not a freedom won in battle, paid for in blood. Rather, a freedom purchased in shame, a bribe to look away as England is invaded. Our freedom bought with their subjugation."

Washington reached across the table and drew the letter in towards himself. "I think we would find that too high a price to pay, even for so precious a gift."

"But America!" implored Arnold.

Washington's lips pushed up against his mouth. "Like this, Benedict? For this price?"

"Yes and yes, General. It *is* a precious gift, and need I remind you, has been purchased for far worse a price than what is being asked of us."

The general had heard enough. He looked over to Hamilton.

"Mr. Hamilton, what say ye?"

"Nay."

"Mr. Green?"

"Nay, General Washington."

"Mr. Lee?"

"Suh, I fight—and have always fought—with honor. I could not abide by the offer in that letter any more than I could leave that boy or the others like him to be conquered."

"I'll take that as a 'Nay,' then, Henry?"

Henry's lips formed into a playful grin. "I 'spec so, General."

At last, Washington turned to the lone detractor. "Benedict, what say you?"

"I have no love of the British nor hatred of the French, but as we must be united in our endeavors, I, too, vote nay."

Washington smiled and then spoke in reassuring tones to his friend. "We will find another way, Benedict—one that will allow us to sleep better at night, one that will not wrap an anchor of shame around the collective neck of future generations."

Benedict bowed his head slightly.

"Mr. Hamilton," continued Washington, sliding the letter back across the table, "you are to take this letter and burn it. Make sure no one—and I mean no one—ever sees it again."

Hamilton nodded, picked up the letter, and slid it into his waistcoat.

"Gentleman," continued Washington, "I must impress upon you the absolute secrecy of this evening's events. This letter was never here. We never talked of it. We never heard of it."

"And what if Napoleon chooses an opposite tact?" asked Nathaniel. "What if he chooses to publicize it for his own ends?"

"I'm really not sure what good could come of it from his perspective—after all, we turned down his invitation to dance. However, your point is well received, Nathaniel. If the little general chooses to disclose the letter and its contents, then our united response shall be that we never received it."

The warriors nodded their ascent.

"Then without further ado," said Washington, pushing his chair out from the table, "there is a battle to prepare for."

Everyone stood, bowed respectfully, and made their exit into the unusually quiet night.

Washington stood at the tent's entrance, watching as his council fanned out, drawing larger assemblages of subordinates around them as they did, all fast-moving comets with ever-expanding tails. It was the frenzy before battle. He knew he shouldn't like it, knew that the taste of death which now so energized the camp would, on the morrow, do its wretched best to dispirit it.

Washington took a deep breath and then slowly exhaled the moist night air. A half smile etched the corner of his mouth as he spoke into the darkness. "Come in, Major Wellesley."

The major stepped from out of the shadows, a look of consternation plastered across his face. "How did you know?"

"I thought I heard someone and was praying it was you," answered Washington, inviting the officer into his tent. "What did you gather?"

"Everything," he answered tersely. Washington nodded. "Then I must ask of you the same thing I asked of my men."

Wellesley's left eyebrow cinched upwards.

"I presume," continued Washington, "you understand the gravity of the situation—and how critical it is we keep this little conversation to ourselves."

"Yes, General, I do—more than your men, I think. The question is, will *they* keep it quiet?"

"Quiet enough, I pray."

Wellesley's rigid posture slackened, and his head sunk slightly between his two broad shoulders. "Thank you," he barely managed, "for what you did. The British people will never know how much they owe you, General Washington, but rest assured: for what's it's worth, you have earned my unbending loyalty."

"Do not lay thanks at my door, Major. If you must, lay them at the humble dwelling of Mr. Williams."

On Wellesley's look of confusion, Washington added, "Till the lad entered, I was inclined to accept Mr. Bonaparte's offer."

* * *

The Battle of Plymouth was typical of those fought during that period, even if waged in two wholly different styles. The Americans, as usual, were peripatetic—always on the move, always deceptive. The French relied on the tried and true: attacking en masse with the column. It should also be noted that both generals were masters of their game, and as such, the Battle of Plymouth turned out to be a set piece for the entire era, one that would be replayed countless times and argued over in pubs, clubs, gaming tables, and simulated reality engines ad infinitum.

—Introduction to General History:
The Battle of Plymouth as seen through the eyes of Washington and Napoleon
Charles Washington Stanfield
London Press, 2009

* * *

By one o'clock in the morning, the American army was once again on the move. The British cavalry, who'd only just joined them, had never seen anything quite like it. For an army of that size to simply arise, pack all it needed into a few wagons, and depart so quickly was unheard of; that it had been done in such relative silence bordered on miraculous. What the British cavalry didn't know was that the comportment they stood in awe of was honed to perfection against their own army by their once-enemy, General George Washington.

Soon after the Declaration of Rights had been signed back in July of 1776, the British invaded New York with 35,000 men. The colonies had only been able to raise 20,000 men, all under Washington's command. Twice in that campaign the British had cut Washington off and readied themselves to deliver a death-blow, and twice the crafty general had simply vanished, moving his entire army in the middle of the night to a defensible position. That stealth had forced the British to load up their ponderous armies in slow pursuit. At one point, with only 2,000 men left, Washington organized and moved his "army" at night for an attack on Trenton. The brash attack had raised the spirit of the colonies and saved the American cause until the victories of Brandywine and Saratoga, with a newly swelled army, had finally put an end to the war in favor of the Colonies. The Trenton victory had been the result of an extremely mobile army launched from behind a retreat—a lesson Washington never forgot.

The general cut a striking figure, even in the dead of night. His silver-brown hair was pulled back and tied in a queue. Though cloaked in shadows, the white-and-blue waistcoat of the Continental Army looked resplendent on the general's wide, six-foot, four-inch frame. Even the waistcoat's pewter buttons seemed to dance to the movement of Washington's body, struck by wisps of moonlight that had forced their way through a canopy of angry black clouds. Only the sounds of wagon wheels turning, legs tramping, and the occasional whinny of a horse broke through the interminable silence.

Wellesley had finally had enough. "What are we doing?" he whispered tersely.

Washington turned to face the major. There was no life in his eyes. It was, thought Wellesley, as if they were already at the battle, already watching the sacrificial slaughter of mangled bodies and severed limbs.

"Finding a better place to fight," answered Washington. "This is an open field too far from Plymouth." Washington then turned to look behind him and then looked over to Wellesley with raised brow. "Napoleon was right."

"General?"

"If we'd chosen to fight on this field, he would have enveloped and crushed us in a flanking attack."

Wellesley nodded slowly. "So we're running away, then."

"We are running *towards*," corrected Washington.

After two minutes of riding silently in near-total darkness, Wellesley could contain himself no longer. "Yes, but towards what?"

Washington waited until the admonitions of quiet had died down before whispering back. "I'll know when we get there."

* * *

By the early dawn, the French awoke to see that the American army was gone and its camp abandoned. After the revelry of having achieved a bloodless first victory subsided, their army began preparing for what all expected to be a quick march followed by an easy conquest. After all, an enemy that ran in the face of battle was no enemy to fear; it was an enemy—if such a word could even be ascribed to such cowardice—to hunt and slaughter. Only Napoleon remained uneasy. He kept eyeing his maps nervously, repeatedly placing his index finger on the worn map where he thought Washington should be—where he, Napoleon, would have been. *No*, he thought, *Washington is far too cunning an adversary to come this far only to flee.* Though the arguments Napoleon's officers had made were sound—that Washington had arrived too late and knew his cause was hopeless; that the British had not supplied sufficient reinforcements for the American to consider going up against someone of Napoleon's stature and obvious superiority—the French general still paced nervously in his quarters, cracking his knuckles obsessively, tapping at various junctures along the routes of his various maps.

The sound of hooves thrashing towards his tent offered some release. There was news, of course. And that news would either increase the tension the French general always felt before battle or dissipate it, as his staff seemed to be betting on. Napoleon took his seat behind the ornate desk "borrowed" from a local aristocrat and puffed out his shoulders and chest, keeping his eye firmly on the tent flaps. He listened patiently as the guards questioned the messenger and timed to the second his assistant's call to him.

"Yes?" asked Napoleon.

"Message for you, Excellency."

"Come."

The young officer entered the tent, bowed, and then proffered the document. Napoleon took it from the major's outstretched hand and then removed the wax seal. The General's penetrating blue eyes flittered across the page from under an arched brow, and as they did, his mouth formed itself into a half scowl. It seemed the British cavalry were blocking the road between him and Plymouth.

* * *

Margaret Thatcher was elected Chancellor today, making her the first woman ever to hold this post. The votes will now go to the House of Electors, where they will formalize the results. Although Ms. Thatcher's victory is a stunning break with tradition, the Chancellor-elect has signaled that she will rule in conservative Whig fashion. To that end, Ms. Thatcher has indicated that she intends to revive the tradition of newly elected Chancellors going to Arnold & Hamilton Hill to lay a wreath of flowers. The ceremony will be televised on all major channels and is open to the public.

—U.E.P. news release, November 7, 1980

* * *

Wellesley, leading a group of officers, rode up to the top of a small hill where General Washington had been sitting comfortably on his horse, scanning the horizon.

"He knows we're here," said Wellesley, eyes wide, alert, "and he's marching,"—Wellesley glanced back over his shoulder—"fast!"

Washington was sure that the impetuous major had observed the situation firsthand even though he'd expressly forbad Wellesley from putting his or any of his officer's lives needlessly at risk. It had been Washington's unearthly patience, as well as a tight grasp on the reigns of his men's intemperate nature, that had kept the general and his armies around for so long. Washington sighed, knowing it would be hard to train these "new" recruits on the merits of living to fight another day. Still, he couldn't begrudge them their exuberance; he, too, had been young once. He, too, remembered what it was to be enshrouded in the warm and euphoric embrace of immortality.

The general acknowledged the group with a measured tip of the head. "How much time, Major?"

"By my reckoning, sir, two hours." The men behind Wellesley all nodded.

Washington's eyes narrowed. "I see."

"My men are attempting to delay them," interjected one of the other officers. "Firing from behind fences, the tops of hills …"

"… then we ride away and do it again at the next turn in the road," offered another.

"You know," added Wellesley with a good-natured grin, "American style."

The old general's lips curled into a churlish grin. "Indeed. How goes it?"

"Damnably well," replied Wellesley, shaking his head. "They would've been here by now otherwise."

Washington pulled a scroll out from his coat. The swiftness of its retrieval and unfurling was indicative of just how many times he'd performed the action over the course the past few hours and over the course of a lifetime. As Wellesley and his men looked on, Washington reviewed the sketches and battle plan he'd only that morning drawn up with his staff. They were, he mused, an almost exact copy of those drawn up for the defense of Breeds Hill in Boston, Massachusetts—against the very army he was now in cahoots with. Though Breeds Hill had been one of the few battles Washington had not participated in, it was one he'd studied assiduously when he'd assumed command of the Continental Army. He refolded and slipped the document back into his coat with the same insouciant ease as he'd retrieved it. He then rubbed his eyes. *One more battle, and then I can sleep*, he thought. *Hell, I'll sleep for a week, by God!* Washington's eyes opened. The officers were staring blankly at him but with obvious patience.

"My apologies, Major; I seem to have been momentarily swallowed whole by the preparations." He lightly tapped the side of his coat, where he'd only just tucked the plans.

"None necessary, General. The battle is in two hours. May I suggest you get some rest?"

"You may," answered Washington with dismissive charm.

"Really, sir. It would …"

"I can rest *after* the battle, Major." Washington's tone indicated he would brook no further argument; the major promptly ignored this.

"*Which* we will lose if the commanding general is mentally incapacitated. My God, sir, you've been going nonstop since you disembarked nearly three days ago. If in that time you've had even three hours' sleep, I would be amazed. Two hours will clear some of the fog …"

"And give us a chance?" Washington asked.

"Indeed, sir. You yourself have stated that when it comes to marching and digging in, yours is the best army in the world. So I dare say, let them do their job. Oh, look." Wellesley's head turned slightly, noseindicating direction. "There is a tree not ten yards away. There's even a bit of shade and," he added, "even a blanket."

There was no blanket.

Wellesley's eyes became arrows as he fixed his gaze on one of his subordinates. "I *said*, even a blanket."

Two officers quickly snapped to attention. They dismounted their horses, one with blanket in hand, the other with a cloak. They both raced over to the tree, and within seconds, the makeshift bed was ready.

A small laugh escaped Washington's lips as he watched the goings-on.

Once more, Wellesley indicated the tree. "Go … sir."

"Is that an order, Major?"

"Oh, absolutely, General," answered the Major with a grin. "You know we aristos become disconsolate unless given some hapless Colonials to order about."

A broad smile worked its way across Washington's weary face. He laughed, shrugged, and dismounted. "Very well, then," he said as he headed over to the tree. He sat down on the blanket and brushed off his knees. He sat there for a second as Wellesley stared down from his horse disapprovingly. Washington laughed once more and stretched his large body out on the blanket. He was asleep almost before his head hit the rolled-up cloak.

* * *

Washington awoke to the smell of sulfur and the sound of cannon fire. Whether because of experience or simply because his nerves had long since been frayed far beyond caring, he didn't jump to. Not that his old bones would or even could do such an outlandish thing. As was his wont, he simply propped himself slowly up on his elbows, allowing his eyes to flitter open. He viewed his body stretched out: the well-worn jacket, familiar waistcoat and boots. As he pulled himself up to a sitting position, he mused that in his sixty-six years of life he felt he'd not bathed for at least thirty of them. Still, when his aide de camp approached, Washington was fully cogent. He looked past the aide and saw that the sun was well up on the horizon and that his men had done an admirable job of digging in. Three lines of well-fortified pits now surrounded their small hill. The trenches were braced with trees—small and few as compared to those found in the Americas—and, of course, rocks, of which there seemed to have been more than enough. The only things missing, thought Washington with an understanding smile, were soldiers. Or, to be more precise, soldiers primed and at the ready. Most of those surrounding him and even those manning the works were sound asleep. After three days of Herculean effort, they'd finally managed to exhaust themselves, and not even a French army positioning itself for attack would wake them up.

Washington stood, noting just how painful that simple act had become. He then requested a telescope from the aide, and one was produced immediately. He brought it to his eye and scanned the French positions. As he did, he heard the rustle of footsteps behind him and noted that Hamilton, Arnold, and Lee were now also standing by his side. Washington gave them a cursory nod and went back to scoping the lines. Napoleon, Washington saw, was arranging his thirty thousand men in three columns of ten thousand each, to the left, right, and center of the American-held hill. That would mean that an attack was at least an hour away and, with any luck, possibly two. The General would let his men sleep until the bugles sounded or the French began dropping shells into their camp.

"Colonel Hamilton," said Washington, handing the telescope back to the aide, "does this not remind you of the Battle of the Swamp?"

Hamilton's eyes sparkled at the memory as a brief smile escaped his parched lips. "They were *all* battles of the swamp in Florida, General—or so they seemed."

Washington nodded, amused. "Yes, I guess they would. I am, of course, referring to the Spaniard's night attack."

"Oh, yes," answered Hamilton, brow narrowed. "They were going to catch us by surprise."

"Gentlemen," interrupted Wellesley, now taking up a position next to Lee, "I am afraid the only thing *I* remember about the whole Spanish-Colonial War is that the Crown was against it and you chaps had the audacity to win it without our help."

Washington smiled easily. "It was a little more complicated than that, Major."

"Really?"

"Life in the colony of Georgia," added Arnold, "had become untenable due to the constant attacks by some of the Indian tribes, including a split in the rather large and influential Cherokee Nation."

Wellesley's eyes grew wide, whether as a result of the imparted information or the uptick of munitions being traded between the two armies. It was hard not to notice the bullets that were starting to buzz about the hill; the sound as they struck the well-turned soil was very much like the errant *plunk* of thick raindrops prior to a downpour. Washington, as well as the rest of the group that had now formed a protective circle around him, barely acknowledged the pernicious intrusion. There was an aura of complete calm about the place that, Washington knew, emanated from him. *Of course*, he thought with a wry grin, *the fact that half the men are asleep probably has something to do with it.*

"I say," continued Wellesley, "these Indians you speak of,"— the major's eyes darted over to a particularly dark-skinned group of men who'd taken up a position just a few yards away from where the group had situated itself—"do you mean to tell me that *they* …" Wellesley couldn't finish his thought.

Washington chuckled at Wellesley's unmasked incredulity. The Europeans' abject fascination for anything Indian related never ceased to amaze him.

"Yes, *they*, Major," answered Washington, now eyeing the same group of men Wellesley had just ogled. "Make the best scouts, after all."

"Well," added Lee, left eyebrow slightly raised, "the ones not trying to kill us 'n all."

Wellesley didn't laugh. "I never have understood the nature of your relationship with the savages."

"Savages they may be," answered Washington evenly. "I myself have witnessed a few of their more gruesome attacks—unspeakable," he uttered in barely a whisper. "But be that as it may, Major, these savages happen to be *our* savages, and as such, I prefer you refer to them as either *soldiers* or *Indians*. As to which—I'll leave that to your discretion."

All eyes fixed on Wellesley, whose cheeks flushed momentarily.

"'Indians' it shall be, sir."

Washington nodded. "Very good, Major. The first thing you must realize is that there is no *one* Indian, much like an Englishman, Frenchman, or American. It's more like the situation thirty years ago, where we had thirteen separate colonies. Only imagine, if you will, *hundreds* of colonies, each with their own identity, language, religion, and customs, all of which can best be described as vaguely related."

"Why, General," answered Wellesley with an impish grin, "I do believe that you're describing Europe!"

"In a way I am, Major, and you know how peaceful *that* continent is."

Serendipitously, the sound of light cannon fire—mainly of the harassing sort—could be heard coming from behind the Americans' lines.

"And yet, General," continued Wellesley, once more glancing furtively over towards the nestled group of dark-skinned men, "they seem to have made peace with you chaps."

"Some," interjected Hamilton. "There were those who wanted to come to an accommodation with the Colonies and those who did not. The Cherokee,"—Hamilton indicated towards the men with his head—"are the best example. They're a vast and advanced tribe in the Georgia colony. Most embraced our way of life, going so far as to adopt our alphabet, farming techniques, and even our religion, of a sort. But that acquiescence caused a particularly vicious civil war."

"Enter the Spanish," added Washington, voice thick with disdain.

Hamilton smiled curtly. "They let it be known that any Indian tribe or rebel force willing to do us damage would not only receive a steady supply of advanced and, I might add, *free* weaponry but would also, should the tide turn against them, receive safe harbor in Florida. We had no choice but to put an end to that meddlesome threat."

"The Florida invasion?" asked Wellesley.

Washington nodded. "Helped in large part by the likes of those gentlemen you see there. Wasn't long thereafter that the first Indian delegates to the Continental Congress were sent and seated."

Wellesley's eyes lit up once again. "You allow sava—Indians to make your laws?"

Washington gave a half smile. "Well, I would hardly call Congressman Reindeer a savage. His Latin is better than mine."

"That's not saying much," said Arnold with a slight sparkle in his eye.

"*Mea Culpa*," retorted Washington, and then continued, "In a democracy, Major, you must represent the people under your control, which most of the Indians are. Had we not let them in, we would've had to kill them or drive them out—an unpleasant endeavor by any stretch of the imagination."

"Much easier to give them a vote," added Lee, "and *then* tax the hell out of them."

Wellesley put his fingers to his chin. "An invaluable insight, sir."

"Which," laughed Washington, "we learned at your expense."

"Ah. The proverbial chicken coming home to roost. Touché, General. You mentioned something about the Battle of the Swamp?"

"Oh, yes. Very similar to this situation, Major. We'd positioned ourselves on a hill, and just like the French are preparing to do now, the Spanish tried to attack us in three columns."

"Well, not exactly like that," chimed in Arnold. "The Spaniards were attacking from a swamp at night; they did not outnumber us at all, let alone three to one; and they were exhausted after marching to attack us in a position we'd had a good three days to dig into to. Other than that, it is *exactly* identical, Major Wellesley."

"Thank you for clarifying it for me, Colonel Arnold."

"Always at your service," answered Benedict in a tone that belied the words.

At that moment, the tempo of the dirt piercing seemed to pick up. The smells of saltpeter, sulfur, and charcoal blew through the camp, unseen eddies in a roiling mass of gunpowder. Washington looked around, sniffed the noxious air, and then fixed his gaze on Wellesley.

"Major, you should get going."

All jocularity within the group vanished with the heightening situation and Washington's order. The old man, most knew, had a feel for these sorts of things, and most of those present had managed to stay alive by trusting those feelings.

Wellesley saluted stiffly. "At once, General Washington." Washington returned the salute as the young Brit made his way to a group of horsemen at the base of the hill.

"I don't believe I'm saying this," said Benedict, shaking his head ever so slightly, "but I'm actually sorry to see him go."

"I seem to remember a time," piped in Colonel Lee, "when watching a redcoat in retreat was all you could ever ask for."

"Exactly!" exclaimed Benedict, glad for the empathy. Then he moaned, "Oh, how the mighty have fallen."

Henry Lee looked over to Washington. "Are ya sure it whas the best thing to let those two thousand redcoats go, suh?"

"Sadly, Colonel Lee,"—Washington's mouth drew itself into a perfectly straight line—"yes. They're cavalry and not well versed in the sort of battle we're about to fight. Anyone but Napoleon probably would've waited a day or two trying to decide what to do next. And maybe the British army, sitting on their asses in London, would've been able to join our little party."

"Not damned likely," scoffed Benedict.

"Indeed," confirmed the General. "Pure speculation, of course."

"Never thought in a million years I'd be sitting on a hill in England actually regretting the British army's absence!"

"Two for two," quipped Lee.

Benedict responded with a snarl.

"Hell," continued Benedict's tormentor, "I should be taking bets at this point."

"Way I figure it," said Nathaniel, "all the frog has to do is leave one third of his army here to block us on this hill and then go and attack Portsmouth with the twenty thousand men under his control."

"And," said Washington, "that is exactly what he *should* do. It's certainly what I'd do. Portsmouth would be his by the afternoon at the earliest or on the morrow at the latest."

"I see," said Benedict.

"I'm not sure that you do, Colonel."

Benedict tilted his head slightly.

"I've studied this man's campaigns," continued Washington. "He doesn't like to split his army. Before any encounter, he'll spread his troops like jelly over bread, but on the day of battle, he invariably reconstitutes."

"To what end?" asked Lee.

"Overwhelming force."

"Doesn't trust his troops?" asked Benedict.

"More for insurance, I suspect," answered the General.

All nodded with grim acceptance.

"And I sincerely hope," continued Washington, "that he stays true to form."

"Behold," intoned Hamilton opening his arms in a symbolic gesture that encompassed the gathered warriors, "the martyrs of Portsmouth."

"Not just yet," cautioned Washington, who then allowed a mischievous grin to emerge on his weathered face. "Napoleon is a man used to springing surprises; now we've gone and turned the tables. And by doing so have both delayed and hampered his efforts."

"And injured the Frenchie's pride," added Hamilton, suddenly aware of the game afoot.

"Now," continued Washington, "if we can only add a little more insult to the injury, we may just rouse him to an all-out attack."

"Which is what we want," said Nathaniel, more curiosity in his voice than conviction.

"Unless you'd like them to secure Portsmouth, Colonel—in which case, our Herculean endeavor will have been for naught. No," the old warrior said, surveying the fortifications, "history will … *must* be made here. Destiny insists on it."

"This insult, suh," asked Henry, "What exactly did you have in mind?"

In reply, Washington gestured to his aide, Lieutenant Bergen, who saluted and ran off to where the American flag, ordinance zipping around it, flapped angrily atop a long makeshift pole. Bergen gave a command to a sergeant, who removed the stars and stripes and hoisted a Union Jack. An hour later, all three columns of French army attacked.

* * *

"I was created Duke of Wellington by our Majesty himself; was the third Chancellor of the British Empire, serving for two terms; and commanded the British army when we took the Iberian Peninsula away from Napoleon and his brother. I arranged the peace between Napoleonic Europe and ourselves in 1820, helped oversee the beginning of the Suez Canal, and have been befriended by Her Royal Majesty Queen Victoria, may she reign forever and a day. This is not even a tenth of my accomplishments, and yet, what is it that almost everyone who meets me for the first time asks? Whether they be simple Kentucky farmers, California miners, Indian princes, and, yes, even the Czar of all the Russians, the question is always the same: You knew HIM? I have

always known the 'him' to whom they refer, and I have always been proud to say, 'Yes.'"

—Excerpt from the Duke of Wellington's last speech,
given to the Royal Academy of the Sciences
May 12, 1853.

* * *

"Conserve your ammunition!"

Washington's order could barely be heard above the din, but somehow the fire reduced markedly as the French pulled back from their second and, rued Washington, even bloodier attempt to take the hill from the Americans. The army likewise was now defending its second line of defense, the first being too mangled and the men too few to defend it properly. But that was the least of Washington's concerns. The problem was ammunition. The colonial reserve had boarded the transports with enough musket balls and powder to give each man one hundred rounds. It was an absurdly high number for an army going on duty in a foreign country with little prospect of battle and with the intention of being supplied by the host government. If the Americans had been going to battle in Ireland instead of garrison duty in England, he would have carried more. Even a hundred rounds had seemed a lot for patrolling a peaceful countryside. However, Washington had learned over the course of as lifetime that it was best to be over-prepared than simply prepared and so set the numbers high.

"I should have carried a thousand," he muttered.

Between Napoleon stealing all he could get and the British government shipping all they had to an army now uselessly centralized in London, there was not a lead ball or beaker of powder to be had in all of Southern England except for what the Americans had brought with them. And now what little they had left was being depleted quickly. Washington saw that his men were stripping the dead, both French and American, of any powder and shot they could find, but he knew the lot of it couldn't hold off the French for long.

It was at that moment that a barely recognizable Lt. Bergen came rushing over to him. The lieutenant's arm was in a makeshift bandage pulled from the fabric of a blood-spattered waistcoat, and his face was covered in grime so thick only the whites of his worried eyes indicated trouble. Saluting clumsily, he said, "General Washington, it's Colonel Arnold; you'd better hurry."

Washington's face registered momentary alarm but then quickly comported itself. Seeing that it would be at least another half hour before the French could launch a serious attack, the general followed his aide up the hill to where the wounded had been moved.

It didn't take him long to spot his friend. When Arnold saw Washington, his eyes lit up.

"So," asked Washington with such alacrity it caused his young aide's brow to cinch upwards, "is this really the day you've chosen to die?"

"And defending England, no less!" sputtered Arnold, incensed.

"You survived India and you fought for England then; you'll live now," Washington lied.

"I fought for America then. To learn what the …" Coughing mixed with blood interrupted Arnold's rambling. "… what the British knew of fighting. I figured that I could use it for when we were ready to try again. But we never did." He wheezed painfully. "General, is … is the surprise ready?"

Washington nodded. "We have them moved, Benedict. We have enough ammunition for one more attack. If we do not break their will now, we'll be in for a bit of difficulty."

"You'll win," answered Benedict with absolute certainty. "And when you do, you must use your prestige."

Washington eyed his friend warily. "What in the world are you talking about?"

Arnold's blackened hand grabbed Washington's coat sleeve. "Damn it all to hell, General, I don't have any more time! When you win this battle, the British will owe you. Make them return on the debt—*independence*! You were right; we couldn't take it like a thief in the night. But we can win it on the battlefield—on *this* battlefield. Promise me, General. Promise …" Benedict's voice faded.

"General, the French …" prodded Lt. Bergen.

"Let them come," said Washington, watching sadly as his war-weary friend fought his very last battle.

* * *

"I'm worried about young Lafayette, suh."

"Tell him—and let him know it's direct from me—that he'll get his chance. When it comes, he'll know."

"I'm not so certain, General Washington. One Virginian gentleman to another, he has a powerful thirst for vengeance."

Washington's face was grim but resolute. "It will be quenched this day, Mr. Lee. One way or the other, it will be quenched."

Colonel Lee saluted and headed back down the hill.

It took the French over an hour to organize the attack. They would've done it sooner, but their officers were getting killed almost as soon as they stood up to organize it. The French troops had faced a number of adversaries in their many campaigns, but nothing had prepared them for Kentucky Riflemen. Washington had refrained from using his expert riflemen, partially for honor and partially for effect. Now that the French officers were being dropped piecemeal in front of their soldiers' eyes, it was bound to plummet their morale. At least, that's what the old general was hoping. It seemed to be working. Washington looked through his telescope; the French were organizing their attack from farther away, and the more canny officers had taken to lighting small fires, fanning the smoke, and organizing under the limited cover provided. But the stress was showing. After two failed assaults, they were starting to get discouraged. They weren't used to setbacks of this nature. Washington watched as one of the enemy officers went down screaming, clutching at his leg. The shot had been landed at extreme range and, noted Washington, through the smokescreen. A whoop went up from a group of men not more than ten feet from the general. He noticed a much older one being patted on the back. Washington smiled when he realized who it was.

"Excellent shot, Mr. Boone," he said with an amiable grin.

"Anything to make the French feel welcome, General."

At that moment, the sound for a general attack was trumpeted from the French position, and their army rose as a gargantuan beast and suddenly struck with all three columns. Washington quickly made his way down to the front lines, making sure whatever was left of his troops held their fire. The old General waited as the massive French body of crimson, gold, blue, and gray converged on the second American position, a large wall advancing implacably on a small but determined knot of men waiting to die. But, Washington knew, his men were waiting for no such thing; that they were, in fact, waiting to unleash the angel of death rather than receive him. The General looked up to the top of the hill and stared momentarily at the neat rows of canvas-covered logs jutting out from the pulverized ridge, an ominous silhouette against the turbid skyline—death's harbingers waiting orders to rain down their own indiscriminate salvation from on high. But the crews manning them, like the carved ruses themselves, were only there for show. The real artillery, fifty Howitzer cannons in all, had been quietly moved during the frenzy and confusion of battle and were now in the hands of the same determined knot of men staring into the implacable faces of the approaching enemy. The newly positioned cannons had been arrayed to cause widespread damage. Given what the Howitzers' normal ordinance had recently been replaced with, their sting would be even more painful. Washington sniffed at the air and stared down the approaching horde. Furtive glances from his own men only added to the pressure. But this was where soldiers were made. This was where Washington knew that he, more than most, excelled. Anyone could plan a battle on paper, but there were precious few who could direct its ineluctable slip into anarchy. The General turned his eyes from the French and fixed his determined gaze on Colonel Hamilton.

"Now, Colonel."

"Give Fire!" ordered Hamilton, who'd not once taken his eyes off his acting commander through the whole world of muskets, sharpened steel, and the tension-filled clamor of war that had been bearing down on all of them.

A cacophonous symphony of cannon fire, rifle shot, and bloodcurdling screams suddenly erupted. Between the grapeshot—

masses of loosely packed metal slugs loaded into canvas bags—shards of glass, rocks, and loose strands of chain exploding from the impossibly close Howitzer array, the first part of the French army simply disappeared into a bloody miasma of smoke, torn flesh, loose appendages, clumps of dirt, and the gut-wrenching wails of the mortally wounded. Yet still the French managed to advance—over the corpses of their comrades—into the American lines. They were immediately met by the jutting bayonets and bullets of the Americans. After what seemed an eternity of fighting, Washington ordered his army to fall back to their third and most heavily fortified position.

The French, finally too weary to advance, started to fall back. Washington, ignoring the pleas of his men to put himself out of harm's way, watched with great satisfaction as the French began to retreat in abject disarray. The pullback itself was not what gladdened the old general's heart—rather, it was the way in which it unfolded. In confusion lay victory, and the French seemed very confused indeed. There were all the telltale signs of breakdown: the burgeoning panic and fear, the tossed weapons, the pitched voices battling for authority amongst the survivors, the fear of being so close to death that the cruel winds coursing through the battlefield might very well be the malevolent breath of Azrael himself. Add to that the blessed silence of the one thing that could turn chaos into control: the fife and drum regiment, key to any large army's orderly movements. All of it, knew Washington, would overtake and ultimately destroy the French before they could pull themselves together. All that was left was deciding when to strike the deathblow. Too soon, and the French might rally; too late, and they'd escape to fight another day. This was where experience counted most, so Washington stood his ground and watched ... and waited.

It was then that the old general heard a sound that sent a shiver up his spine—a lone fifer playing somewhere in the distance. The purposeful rhythm was unmistakable—it was a call to retreat. But, prayed Washington, it was only one and perhaps too late. The General knew that his best marksmen were frantically trying to spot the fifer, but with the dust, smoke, and pandemonium on the field, their task would be nigh impossible.

The lone fife was soon joined by another, farther away, but close enough that their combined sounds melded as one. Shortly thereafter, the two fifers were joined by the rhythmic staccato of clacking drums. *And that*, thought Washington sadly, *was that*. The French, drilled to perfection, began to act on training rather than instinct. They ceased their cries of panic as order replaced anarchy. The impending rout had just been turned into an orderly retreat.

Washington took a deep breath, pursed his lips tightly together and turned his back on what was supposed to have been a crowning achievement: Napoleon Bonaparte's ignominious defeat at the hands of "the Great" General George Washington.

"Damn to hell the man with the sense to rouse that fifer!" bellowed Washington as he made his way through the ranks of the wounded and dead. It was then that tragedy struck again. The second he saw the large crowd gathered around the prone figure, he knew, by proximity, who it had to be.

"Alex," whispered Washington, slowly reaching forward with his hand as if in the reaching he could somehow halt the sad tableau playing out before him. The crowd parted.

"Sir," offered one of the men choking on his own words, "he ... he died bravely." Washington took off his tricorne and held it to his chest, staring forlornly down at the corpse. "Held off three of the Frogs himself, he did," sputtered the soldier. "Gave us time to plug the hole in the line ... may have saved the army, General, sir. He was, he was ..." the man's voice drifted off when he saw his words were having no effect whatsoever on the stolid figure standing mute over the body of his friend.

Washington finally looked up and around at all those who'd gathered to pay their respect. "Colonel Hamilton was a hero. Let us see that his sacrifice was not in vain."

* * *

The Emperor never explained that battle. What possessed him to make that third charge? Not in all his memoirs or discussions with his friends, heirs, or family was he ever heard to utter so much as a word about it. Although he would go on to achieve much greater victories of far more significance, that battle, above all others, was the one that seemed to haunt him the most.

—From *The Battles of the Emperor*
Col. Renee-Javier Ternot, Retired
Paris: Imperial War Academy, 1877

* * *

Of Washington's original command staff, only Nathaniel Green and Light-horse Henry Lee remained. And of the ten thousand hearty souls who ventured forth from the Americas to help their British brethren, only seven thousand survived.

"If there be a hundred shot left in the whole army," groused Nathaniel, spitting a chunk of mud out of the left side of his mouth, "I will be surprised."

Washington acknowledged the comment with a sidelong grin. "And the men?"

"In remarkably high spirits for an army on the verge of oblivion, sir," he said. "Damn! If we'd only packed twenty-five more rounds per man, we could win this battle!"

"Victory," groused the old general, whose mien was now one of pure determination, "is still within reach, Colonel."

Nathaniel shook his head, surveying the wanton destruction. "But how, sir?"

"First things first. See that the last of the shot is given to our Kentuckians. They'll make every musket ball count, I am sure. Second, get to your men and be seen. Let them know that we have a plan to win this."

Lee shot Washington a look.

Washington returned his gaze with a knowing grin. "Go, gentlemen."

It took over two hours for the French to organize their last attack. Though Washington saw immediately that they had no fight left in them, that in fact, they were preparing to die, it offered little solace. The French discipline was damnably holding as they marched slowly up the American-held hill to the beat of fife and drum. Washington kicked at the dirt and grimaced, wracking his brain for a way to stop the assault. He could feel the eyes of his men upon him, smell their fear and desperation. It was only when the armies were within musket range that the General's answer arrived in the clarion blast of a distant bugle.

* * *

"I was at Wellesley's charge."

—Inscription on William Williams' tombstone.

* * *

Washington turned in the direction of the sound and was astonished by what poured into view: thousands of cavalry charging out of the west and towards the base of the hill. Despite the unceasing, rhythmic pace set by their musicians, the French hesitated for a mere moment as they looked back at what was coming. But that moment was enough for Washington to work with. He knew the French only needed a push to fall off the ledge and just as suddenly knew exactly what that push would be.

"Fix bayonets!" he roared over the din.

Washington drew his sword, and his command was repeated up and down the American lines.

"Charge!"

As if possessed, the Americans poured out and ran directly at the stunned French, yelping like the Indians they'd fought with and against for so long. The French, only moments before a cohesive and unrelenting wall of steel and grit, were soon a mob trying to escape the battlefield by any means necessary. The few officers who did try to regain control were quickly trampled underfoot. The British cavalry helped out by driving against any stragglers they could find. In fifteen minutes, the field belonged to the Americans, Napoleon was nowhere to be found, and Major Wellesley rode up to find Washington leaning tiredly on his sword in the middle of a cheering army.

"I heard," Wellesley said, grinning through a mud-spattered face, "you were having a party. When I found some friends coming down from London, I figured we just *had* to attend. I hope you don't mind that they came uninvited."

"You and your friends are always welcome, Major," answered Washington, surveying the battle's aftermath. "Now we must get this army to Portsmouth while the French are still running. By the time they recover, no channel port will be vulnerable, and the London army should be here to finish off the remainder." Washington then stood up and placed his sword back into its scabbard. "Let us away, gentlemen."

* * *

Napoleon's disastrous outing had little effect on France as a whole. Not even the abandonment of his army nor his hurried—and many have argued, humiliating—escape on a fishing boat in the dead of night could bring the French to try their most famed and beloved warrior. Instead, Napoleon was declared a hero who had brought real and sustained battle to England for the first time since the Hundred Years' war. Not only that, but he'd made the damned English howl. Losing to Washington, the polity seemed to have decided, was acceptable. Soon Napoleon would rule an empire that would unite Europe from the Pyrenees to the Russian border for the next one hundred years. But the changes that Napoleon's outing had caused in the British Empire were nothing short of astounding!

—Excerpts from *Britain & France: Eternal Enemies*
Trevor Kent
San Francisco: Harper Press, 1932

* * *

It had been a very busy week for Washington. He'd had to secure the channel ports and organize the units coming from London. Although he was not in command of the British army, he was made commander of all British forces in Southern England for the purpose of mopping up those French still left. That task had been quickly assigned to young Lafayette and Major—soon to be Colonel—Wellesley. Of the ten thousand men Washington had come to England with, a little less than eight thousand would be returning. And of those, only about six thousand were fit for combat. But the prospect of renewed battle, Washington knew, was as unlikely a prospect as … *As what?* he thought to himself. *As Napoleon invading England?* The thought brought a knowing smile to the old fox's lips.

To great fanfare and excitement, ten British ships of the line soon appeared at Portsmouth under the command of Admiral Nelson. Washington made sure to be there for the Admiral's disembarking, and when the two finally shook hands, it was to thunderous applause; the channel was secure and England was safe. Not coincidentally, it was also on that day that a letter came relieving Washington of his command. He'd been summoned to London to greet and advise his royal majesty, King George III of Great Britain, as well as receive the gratitude and rewards of his service to the crown.

What should have been a quick trip of at most three days turned into an exhausting weeklong extravaganza. The general, too polite to turn down the pleas of those wishing to do him honor, was determined to abide by every town's request to pay a brief visit. Inevitably, Washington would be showered with gifts in the form of food, clothing, and other sundry items—all of which were quickly distributed to the soldiers. And because he was traveling with his guard of Kentucky riflemen with their long muskets and his exotic cadre of Indian scouts, the crowds seemed always abuzz with excited murmurings. But it soon became apparent that the general's largess would be viewed as an impertinence to the King. Washington, in military-like fashion, soon found himself sneaking around numerous population centers in the dead of night.

By the time he arrived in London, the general was spent, almost as exhausted from the revelry as from the actual battle itself. Having no patience or energy for the King's court, Washington begged off staying at the palace, choosing instead to reside at Ben Franklin's old quarters in London. The General had used his poor health as an excuse to turn down the palace invitation. That excuse had been readily accepted by the King, not only because it had been politic to do so but also because it hadn't been far off the mark—Washington *was* old and in questionable health. At Franklin's residence, Washington did nothing but sleep, eat, and write letters. At first they were to the Continental Congress, giving an accounting of his campaign; then to his wife, assuring her of his health and safety; last but not least, he wrote to his friends. On the third day, the old man awoke only to be informed that he would have a royal audience with His Majesty the King that very afternoon. The timing of the meeting indicated he'd be having tea with the royal family as well. He was having a suit fitted out when he heard a gentle knocking at the door. Jeffery, one of his former slaves, excused himself to answer. He returned in a moment.

"General, a gentleman wishes to see you."

Washington's brow raised slightly, but he remained stiffly in place as his tailor measured his arms with punctilious resolve.

"He did not say who he was," continued Jeffrey, "only that he hopes you remember his father, whose public declarations of friendship for the Colonies bore no equal."

A smile worked its way across Washington's face. "I think I know of this gentleman, Jeffery." Washington looked down at the tailor and nodded. The tailor bowed gracefully and began to collect his things.

The general, lowering his arms and padding down his shirt, then looked back to Jeffrey. "Send him in."

Moments later, a middle-aged gentleman entered. He was dressed in a simple coat, white shirt, brown leggings, and white socks. His shoes looked serviceable but not extravagant. He could, thought Washington, very easily be mistaken for a hardworking clerk looking to improve himself and not the son of an Earl that he was.

"Mr. Pitt, it is an honor to meet you. I knew of your father well."

William Pitt, known as "the Younger," tipped his head respectfully towards Washington. "It is *I* who am honored, sir, and I thank you for seeing me on such short notice."

On Washington's brief look, both Jeffrey and the tailor exited the room. Jeffrey pulled the door quietly closed behind him.

Washington bade Pitt to the parlor chairs. "To what do I owe the pleasure of your company, sir?"

"May I first offer you my congratulations on a magnificent victory?" said Pitt, taking the offered chair across from where the General now sat. "There are many in government today who are glad that you're a loyal subject—"

"As opposed to the successful leader of a revolution?" interrupted Washington with a bit of the sprite in his eyes.

Pitt nodded, lips upturned.

"No doubt," continued Washington, "many of those same men were calling for my execution not so long ago."

"No doubt, sir, but in that regard they were about as successful in getting your head as was Napoleon."

Washington grunted appreciatively. "To business, Mr. Pitt."

Pitt, unused to the American penchant for forthrightness, looked somewhat taken aback. But he quickly recovered.

"I was wondering if, per chance, you would consider entertaining a notion of mine."

"And that notion would be?"

Pitt smiled demurely. "Could you go to the window, please?"

Washington stared at Pitt dubiously. The window's shuttering had been purposeful, offering the General a modicum of peace and quiet from the large and ever-present crowd that always seemed to be camped below. What light Washington did have, which seemed to him plenty enough, had come from the few skylights above.

Pitt was already on his feet, beckoning the general. Washington, seeing the earnestness with which the Younger moved, reluctantly unfolded himself from the chair, made his way across the room, and pulled the curtains aside. The sudden flood of extra light was accompanied by the deafening roar of a mob. Everywhere he looked, he saw the street filled with people standing shoulder to shoulder. Men, women, and children were hanging out of windows, standing on boxes while waving and shouting in a cacophonous roar. When Washington waved back, the roar seemed to double in volume. He looked back at Pitt querulously.

"Perhaps a small speech, sir."

Washington made to protest, but Pitt seemed adamant. "It's all part of the notion, sir. I beg you for my father's sake."

Washington sighed and once again faced the crowd. He managed a slight smile and motioned with his hand to speak. The roar subsided to a murmur as the old general cleared his throat. He gave them his usual stump speech, thanking them for their bravery during the recent difficulties and reminding them that it was their tenacious defense of London that had given him the time he'd needed to win his small victory. And finally he bade them farewell, exhorting them to go about their business as he would soon be meeting with the King. With one last wave, he closed the window and drew the curtain. The noise was so great that even the closed window could not prevent the din from entering into his modest chamber. Washington motioned for Pitt to follow him into an adjoining sitting room. With the door firmly closed, they could once again continue their conversation in relative quietude.

"And the point?" asked Washington, sinking into the sofa with an exasperated sigh.

"That they love you, of course."

The look on Washington's face acted as a cool rebuke to Pitt.

"Yes, yes ..." stuttered Pitt, "I realize I'm overstating the obvious. But implicit in that love, sir ... and perhaps what you fail to realize ... is that it is not wholly for you ... the love, that is ... but rather for what you represent."

The last words tumbled out of Pitt like crumbs emptied from a pocket. The young man waited, face taut, gauging the general's response. Washington's brow had narrowed, and his shrewd eyes took stock of the Younger, but the old General kept his tongue.

Encouraged, Pitt continued, "Your name has always been associated with freedom, General. For many, present company included, it was believed that the cause of freedom both for the English and the Americans would be best defended in your hands."

Washington eyed Pitt warily. The young man was wading into dangerous waters.

"That belief," said Pitt, either oblivious to or uncaring of the consequences as he delivered his coup de grâce, "has now been made manifest."

Washington leaned forward on the sofa, straightening his back, making his already broad shoulders that much more formidable. "You do realize the precariousness of your position."

Pitt nodded stiffly but said nothing.

"Look at the little fellow, Napoleon," continued Washington, moving off the topic of treason. "All he needs is a couple more victories to make himself ruler of all France."

"You are no Napoleon, good sir. And it's patently obvious to any that have followed your storied career you would sooner live on a hill in China as become a king."

An uneasy smile appeared on the general's lips at the truth of Pitt's words.

"But you are right that you have an enormous amount of power now. What do you intend to do with it?"

"Do with it?" laughed Washington "Why, nothing. Power is temporary, young Pitt. The more I abuse it now, the more it will be resented later."

"But surely, General, there's something you would ask for. The King would expect no less. Even the people speculate."

"Really? And about what do they speculate?"

"Your independence from the mother country."

Washington's lips thinned with a forced smile. "You appear to have given this much thought, Mr. Pitt."

William the Younger nodded solemnly.

"Indeed," continued Washington, "now *would* be the best time for the colonies to achieve their freedom. We're a new nationality in dire need of a new nation. And I believe your assessment to be correct. After the events of this past month, I do not think the British people will begrudge us our new nation."

"No, sir, I imagine not. Especially if you make it clear that you would continue to be allied with the mother country in matters of foreign policy and military assistance. I'm confident that the bonds of language, culture, and history would keep us very close indeed."

"Ah. So *that* is why you are here, Mr. Pitt." Washington leaned back into the sofa. "You wish to discuss the details of the separation of our two countries. But I must warn you that this would be improper. I am not a member of Congress at this time. A delegation from that body would be empowered to make such an arrangement. Also, not to put too fine a point on it, you do not hold a portfolio in the current British government."

"I am a member of Parliament."

"I did not know that members of Parliament could hold such high-ranking discussions."

William smiled politely. "Allow me, sir, to clarify some points. The little matter of being invaded and almost conquered has given rise to a certain loss of confidence. In short, the current government is finished. A new Prime Minister will be chosen to form a new government."

"I understand. And that man will presumably be you?"

This time it was William's turn to play coy.

"You will follow in your father's footsteps," said Washington.

"My name is the one being put forward before all others," agreed William, "but mine is not the only one."

"I do not understand, sir." Washington's relaxed pose suddenly took on a studied formality. "If you want my help in securing you the office of Prime Minister, I must refuse. That would be an unconscionable interference in internal British affairs—something I can assure you we would not take kindly to if you were to attempt such an action in our congressional elections."

"You misunderstand me, sir," answered William, eyes narrowing. "I do not want your help in making *me* Prime Minister. I want you to accept my help in making *you* Prime Minister."

Washington's lower jaw dropped. "I'm the *other* name?"

William nodded enthusiastically.

"Are they mad? I'm an American!"

"It's not an insurmountable obstacle. I admit that on your own you could never hope to achieve or use the position with any success. But that's what I came here to tell you, General. You would not be on your own. It would be my honor to help you."

"You wish to give me your position—a position that your father had before you?"

"Yes."

"But why?"

"Because this is a rare opportunity. Your victory has opened up a window, small but serviceable. With your help, we can transform the whole of the Empire. Think of it, General: a world empire that runs with the consent of the governed, not England or Scotland or Virginia, but a Britannic Empire."

"I am honor bound to think in the best interests of America, Mr. Pitt. This is all very well for the British Empire, but what of America?"

"Do you think I would ask if I did not know this was in America's best interest as well?"

Washington looked at William askance.

"When you were born," continued William, "how many Americans were there?"

"I fail to see the …"

"Please, General. Humor me."

"About one-half million or so."

"How many now, sir?"

"Over four million."

"Of those, General, how many are under the age of sixteen?"

"I would reckon about half, Mr. Pitt."

"Which means that if we achieve a true political union with the American colonies, in about fifty years you will be running the Empire. In a hundred years, the American continent will *be* the Empire."

"I do not see why we would need you to help us in this. What you wish to do with us we can, in the fullness of time, achieve on our own."

"Not, I should think, as quickly, as safely, or as well. Also, General Washington, there *is* the slavery issue. I noticed that you have a Negro manservant."

"He is a free man."

"Because you freed him."

Washington hesitated. "Yes."

"You have freed a number of slaves in the past few years."

"As a matter of fact, I have."

"If you don't mind my asking, why?"

Washington looked warily at the young man but chose to answer regardless. "As my economic circumstance has improved, I've been able to free more of the slaves I inherited by marriage to my wife. I hope to be able to free them all in my will."

"How do your fellow Virginia gentlemen feel about your generosity?"

"That is a matter for America to deal with, Mr. Pitt."

"Oh, I agree. But *how* will America deal with it, I wonder? Already some colonies have declared themselves to be free while others are calling for stricter slave laws. You yourself feel that slavery must end, I hope."

"Slavery will end someday, Mr. Pitt."

"I agree it is an offense *and* against the natural laws you have so eloquently stated in the Declaration of Rights. But will it end peacefully or in blood? As part of the Empire, it will end naturally and under the guidance of law in its proper time. Can you say as much if America is its own country?"

Washington didn't answer.

"That is not the only reason for union," continued William. "We have a fleet, an army, and bases all over the world. And that translates into a marketplace that only members of the Empire have access to. As this latest battle has shown, we need each other. And yes, maybe we need the Colonies more, but still, the great Franklin was right."

"Franklin?"

William Pitt took out a small pamphlet from his breast pocket. He handed it to Washington. It was on old proposal of Benjamin Franklin's going back to 1754. A proposal for an Empire in which the Colonies are given full political rights. It had been ignored and eventually forgotten by almost everyone.

"Even back then he knew," whispered Washington.

"We can work out the details later, General, but we must begin now. Which road do we take: Independence or Union?"

"I need more time. This is far too great an issue for one man alone."

"Is it, now?"

"You, sir, are asking me to decide the fate of nations, continents, and possibly even the world."

"General, you've been deciding that since you started the Seven Years' War back in the 1750s. It's a little late to complain about it at present. Besides, the timing is right. I can sway my supporters to you now. We can make real, needed changes to the government with your prestige as a lever. Otherwise, it will take decades to achieve true reform."

"Without the threat of American secession …"

"We will not get Parliament to change its stockings, let alone the structure of government. But now it is obvious to anyone that we need the Colonies very badly if we are to win this war against the French. We need your Colonies so much that we can finally do away with all the rotten boroughs and vestiges of the Middle Ages and have an enlightened government."

"Mr. Pitt, might I remind you that you are a product of the British system? You stand to gain the most if the system stays the same. Your actions are illogical."

"I'll be honest, General Washington—a great part of me wants nothing better than to go with you to the King, watch as you have tea and crumpets with His Majesty, and sail off into the sunset with America tucked under your arm while I become the next Prime Minister of this great nation. If the Colonies were not a part of the Empire, I *would* be Prime Minister. But you and the colonies are our future. A great future, if we are willing to sacrifice. Britain must eventually give up control of its Empire to North America if this works out. That is a sacrifice. You must give up the rest of your life and privacy to the necessities of power. That is your sacrifice. I must give up becoming the Prime Minister. That is my sacrifice. America must give up the dream of independence. That is a mighty sacrifice, the greatest yet mentioned. But what we will create will be greater still. The United Empire will be the greatest achievement ever put into practice by the will of man. It is a greater dream, and it will be worth all the sacrifices we give to it."

The two men sat in companionable silence for some time before Washington chose to speak. "How long have you been planning for this, Mr. Pitt?"

"This particular circumstance I did not plan for. I can assure you that I had no desire to see Napoleon or the French invade my country. But the United Empire? Ever since those idiots in power almost lost you in the Colonies to utter stupidity. I knew that the government would have to change if we were to keep you. Mr. Franklin saw that in the 1750s. It just took me a little longer to see it as well."

"Those 'idiots in power' are not likely to desire this great change you seek to make."

"Power is conservative by nature, General. Without new circumstances, they will not change. But *you* are that new circumstance. The King will see you today. My people are ready today. The citizens of London are ready to back you today. Like it or not, providence has made the choice yours. Independence or Union: What is your will, General Washington?"

* * *

The convention was really a smoke screen. Originally called by Prime Minister Washington, it was only empowered to discuss ways of bringing the delegates of the Continental Congress into the Parliament. At that moment in 1799, that is what most people thought union *meant. But the founding fathers had a different goal. They set up the convention in Plymouth, far from the distractions of London, and sent the best men the Empire had to offer: Burke, Pitt, Adams, Smith, Madison, and many others. The first thing that they realized was that the old form of government could not work for ruling a worldwide empire. So they chucked the whole thing and came up with the three-tiered system we have to this day. Exactly like theirs, it had two houses of the legislature, an executive, and a judicial; the Chancellor to be elected by a house of electors; etc. It was a very practical form of government. But it must be remembered that those who made it were very practical men. This was a form of government that, once drafted, would have to be accepted by King, parliament, and populace. The founding fathers were hardheaded practitioners in the art of politics and so made a document that would function and grow, and grow it has. The Empire now controls large portions of the Earth, including two whole continents, innumerable islands, and an unprecedented amount of land in Africa and Asia. Although some of this empire is held as a protectorate or colony, most of the Empire is represented in the Imperial Parliament and votes in the Chancellor elections. Indeed, what the men in the Constitutional Convention of 1799 developed was nothing less than the blueprint for a functional world government. Given time, we may see that dream fulfilled.*

—The Art of the Possible Past, Present, and Future
Michael Wellesley, IX Duke of Wellington
Ann Arbor, Michigan: Ann Arbor Press, 1999

* * *

"They're almost seated, Mr. Chancellor."

Washington waited nervously. He would have paced in the halls outside the still-being-constructed Imperial Parliament Building, but that would not have befitted his new office. So he stood and waited as his secretary and aides attended to all the last-minute details, a speech that he and William Pitt the Younger had written for this day shifting nervously in his hand. The long months of campaigning, bribing, promising, and toiling ceaselessly had finally paid off. When the Parliamentary Seat of London had voted to accept the Constitution, the King had signed it into law. Elections were held, and Rhode Island Colony, the last of the parliamentary seats, had accepted the inevitable and joined the United Empire of Britannia. The UEB was born. An Imperial Parliament was now in session in London, and the first chancellor was about to give his first speech. Every gesture, every action, and every word was going to be watched. Everything Washington did was a precedent, and he knew it. His life was not his own and would not be for the next four years—eight, if reelected. But Washington would do his best for this strange new country that he had helped to create. He could do no less. It was his destiny.

DAY BY DAY

December 21ˢᵗ, 2012
Day 182,503: 8:30 AM

Alastair M. Ignacio began the morning of December 21ˢᵗ, 2012, the way he began every morning: he bounded out of bed and, stark naked, leapt out of his seventh-story window. And it had only taken him one hundred and twenty-seven days to figure out the best way to do it. After the first hundred extremely painful falls to the pavement below, he was beginning to think he'd simply have to run down the seven flights of stairs after all. But he hadn't been in the best of shape on Day 1, and that had cost him. No matter how many times or even how fast he made it to the street via the traditional method, he arrived exhausted and gasping for breath. It was out the window or nothing. So after his last disastrous fall, Alastair resolved to take a day (it's not as if he didn't have plenty of them) and scale slowly down the side of the building. The day he'd set aside ended up needing another as he'd lost his grip and was sent hurtling, once again, to the pavement below. But on that second day of trying, Alastair was more successful. He found an open window with a fan perched on its ledge. Even better, the fan's cord was tangled around the leg of a nearby table. The next day he leapt out the window and aimed for the fan. He found that by grabbing the fan he was able to not only slow his decent but also slightly change its angle—which led to other open windows, which led to other things he could grab to slow his decent even further. After that, he only needed twenty-five or so more days to figure out the best way to land on the sidewalk and on his own two feet. For everyone else in the world, his actions were not only pointless—all actions were—but positively deranged. Alastair M. Ignacio, however, couldn't help himself. In a world with nothing but time, he was the last man in a hurry.

December 21st, 2012
Day 2: 8:30 AM

Alastair woke up, stretched in catlike delight, and then shuddered in abject surprise—he was stark naked. That was the first clue that something was seriously amiss. He distinctly remembered putting his pajamas on the night before, if only for the fact that he'd tripped while attempting to slip into the silk bottoms while bouncing around his bachelor pad on a single leg. Feeling just above his left eye, Alastair was surprised to discover that the extremely tender bruise created as a result of the previous night's accident was gone. More to the point, he *always* wore his pajamas to bed and had only slept in the buff once in recent memory—just *two* nights ago on a dare elicited via a phone call from his girlfriend. She'd chided him into the deed, which had proved a disaster. His body greeted the unfamiliar sheets as if an unwelcome guest. If the tossing and turning hadn't been enough to convince him, the loss of a few precious hours of sleep had. Alastair always was and always would be self-conscious about his body—it was simply pudgy in all the wrong places, and until he shed the twenty pounds he'd been swearing to since college, he'd continue to keep his pj's on, thank you very much.

Alastair rose slowly from the bed, eyeing his small bachelor pad warily for any signs of an intruder. Everything seemed to be in place—except for his pajamas, of course. Not for the first time, he noted the brilliance of the sunlight streaming through the room's two-panel tenement window; only in his present state of heightened alert, the light somehow seemed more menacing—a blade cutting through oneiric wisps of dust. His ears were also attuned, listening intently for anything out of the ordinary. The building was murmuring to life in typical fashion—muted voices trailed along hallways, pipes shuddered, and the occasional open door belched morning newscasts by somber anchors or the chirpy, vacuous drivel of morning show hosts. After determining that nothing he could *sense* was out of the ordinary, Alastair suddenly burst out in a fit of laughter. Of all the reasons for him to be naked, a thief so dedicated yet stealthy enough to remove the pajamas from a sleeping man was probably not one of them.

His bedside phone rang; the shrill sound of it hit him like a bucket of cold water. Before he answered, he dashed over to his dresser, pulled open the top drawer, and was immediately struck again. There, perfectly folded and obviously un–slept in were his favorite pair of silk pajamas. The phone's fourth insistent ring reminded him that one more would send it to voicemail. He dashed back to the bed and snatched it up.

"Hello," he said, eyes still fixed pensively on the open dresser.

"Alastair," shrieked the frightened voice of his girlfriend.

"Madeline? What's wrong? Where are you?" It was hard to hear her over a PA system blathering in the background—in Chinese.

"I'm … I'm … at the airport!"

"What? Which airport?"

"Taiwan International!"

Alastair's brow curled up slightly. "Come again?"

"Yes," she affirmed, voice laced with trepidation.

"How did you … *why* did you?"

"I *didn't*," she sputtered. "That's what I'm trying to tell you!"

Alastair scratched his unshaven chin, finally taking his eyes off the dresser. "I'm sorry. I've been a little distracted. I'm naked."

"Alastair, this is neither the …"

"No, no," he interjected, "I woke up without my pajamas on, and …" He shook his head. "Never mind. Please," he encouraged, "what were you saying?"

"That … well, I know it's going to sound crazy …"

Alastair looked down at his naked body, then back over to the dresser. "Try me."

"It's just that … well, right now I'm about to board the same plane I was on yesterday at Taipei International!"

Alastair's eyebrow formed into a V. "You're telling me you're coming *back* to LA … *again?*"

"That's what I'm telling you." The fear hadn't left her voice. "And it's not just me, Alastair. Everyone here is looking around at each other. I think they're all just as surprised as I am. We're all scared, baby."

"Alright," he reassured. "Just calm down. Take a deep breath."

"This *is* calm, Alastair. You should've seen me five minutes ago."

Phone cinched firmly between his ear and shoulder, Alastair went over to the dresser and pulled out the silk pajama bottoms. He'd be getting dressed in an hour and could've easily put on his jeans, but for some reason he now felt the need for the reassurance of his sleepwear. "How is that even possible?" he challenged. "I picked you up at LAX not nine hours ago and drove you back to your apartment."

"I know."

"Even if you wanted to, there's no way you could've flown back to Taiwan in so short an amount of time. It's a fifteen-hour flight!"

"I know that too. Don't you think I know that?" she restated in a voice barely brought under control. "What I don't know is how one moment I could be in my own bed in LA, falling asleep after a particularly horrible flight and the next moment be here, awake and walking with my carry-on to my terminal."

Alastair checked the time on his phone. *That's odd*, he thought to himself. *Date's off by a day.*

"Hello?" Madeline said in frustration.

"Sorry, honey. It's just that …" Alastair continued to focus intently on his phone.

"It's just that what?" repeated Madeline.

"What's the date on your cell phone?"

"Really, Alastair. Of all the stupid …"

"Just tell me!" he demanded in voice firm enough to inspire action.

"It's …" she paused. "Why, it's December 21st."

December 21st, 2012
Day 182,503: 8:32 AM

The car with the key still inside turned out to be a red Corvette convertible. Even better, it had a tank full of gas. Alastair had never really gone for that type before, always having preferred a more sober driving experience, but over the endless days, he'd come to appreciate speed. Not for the thrill but for the expediency. There were only so many hours in a day, and he'd need to use each and every one of them to maximum efficiency. He'd become rather good at driving the route from his Westwood condo to LAX. He'd take Gayley Blvd. to Wilshire. Wilshire to Sepulveda, then a straight shot down Sepulveda to the airport. The 405 freeway was absolutely off limits—every car on it was either stalled or crashed. But Sepulveda had its own problems. He ran the lights, of course. Everyone did. But since there was really no point in going to work, the only people still on the road were those that had been there when the fateful day had started. It was a calculated risk. Alastair could live or die with the occasional collisions; they were purely random, but as his driving skills improved, so did his survival. There was, however, one part of Sepulveda that was never random—the Green Valley Circle overpass. It wasn't listed as such in any GPS guide or manual, but it was in Alastair's mind (for the simple reason that it was the first overpass right after Green Valley Circle Drive). On any other day he'd be able to zip under the 405 freeway with nary a thought. But this wasn't any other day; it was the *only* day, which meant one thing—Harold would be waiting.

Alastair knew him well: a man in his thirties, not particularly good-looking nor ugly, for that matter, not overweight or in good shape. Just average. The type of guy, Alastair often mused, who in the old days could've gotten away with murder because no one would be able to remember him or pick him out of a lineup. Everyone, that is, but Alastair. Over the course of the endless days, he'd spent a lot of time with Harold trying to prevent the guy from killing himself. Not that Alastair was against suicide. It was as pointless as every other activity. But Harold had insisted on committing suicide the same way every day—by jumping on Alastair's car as it went through the overpass.

Alastair had considered using a different route but learned early on that there really wasn't one. Given the nature of the Earth's day-by-day existence, most cars simply stopped or crashed where they were when the day of days began again. It also didn't help that it had been rush hour when the whole damned thing had started. And so, as fate would have it, if Alastair was going to get to LAX as quickly as possible, he'd need to take the Green Valley Circle route. And that meant that Harold would be waiting.

The game was simple. Harold tried to jump on Alastair's car as it came to the overpass, and Alastair would try to avoid him. The problem was Alastair didn't know if Harold was going to jump as he entered the overpass or as he left it, nor what angle of fall Harold would select. Worse, after thousands of days, the little shit had gotten very good at timing his jumps. But Alastair had gotten equally good at avoiding them. Of course, there were days when Harold would "cheat," as it were, and wait somewhere on Sepulveda Blvd in order to jump in front of Alastair, but those days were very rare. It required that Harold care enough to leave his perch above the overpass, and most days he didn't. Alastair had only found out later that Harold had come to the overpass with the intention of killing himself, wanting to avoid whatever fate befell the world on that prophesied day. The sad irony was that he'd succeeded. Alastair had made the mistake of laughing when Harold had related the story. He'd laughed at the utter absurdity of it all, not at Harold personally. But it didn't matter because the poor schlub had taken it personally. Harold now seemed to have only one purpose left in life—jump on Alastair's car and mess up his day.

As Alastair pulled back on the emergency brake and spun out of the overpass Harold's body whooshed down and hit the side rear panel, busting out the left tail light.

"See ya tomorrow!" shouted Alastair as Harold's shattered body barrel rolled along the pavement. Of course, Harold couldn't hear him; he was probably already dead or would be as soon as the internal bleeding finished him off, but it was all part of the macabre dance they'd worked out over the span of thousands of such attempts. Alastair glanced at his side-view mirror. The Vette was only slightly damaged. He'd make it to the airport in good time. It was only after he'd made his final right turn onto 96th Street towards LAX that, right on schedule, he saw the baby.

December 21st, 2012
Day 27: 9:30 AM

As his taxi made the final turn onto 96th Street towards LAX, Alastair saw a baby propped up in one of those strollers that looked more combat ready—with its generous aluminum tubing and wide, knobby tires—than baby friendly. But none of that mattered at that moment; it was clear that the child had been abandoned.

"Stop the taxi!" demanded Alastair. The driver, in automaton-like fashion, did as he was told. Alastair leaped out of the cab and approached the wailing child. He unbuckled its straps and, patting it gently on the back, pulled it to his chest. He then grabbed whatever accessories he could from the stroller, including a diaper bag, and returned to the cab. As Alastair pulled a bottle of already-made formula from the bag, he ordered the driver to turn the car around. Within minutes, the baby's screaming had transformed to coos as its belly was filled with sustenance and its body was embraced by warmth. Its gentle gurgling was a marked contrast to what had befallen the world. Alastair used his newly acquired authority with the Federal government to ensure that a social worker appeared daily on the corner of Airport and 96th. The world may have gone to hell in a handbasket, but the child would be well cared for.

The first week of the "Groundhog Effect," as the event was being billed, had been utter pandemonium. Unlike the eponymously named movie where a single man watched the world reboot on a daily basis, this phenomena worked in reverse—everyone was aware. Worse, the world might not have been able to move forward, but oddly enough, everyone's memory could.

There'd been riots and parties and felonies and prayer. Crime had skyrocketed in the first two days and had collapsed to record lows thereafter. What was the point of stealing a large screen television if it was going to be right back where you'd stolen it from the very next morning? What was the point of trying to prevent any crime, really, given the same fact? Even murder had become a mere inconvenience. Rape was still a problem given that its effects were as much mental as physical, but some rather widely reported acts of vengeance had a salutary effect on future would-be rapists.

What impressed Alastair the most, however, was how quickly society had pulled itself back from the brink. The lame duck President and President-elect had met in the White House and issued joint broadcasts. It was decided that on the day that *would have been* January 21st, power would transfer to the President-elect. It would be a bit awkward, as the defeated President would continue to appear in the Oval Office and the newly elected President would continually be waking up in his vacation retreat in Montana, but both parties were dedicated to making it work. Transfer of power needn't, all had decided, mean transfer of location.

Within two weeks, some semblance of order had been restored. Police returned to policing, firefighters returned to their stations, and pretty soon everyone was trying to do their jobs as best they could under the circumstances while the "experts" tried to figure what had happened and how to correct it. String theorists and quantum physicists were suddenly the rage.

Beneath the stratum of calm there still lurked a deep sense of foreboding, and as such, fissures would constantly appear. On the one hand, the supermarkets were always full, electricity would always be on, and the utility companies and the IRS could go screw themselves. On the other hand, that deeper sense of foreboding convinced many that the Groundhog Effect was part of some sort of divine plan—whether as reward, punishment, or purgatory was still being hotly debated. However, in those early days of the day, a great majority of people wanted things to get back to normal, and so it was that Alastair was given a call.

He was surprised he'd even been considered. But then he found out why: Alastair M. Ignacio was a PhD in Meso-American civilization specializing in Mayan culture with an emphasis on religious ritual. So for the past week, his day began with a limo ride to the airport, where he and the other important people would board a special 747 and be flown to Washington, DC. Once there, all the experts would convene, break up into fields of expertise, and propose ideas, no matter how outlandish they seemed. The irony was that his true interest had lain in early Mongolian civilization and he'd only switched to Mesoamerica because he couldn't drive to Mongolia, boats took too long, and he really hated to fly. Now he was flying every day and, but for the greater good, was hating every minute of it.

His relationship with Madeline had necessarily come to a halt. It certainly didn't help that she was half a world away and even on days when a few errant planes bothered to fly to LAX, the three times she'd managed to make it back amounted to her complaining about how horrible it was having no home, no friends, and nowhere to stay but at an airport. Then she'd fallen asleep. A week ago he got the "Dear John" email. She'd decided to catch the flights to the Philippines or Australia. They were shorter and gave her more time to adventure out. Alastair felt sorry for her, imaging what it must be like to wake up every day walking towards a plane that could never really take you home. He'd even felt a few pangs of guilt for having lucked into the luxury of getting to at least wake up in his bed every day, even if naked.

But none of that mattered now. He was part of the Historical Mayan Data Reclamation Team that reported to the head of the Cultural Affairs Department who reported to the Secretary of the Interior who reported to both the present and future President of the United States. He desperately wanted to believe that all these people were going to solve the problem and, hopefully, solve it soon.

December 21st, 2012
Day 182,503: 9:00 AM

Alastair continued to be amazed that the baby carriage was never in a different spot. The law of averages alone should have had someone move it, someone try and help the crying child. The fact that no one had was a sad testament to the malaise that had pervaded every corner of society.

It had gotten to the point where he could hit the brakes and donut perfectly around the waiting carriage. Then, as he'd been doing for more days than sanity would let him contemplate, he'd hop out of the car, disconnect the carrier from the carriage, and quickly retrieve the two items he knew he'd need—the baby sling and fully stocked diaper bag.

"Good morning, Professor," greeted Alastair. "Ready for our plane ride?"

The Professor farted and then began hand tapping against the carrier's edge. The purposeful and articulated taps were either interrupted or emphasized with cries of distress, annoyance, or exuberance.

"Oh, come on," protested Alastair as he strapped the carrier into the front seat, "you can't seriously believe that Gibbons and Einstein had anything in common."

The baby Alastair had named "Professor" was not about to be contradicted. As Alastair hopped back into the driver's seat and sped off, there followed another furious *rat-a-tat-tat* on the carrier's small tray with the occasional exhalations of breath.

Though he was driving at blinding speeds, Alastair shot the baby an unqualified look of disdain. "I will not for a second consider Xian's application of the theory of relativity to the Empire's decline. That was never properly vetted, and by then Xian had gone a little off the pot."

The strange yet passionate discussion continued all the way to a private security gate just astride the tarmac. Alastair input the override code and the gate swung open (too slowly for his liking), which allowed him to drive directly up to the waiting Boeing 787 not two hundred yards away. Still naked (getting dressed would've lost him two extremely precious minutes), Alastair leaped from the car with the professor in the carrier and the diaper bag slung over his shoulder. He then bounded up the stairs into the primed and waiting airplane. As he entered, he was not at all surprised to see the cockpit empty and the plane, with the exception of a single open seat in first class, filled to capacity.

Alastair quickly flung the baby carrier into the co-pilot's seat and strapped the professor in. He then placed a headset on the professor's head and tightened it in place with a stretch of duct tape he pulled from a nearby panel. It wasn't a perfect fit, but then again, it didn't have to be. Communication through gurgling wasn't nearly as effective as tapping *and* gurgling, but it would suffice. On the Professor's non-complaint (too tight a fit would've elicited two short "*dah*" sounds), Alastair took his place in the captain's chair. As his hands began working their magic on the plane's complex control panel, he activated the public address system.

"Hello, passengers." He then looked over to his copilot. "Say hello, Professor."

The baby gurgled happily into the headset.

"As you all know," intoned Alastair, "this plane trip will end rather badly. So all of you who hadn't planned on dying today should leave now." He didn't know why he bothered. He simply could not remember the last time anyone had acted on his words. The passengers of this plane were indicative of the overwhelming majority of the human race. Beyond fear, loss, anger, or any emotion, they just sat like sheep being led to the slaughter. With the experience of long practice, Alastair sealed the doors, taxied to the runway, and gently lifted the beautiful bird off the ground, heading east across the continental United States.

December 21st, 2012
Day 834: 9:15 AM

Alastair had no idea how to fly a plane, but it was getting harder to find pilots willing to come to work. The same held true for the "experts." What had started out as a group numbering well over five hundred had now been reduced to six. He'd witnessed its inevitability hundreds of times. Passion gave way to impatience, which eventually gave way to doubt, which ultimately succumbed to apathy. All of which was why he now found himself sitting in the copilot's seat of a Lear jet about to take off for Washington, calmly listening to the instructions of the captain.

They arrived at Dulles International, where a car was waiting for them on the Tarmac. Alastair had already begun to plan for the day when even that small convenience would be a thing of the past. The I-495 was kept blessedly clear (the army had seen to that), so the limo was able to make the twenty-six-mile trip in just under forty minutes. Alastair was waived through the gates and then dropped off at a secure entrance. They'd dispensed with the Draconian security measures in an effort to save time. He was pointed in the direction of a new, smaller meeting space—no secret as to why. When he stepped through the door, he saw the six experts from Southern California, forty-four from other parts of the country, plus a smattering of government representatives.

The group's designated leader, Professor Marcus Scartallo, acknowledged Alastair with a slight nod and began the meeting. "We've just received word that President Martin is refusing to leave the White House."

"He can't leave; he wakes up here every morning," interrupted one of the experts, a Venezuelan named Bastian.

"Yes, yes," agreed Scartallo. "I meant to say he's refusing to cede power back to Sorenson."

"But Sorenson's been in power for over two years," protested another.

As the conversation degraded into a free-for-all, Scartallo was forced to raise his voice above the din. "It doesn't matter who says they're president! We could report to the ayatollah for all it matters. Even if it's to the 'wrong' president today, we'll end up reporting to the 'right' one tomorrow. The bottom line is that over two years have passed, and the only thing we know for sure is that the cycle repeats when the sun rises over the Yucatan peninsula."

"Or anywhere along that band," added another official wearily. "It could be when the sun rises in Pensacola, Florida, or Chicago, Illinois."

"Logic demands that it's the Yucatan," countered Alastair. "The Mayans told us when it was going to happen."

"The bastards could have told us *what* would happen," groused Sheng Chen, a Chinese particle physicist.

"Maybe they did," suggested Alastair with renewed enthusiasm. "But so many records from that time were destroyed and looted. There are, however, some tantalizing clues."

"Oh, God," protested a theoretical physicist from Cornell University. "Not the glowing artifact theory."

Alastair's mouth tightened through a stiff smile. "It's the only reference there is," he offered. "I'm not putting it forth as a solution or even *the* solution; I'm only restating the facts. A number of the rectangular lumps of plaster, paint chips, and collected shards unearthed at the Mayan archaeological digs in the city of Palenque are shown to have been from their codices, most of which were destroyed by overzealous Spanish priests. One such shard spoke of a glowing disc of crystal held in place by a golden, tri-cornered handle. It supposedly had an inner light that never dimmed or wavered."

"You got all that from some shards?" quipped a voice from down at the end of the table.

"And from some references in a journal made by the reigning priest of the time, Bishop Diego de Landa," offered Alastair.

"The Mayans also wrote that the Sun and Moon were created from twin brothers," added another, to a smattering of laughter.

"Yes, they did," agreed Alastair. "However, other pieces of evidence found in the hieroglyphics of the Temple of Inscriptions at that very same dig seemed to indicate that this disc, or whatever you want to call it, plays a key part in the prophecy of December 21st, 2012."

"And if only we were to find this disc," mused Chen, "the Groundhog Effect would stop?"

Alastair sighed. He didn't need to fly all the way to Washington to be viewed as a lunatic; he could do that easily enough in LA. "I'm not suggesting that at all, Professor Chen. I am merely stating that none of our translations can pin the object itself symbolically to any mythological or astronomical event, as we can for most of the other symbols found on the Mayans' walls or in their writings."

"And the famous Lid of Palenque—didn't it have some kind of astronaut image?" asked the professor from Cornell.

"Yes, but the lid and all its imagery have since been deciphered. It was not an astronaut or any such nonsense, contrary to a number of popular books insisting that it was."

No one said a word, waiting instead on a plausible explanation. Alastair was tempted to deny it to them, but he had to admit that for once, it was nice that they were finally coming around to his area of expertise—and it only took the loss of 450 experts for that occur. He sighed and pressed on.

"It was meant to show the king at that time, King Pacal, falling backwards and into a gateway to the afterlife."

"So, then, this object ..." probed Scartallo, purposely leaving the sentence unfinished.

"Most likely the disc is an actual object as opposed to the representation of an idea." On the group's silence, Alastair continued, "If a reference was made of it on a wall of the largest temple in Palenque—a temple, mind you, built to honor the king—and if references to it were found on other materials at the dig as well as in the journal of the man responsible for the destruction of most of the codices, it means—based on statistical analysis, not crazy theories—that there had to have been a lot more written about it at the time." Alastair now leaned back in his chair and crossed his arms. His eyes moved purposely and slowly, making visual contact with everyone in the room. "Whatever this object is or was, it's clear from the hieroglyphics that it's somehow tied in to the prophesied date. To what end, I have no idea."

"Assuming for a moment this is true," observed Chen, "where would we even begin looking for this thing?"

"I'd start with the Spanish," offered Alastair. "They looted pretty much anything of value."

"Mr. Ignacio." Scartallo's face looked like it had been chipped into an expression of studied impatience. "Are you really suggesting I go to the President," he paused momentarily, "or presidents and propose that A) we believe the Groundhog Effect is somehow related to some broken shards and ancient hieroglyphics, and B) that we'll need to start searching for a mysterious object described in said artifacts whose trail has run cold by a good five hundred years?"

Alastair nodded. "As incredible as all this sounds, what else have we got?"

No one spoke because the answer was already self-evident.

"What else makes sense? We've heard from string theorists, quantum theorists—every scientist worth his salt. No one's come even close to offering a valid explanation. No one except the Mayans. They knew the exact date the shit would hit the fan. Whatever that object they spoke of is, however it is the Mayans came to possess it, matters not one iota to me. What does matter is that it appears to be some sort of key. Call me crazy, but I have to believe it's a cutoff switch."

"What makes you say that?" asked Chen, now quite serious.

"Because of the images surrounding it on the Temple of Inscriptions."

Alastair removed some photographs from his briefcase and slid them across the table. "See that scary-looking figure in the center of the picture—the one surrounded by the wall?"

The heads around the table all nodded in unison.

"He's the son of Gukumatz, a feathered serpent god who, the Mayans believed, together with the god Tepeu, created humanity."

"Why is he separated from the others?" asked a voice from midway down the table.

"Because the other Gods, including his own father, banished him to Xibalba—loosely translated as 'place of fear,' but for our purposes, hell."

"Any particular reason?" asked Scartallo.

"Yes, in fact. He was banished after attempting to upend the world." Alastair paused to let that rather salient detail sink in. "Anyone notice what's keeping him from escaping Xibalba?"

No one said a word as those closest to the photograph puzzled over the details of the picture.

"Besides the great big wall?" asked one of the professors.

"Yes," agreed Alastair. "Look closely at the base of the structure. Where the entry to Xibalba appears to be."

"The glowing disc," whispered the Cornell professor with some reluctance.

"Exactly," agreed Alastair.

The Cornell professor pried her eyes off the image and looked up at the Mayan expert with grudging respect. "Out of morbid curiosity," she asked, "what's the name of this banished deity?"

"Toltex, God of Chaos."

December 21st, 2012
Day 182,503: Midday

As the plane flew on autopilot over the Atlantic, Alastair unstrapped himself and the Professor from their seats and went to take a nap in the first-class compartment. Technically, they didn't need it. Their physical bodies woke up completely refreshed from a good night's sleep no matter what they did. This, at first, was a benefit compared to those who started their cycles on the other side of the world. Those poor bastards would awake in bodies that were physically drained. Of course, most of them simply learned to go to sleep anyway. But the ones who lived in the western hemisphere soon came to realize that though they could drink enough caffeine and far stronger stimulants with no physical effects on their bodies, their minds still needed downtime. If they were going to function, they'd have to find a few hours of sleep in the twenty-four-hour period or risk the madness inherent in experiencing continuous sensory exposure. Of course, given that the alternative was going mad slowly, most didn't end up caring. But for those who wanted to maintain some grip on sanity, sleep was essential, and since it was a long flight to southern Germany, Alastair and the Professor took this opportunity to actually get some.

An alarm went off, indicating that there was one hour left before they were to arrive over their destination. As usual, Alastair slept through the plane's too-sonorous chime, and as usual, the Professor had to scream while thumping on Alastair's chest to get him to wake. Occasionally a passenger in first class would have pity on the crying child and help out by giving Alastair a nudge, but most were so far gone that even the shriek of a baby couldn't compel them to act. At least Alastair no longer flipped onto to his front side while sleeping. Due to the bed's narrow width, he'd twice rolled over and inadvertently suffocated the Professor to death. Each of those times, the aged infant had spent a week trying to pee on the best and only friend it knew. Fortunately, Alastair had been guilt ridden enough to train himself to sleep with his back to the mattress; the Professor nestled comfortably on his chest, wooed to sleep by the steady and assuring beat of a best friend's heart.

The shrieking seemed to work, and Alastair's eyes popped open to the Professor's red, tear-streaked face.

"Sheesh," he exclaimed. "I'm up. I'm up."

Rising from the bed with baby in tow, Alastair made his way to the plane's private bathroom and showered the both of them off, then quickly got them dressed with clothes he'd snagged from a few different carry-ons. With baby firmly under arm, he grabbed an oxygen mask normally used for preflight demonstrations and then made his way to the back of the plane. Once there, he pulled up on the carpet, opened the hatch to the cargo hold, and slipped down, via ladder, into the belly of the plane. He quickly yanked out a duffle he knew to contain a couple of parachutes, goggles, and a large gym bag, which he then proceeded to unzip and stuff with clothes. He placed the Professor into the open bag while he went to grab a small oxygen canister and some duct tape. He returned, smiling broadly at the Professor, and began to jury-rig the goggles, oxygen mask, and canister to the tiny face. It was done expertly and quickly, given the long practice.

As Alastair starting zipping up the gym bag, the Professor gave a peremptory burp. Alastair paused, lips formed into a sardonic grin. "Of course I remembered to turn on the oxygen." He continued zipping the bag, only to be interrupted once again by a sound that was a cross between a happy gurgle and a snort. "Oh, please. That only happened once in how many thousands of days?" This time the Professor's snort had no happy gurgle to it at all. "Okay, twice," conceded Alastair. The baby simply stared at him with a look that managed to combine contempt, disbelief, and affection all at the same time. "Fine. *Three* times, but I can assure you, this is not one of them." The Professor began to make another sound but was interrupted. "Don't tempt me to make it a fourth!" threatened Alastair. The Professor's eyes narrowed, but no more sounds emanated as the bag was zipped shut.

Alastair attached the parachute to his back, the gym bag firmly to his chest, and the goggles around his eyes. He then climbed back up into the passenger section and made his way back to cockpit, where he put the plane into a slow, declining spin that would bring its speed to under 150 knots and get it well below 18,000 feet. It had taken Alastair a little while to both learn and practice how to open a hatch while the plane was in midair, but now he could do it practically blindfolded. As the air rushed out of the plane, he shouted to the apathetic passengers, "*¡Hasta mañana!*" and leaped. He reveled in the fact that after the thousands of jumps he'd already made, it still never got old. After some tricky tucks and rolls to escape the turbulence of the now-distressed airplane, Alastair opened his chute and began his gentle descent. He then unzipped the gym bag wide enough for the Professor to watch as the 787 plummeted headlong into the Earth with an amazing display of pyrotechnics.

December 21st, 2012
Day 2,004: 8:30 AM

Alastair awoke from a restless sleep. He sighed and lifted himself out of bed, then ambled over to his dresser. He then slipped into a pair of comfortable jeans, a sweater, and a pair of Ugg boots. *I need a day off,* he thought to himself as he reviewed the morning's schedule. It was, given the circumstances, rather ironic. He'd do the same thing he'd been doing every day since the beginning of the Groundhog Effect—go to Washington, DC, in order to figure out what the hell was going on. He'd been the only one flying the daily Lear jet from Santa Monica Airport to Washington, DC. And he didn't really count as a passenger since he was the pilot and had been for at least the past fifty days. Alastair wasn't sure why he bothered anymore, being the only one of the twenty left still flying in from abroad.

He also knew there wouldn't be a driver waiting for him this morning. They'd stopped showing up three months ago.

He decided to amuse himself by going over to the Barnes & Noble on the corner of Westwood and Pico Ave. He took his own car, an old but well-maintained Japanese import. The door to the bookstore was locked, of course, so he smashed in the window, knowing no one would mind. This set off the interminable alarm, but he already knew where the cutoff switch was in the manager's office. Ten minutes after breaking in, he decided to leave. The books, the magazines, the newspapers were all the same and always would be. Alastair had slowly come to realize that the joy he usually found in bookstores was in the search for something new by a favorite author, and other than the ethereal serials currently being put out on the net, there'd no longer be any long form. Yes, he could bide his time reading all the store had to offer—even do the same at the libraries, depending on if they'd been burnt down or not, but it wasn't the same. The place brought him down. So he went to the Starbucks next door, found a comfy seat, took out his laptop, and began to surf.

He knew which websites were still current. There'd been an interesting debate at the beginning of the crisis as to whether or not to update the sites with the date it would have been or keep the date static and count up from day one. Eventually the latter convention took hold, if only because everything was so manifestly December 21st, 2012, no matter how much anyone may have tried to pretend otherwise.

There were, of course, no new movies or video games due to their development time. The Victorian concept of the written serial had been revived but with only limited success. It was impossible for new readers to catch up with a story and just as difficult for authors to look back and review what they'd done. And while there had been some rather excellent work in the past two thousand days, notably by established authors with a strong command of their craft, it was cursed to fade away over time due to imperfect memory. The social media sites were, without a doubt, the most successful survivors. True, any new friends or followers a person added during the day would be gone the next, but if that user was fortunate enough to have had decently sized groups of both to begin with, then he at least had a community to go to. And even those who'd never taken the whole format seriously and therefore had few if any established friends or followers online could always glom on to the friends of their friends. It wasn't ideal, but it was manageable. Social media was perhaps the closest thing to randomness the world had at the moment, and as such, the bandwidth strained daily to absorb all the new users who'd pile on, hoping to hear or see something— anything—they hadn't already heard or seen before.

Television was another story altogether. Strangely, the medium everyone assumed would do great—reality TV—tanked within weeks. Reality was harsh enough without audiences having to be reminded of the fact. To the surprise of most was the unparalleled success of the soap opera. The few that had been on found that their format was perfectly suited for a twenty-four-hour turnaround cycle. It needed a little tweaking, but only just. Sadly, most of the soap operas had been canceled by the time 2012 had rolled around, and thus only those shows that had sets and actors ready to roll could make a consistent go of it. The bad news was that a good number of the medium's industry folk had been away on Christmas vacation when the crisis hit. The good news was that the economy had been so bad that most of them had stayed local. Currently, the shows were being maintained out of a sense of communal good. But that, Alastair suspected, would soon change as the cold, hard truth hit Hollywood as it already had the rest of the world—how could someone expect to keep on working when work lost all its meaning?

After less than an hour of bouncing between his social streams, newsfeeds, and a few active sites, Alastair's stomach began to grumble, so he crossed over the street to Junior's Deli. He wasn't surprised to see full, untouched plates of food, half-full glasses of orange juice, and a slew of orders still dangling from clips waiting for a cook who, like everyone else, saw no need to stick around once wakened. The desolateness didn't bother him; he was just glad to see the place still standing. It had gone up in flames more times than he cared to admit. A while back, there'd been a wave of arson that made life rather inconvenient. But even arsonists got discouraged when the buildings they'd continue to burn reappeared the next day, unscathed. The police didn't bother trying to stop it, let alone prosecute the offenders.

Alastair prepared his own breakfast in the kitchen and then sat down in his favorite booth. After two cups of coffee and some time spent reading the latest serialized adventures of Captain Rocket and the Rocket Men on his smart phone, he still felt disquieted. And then, without understanding why, he returned to the kitchen, turned on all the burners, and left, making sure to drop ten dollars on the counter before he walked out the door.

*   *   *

Alastair found himself standing in front of the Los Angeles County Museum of Art. It was only when he traversed the long walkway and entered the main building that he realized what had brought him there. In a museum, nothing was supposed to change, allowing, if only briefly, an illusion of normality. He strode over to the nearest installation, an exhibit on European dress in detail from 1700 to 1915. The displays told a chronological story of fashion's aesthetic and technical development from the Age of Enlightenment to World War I. Alastair got lost in the evolution of techniques, lush trimmings and coruscations sewn into a good deal of the garments. He ogled over an intricately embroidered eighteenth-century vest infused with messages relevant to the French Revolution; a silk-embroidered evening mantle enlivened with glass beads and ostrich feathers; and formal wear worn at the royal courts of Europe. There were others pointing and whispering among themselves. It was almost liberating to be among a group of people who, like him, were simply enjoying the museum and contemplating its serene treasures. Alastair was so engrossed in the feeling that he failed to pay attention to the PA system announcing that the interactive art session would be starting in five minutes. And he would have remained pleasantly engrossed had not all hell broken loose at the stroke of noon.

Children descended on the clothing with knives, scissors, and glue sticks. A quick peek around the corner saw other miniature hordes rushing masterpieces with ladders, finger paint, and crayons. But all had the same idea—manipulate the treasures to whatever designs met their fancy. Men and women got in on the act as well, attacking sculptures with hammers, chisels, and chainsaws. Alastair quickly made his way back to the lobby, where he saw a bunch of large wooden poles being set up into a teepee of sorts as Mondrians, Manets and Bruegels were tossed at its base and ancient manuscripts were torn up and used for kindling. As Alastair hurried out of the building, ten volunteers were eagerly being tied to the poles (in the name of performance art, he supposed). He didn't see but definitely heard the unmistakable *fwump* of a giant flame leaping to life and soon thereafter the horrible screams of those whose flesh had begun to melt from their bones.

He fled the scene as if from a crime and soon arrived at where he'd parked his car. It was gone, presumably stolen—and not for the first time. It would be back in his garage the following day. Very few bothered taking their keys with them when they left their vehicles. Without thinking, Alastair simply went to the next car, got in, and started it up.

And then he drove without thinking. He first headed west and then due south along his old route towards LAX. He had no intention of flying but found a certain comfort in the familiarity of the route. As he turned the car at 96th, he was struck by an awful image—the baby still in its stroller.

December 21st, 2012
Day 182,503: Early morning

Alastair and the Professor always liked this part of the day best. They never knew exactly where the parachute would take them. In the centuries of days they'd been at it, it never ceased to amaze. Today it brought them to a gentle landing in the middle of a town they were quite familiar with. They immediately spotted the motorcycle they knew had a key in its ignition. Moments later, they were on their way along the pebble-strewn road towards the village of Unterwellshaft.

Upon their arrival, and after a careful comparison of their mental notes, they began digging once again, only this time in a different spot—the back yard of one Matilda Grechtenspeil. Ms. Grechtenspeil was a person of no importance to Alastair or the Professor. As far as they knew, she'd been of no importance to anyone, for that matter—before or after the event. But they were digging up her backyard nonetheless. To be fair, they were digging up everyone's backyard that fell within a forty-square-mile radius of a salt mine in Bavaria. Even though they'd been at it for tens of thousands of days, they were, by their calculations at least, only one third of the way through. It no longer bothered them that they may not find the object of their search. There were plenty of other parts of the world to dig up, and it wasn't as if they lacked for time.

December 21ˢᵗ, 2012
Day 5,735

It seemed to Alastair that the days of Armageddon were finally on the wane. And thank goodness for that! But when the missiles were falling, he much preferred being in the primary strike zone. There'd be a giant flash, maybe even a scream if he had the time, and the next thing he knew, he was back in bed, waking up naked, then running down the stairs to pick up his now-teenaged, fifteen-and-a-half-year-old baby. But there were also days when the missiles were not always accurate and he'd only be *near* the impact zone. Those days, fortunately few and far between, were horrendous. He'd spend them in excruciating pain, skin half melted off a burnt and blistered body, counting the minutes until the sun rose over the Yucatan. If he was really lucky, he'd still be ambulatory and able to break into a local pharmacy to get some pain meds. But on those days he'd have to fight with hundreds of other "lucky" locals for what few meds could be found amongst the rubble. It wasn't ever pretty. Sometimes he just stayed home in the wreckage and practiced his Zen meditation. He'd think about the Professor and hope the kid was bearing it well. Alastair had done the best he could, raising the child under what could arguably be called the worst of conditions. There was obvious love between the two, and as they both got older and wiser, mutual admiration as well.

The Armageddon days were bad enough. That they'd coincided with the rise of The Brotherhood of the Damned had made them worse. To Alastair, the cult sounded like some stupid, melodramatic vampire wannabe club. But the group's influence had spread quickly because they claimed to have what everyone so desperately needed—certainty. As far as the Brotherhood was concerned, the world had been judged and found wanting. The only thing the human race could do was accept the divine punishment. When everyone simply accepted their fate, the Brotherhood's dogma stated, perhaps after another couple of thousand years of days, mercy would be shown and all would finally—*finally*—be allowed to die.

There were, in Alastair's estimation, plenty of reasons to dislike this new phenomenon. Forgetting their cliché name and laughably predictable wardrobe, they were also downright cruel. So much so that they'd insisted Alastair abandon the baby to its fate and not try to help when it cried out, spouting some such nonsense about thwarting the will of the Lord. In time, Alastair grew to hate them because they'd not only made the loss of hope a part of their dogma, they'd also insisted on believing in a creator who could fathom such cruelty as a basis for belief.

The only thing Alastair and the Brotherhood had managed to agree upon was that the days of Armageddon were not only horrible but pointless. Initially, heroic efforts had been made to prevent the missiles from launching. But after a couple of hundred days, even the heroes succumbed to depravity and instead of preventing the reign of terror had actively participated in it. At its height, the crews responsible for the Days of Armageddon had somehow conspired to create a veritable cocktail of planet-ending destruction, at one point launching nuclear, biological, and chemical weapons simultaneously. It had, of course, destroyed all life on Earth and possibly sea down to the cellular level. That level of complete and utter destruction had been maintained for an entire week until it slackened. Even wholesale genocide didn't matter when it didn't stick.

For Alastair and the Professor, that almost daily and complete eradication of life on Earth was only a minor inconvenience—and not even too painful at that. The better the Armageddon crew got at destroying the place, the quicker everyone would die—and hallelujah for that. It was the amateurs they really feared.

With the days of Armageddon on the wane, the duo's efforts not only picked up speed, they actually bore fruit. Alastair's research was beginning to yield some tantalizing clues, including evidence in a will of an item vaguely matching the Toltex key. Then came their Eureka moment: finding a near-perfect description of the object in the records of a Victorian auction. That had been during their London days. The Professor had truly loved going on the huge Ferris wheel and had once been lucky enough to witness the city's nuclear annihilation from its apex.

December 21st, 2012
Day 182,503

Village of Unterwellshaft, Southern Germany

Whereas anyone else would see a backyard with a single hole dug out, Alastair and the Professor had no difficulty seeing all the holes that had been dug over the years. That was the level of concentration required when the task at hand required digging up a country one section at a time. Memory got necessarily sharper when nothing could be recorded. The downside to that level of attentiveness was myopia. Alastair had become far more interested in particular plots of land than he was in any machinations of the world. But the Professor, having suffered the trauma of early childhood abandonment, not to mention any number of accidental and intentional deaths, had never been quite so trusting. Alastair, the Professor reckoned, was truly the one who needed looking after. So it took a couple of exclamations and a sippy cup bouncing off Alastair's thick skull before he became aware that the Professor was trying to get his attention.

"Watched?" exclaimed Alastair, leaning heavily on the shovel. "By whom?"

The Professor sighed and spit up.

"Right. Stupid question."

After a long series of taps, gurgles, and complex facial expressions, it was decided that a direct course of action would be prudent.

Alastair climbed out of the hole, dusted himself off, and shouted into the bitterly cold Bavarian day. "I know you're out there. We can play this any way you like. It's not as if we don't have the time. But if I'm worth watching, I'm also worth talking to. You're going to eventually, so can we please just get this over with? I'd really like to get back to work." The Professor gurgled in agreement and then farted for good measure.

An audible sigh was heard from the next yard over. A figure slowly emerged through the brush amidst a crackling of branches and paused at the edge of the yard. Alastair eyed the intruder with equal parts annoyance and admiration. "I haven't seen any of your type in … well, forever."

The intruder remained still.

"Well, come on," chided Alastair, "let's have a look at you."

The figure stepped hesitantly forward, dragging the long black robes of a mostly forgotten sect, then reached up and slowly drew back the hood, revealing the face of a young woman. She had exquisitely shaped—dark brown eyes, a tussle of wavy, shoulder-length black hair, and an awkward smile framing a perfect set of teeth that couldn't help but glow against the cascade of dark hues.

The Professor, now staring intently at the woman, tapped methodically and then let out a few hiccups.

"Yes, she is," affirmed Alastair, "though I'm not sure if after hundreds of thousands of days the word *ex* even applies." He then returned his suspicious gaze to the woman.

"Hello, Alastair," greeted a hauntingly familiar voice.

"Hello, Madeline."

December 21st, 2012
Day 10,000

The Kremlin, Russia

Getting into the office of the Premier of the Russian Federated Republic had not proven difficult. Alastair simply had to use the palm print of a high-ranking security official. That he'd got the palm print by cutting off the hand of the official was not even the strangest part of the endeavor. That the official had guffawed at the request, gotten drunk, and handed Alastair an ax was.

Alastair would have arrived at the office sooner but had gotten waylaid by his duties as an educator. The baby was now mentally twenty-seven years of age and wished to pursue a professorship to go along with the moniker Alastair had chosen years earlier. They were trying to decide what would be most suitable: particle physics or Elizabethan poetry. Also, there were the couple of hundred days it took them to learn passable Russian.

But now it was finally paying off. They'd managed to track the mysterious disc from the Victorian era auction sale to a secret buyer in France. They'd then spent thousands of days scouring that country's museums, government offices, auction houses, registries, and wills for anything that might indicate who or where the buyer may have resided. And then they had a breakthrough. The item, it turned out, had at one time been in the possession of the Rothschild family, wealthy bankers whose influence and connections had been well established throughout Europe. That connection had led them to the Nazis, who, during the Second World War, had pilfered anything of value they could get their hands on, which had led them to the Soviets, who in victory had looted the looters, which had led them to the Kremlin.

Once inside the office of the Premier of the Russian Federated Republic, Alastair and the Professor made quick work of the computer—a task made easier by having received the secret access codes from the recent amputee. It didn't take long for them to find what they were looking for. With a shout of triumph, Alastair leapt from the desk and started dancing around the office while throwing a happily gurgling baby up into the air.

The merriment was interrupted by a quiet cough that emanated from the corner of the room. Alastair was so startled that in looking toward the source of the noise, the baby slipped through his hands and tumbled onto the floor. Fortunately, it was heavily carpeted and the Professor—based on the expectorations—was far more annoyed than hurt.

"Oh, damn," groused Alastair, picking up the infant while eyeing the telltale robes of the unexpected visitor, "not another one of you guys."

"Not *one* of the guys," intoned the man in a voice laced with weariness, "*the* guy. Father of the Brotherhood, actually."

The Professor's hands slapped against a slightly bruised forehead.

"The baby says," translated Alastair, "'Oh, absolutely. If we're going to be bothered, it may as well be from the top of the heap.'"

The baby slapped its thigh and then put finger to mouth, spitting out its own version of a Bronx cheer. Alastair frowned. "Now, watch your spelling and don't be rude. He is not frothing at the mouth and yelling at us to accept damnation like the last one."

A hodgepodge of taps and gurgles followed the translation.

Alastair nodded, smiling gamely. "That's true; he isn't trying to light us on fire like the last one either. She *did* have a temper." Alastair then looked over to the robed gentleman. "You're not going light us on fire, are you?"

The man's mouth formed itself into a terse but comforting grin. He shook his head in the negative.

"Blow us up?"

The man shook his head once more.

"Push us out the window?"

The baby gurgled and spit in staccato.

"Oh, I forgot," added Alastair, "I hope no acid. The acid was quite annoying."

The baby farted.

"Sorry. *Really* annoying."

"No. No acid, Mr. Ignacio," assured the man. "No explosions, gunshots, stabs, or heavy objects falling on your heads. I'm here to tell you and your companion that the Brotherhood of the Damned shall henceforth leave you completely alone."

Alastair's brow rose slightly. The baby rubbed its eyes.

"Well, that's rather civilized of you. Why the change?"

"Because, Mr. Ignacio," answered the old man, looking around the room as if sizing up a brothel, "none of this matters—

none of it at all. We're all damned, and our only hope of escaping this damnation is for every single human being in limbo to accept it. But acceptance can't be forced. We've experienced almost three decades of days, and most of the human race now realizes our doom." He spent a moment studying Alastair and shook his head. "But you, sir, do not. You are still striving. You're not the only one still trying to live, to accomplish, to hope, but you are one of the last. So we'll watch and maybe even talk to you."

"What on Earth for?" challenged Alastair, now genuinely puzzled. The baby burped its agreement.

"Because when you begin to feel the edge of despair, we'll be there to guide you."

Alastair's brow furrowed. "To despair."

"Yes. When every human admits their plight, maybe, just maybe, God will relent and let us die."

Alastair guffawed. "You're waiting for me to despair so we can die?"

The old man nodded grimly. "Your actions, your *hope*, is keeping us from God's merciful death."

"You have no proof. How can you despair with no proof?"

The monk looked at Alastair as he would a wounded animal. "We've had ten thousand days of proof. What more proof can you demand?"

"Ten thousand days of a temporal phenomenon is not proof that God, if there is a God, hates us, loves us, or even cares if we exist."

"And has that electronic distraction," snickered the Brother, eyes staring reprovingly at the PC, "told you where to find your Mayan magic?"

"Nope."

"Then why were you jumping for joy?"

"Because it told me it's not in Russia. And that includes the former Soviet Union."

"And for this you find hope?" The man's face had contorted into a ball of confusion.

"Absolutely. I was afraid we were going to have to search the largest country on Earth one square foot at a time. We would have done it, mind you, but at least now we don't need to. We just have to search Germany one square foot at a time."

The baby grinded its teeth and tapped.

"Of course we're going to learn German. What would be the use of going to Germany if we didn't learn German?"

The baby gurgled, tapped, and then began cooing.

"Yes, yes, we'll start with Sesame Street. Don't we always?"

The head of the Brotherhood of the Damned watched the spectacle of the adult and infant unfold, shook his head sadly, and left the room completely unnoticed.

He, after all, was contemplating the larger questions of life while they seemed content to argue over whether or not taking cookies away from the Cookie Monster had been the true portent of the downfall of man.

December 21st, 2012
Day 182,503

"Can we go into the house?" pleaded Madeline. "These robes are not as warm as you might think."

Alastair shot her a quizzical look and then continued his digging. "How many days have you been following us?"

Madeline paused, a look of abject confusion on her face. Questions as to lengths of time had necessarily changed with the crisis. Reasons were far and few as to why someone would even bother to keep track, much less be asked—Madeline being no exception. After a minute of murmuring to herself, brows undulating along her forehead's ridgeline, she answered.

"About twenty thousand days, give or take a few thousand."

Alastair and the Professor looked at each other, then burst into a fit of laughter.

Madeline clenched her teeth, waiting for their teasing to subside. But their paroxysms of laughter only brought about more.

"Oh, will you two just shove it?!" she finally bellowed at the top of her lungs. The shrill of her voice seemed to do the trick, and Alastair and the Professor caught their breath in small measured gasps as they wiped the tears from their eyes.

"Come off it, Madeline," insisted Alastair. "Twenty thousand's a pretty big number." They started to laugh again, much to Madeline's consternation.

"I'm sorry," continued Alastair, "but look at it from our point of view. That's a really long time to be following us—especially all the way from Taiwan. Whatcha flyin', by the way?"

"Jets, though I started with airliners," she explained. "The Brotherhood decided that by crashing the planes, I was sparing the passengers hours a day of purgatory that could be viewed as a sublimation of God's will. So I learned how to fly jets—fighters, actually. Even with landing to refuel, getting here was much quicker."

A half smile formed on Alastair's smudged face. "So let me get this straight—in order to keep us under observation, you learned how to fly a modern jet fighter?"

She nodded.

"You then learned how to refuel it at various locations around the world?"

She nodded again.

"And how many additional languages did it take to facilitate this?"

"Three, but they were relatively easy ones to master."

Alastair tilted his head sideways. "And you managed to track us to the same area of Germany night after night."

"Obviously," she agreed, annoyance creeping into her voice. "What's your point, Alastair? Honestly, sometimes you can be so damned childish!"

"Agreed. I guess what I really find amusing is that in all those days and with all those skills, you never once bothered to pick up a warmer coat. And just in case you hadn't noticed—" He took a moment to purposely survey their surroundings. "—we're in *Bavaria* in *December*, for God's sake!"

"It is for God's sake that I don't," she countered, voice rising to a fever pitch. "It would be against his will."

"To stay warm?" he asked with obvious derision. "Who sold you *that* load of crap?"

The baby tapped and then slapped its ruddy face.

"Right, right, the Brotherhood." And then Alastair climbed back into the hole and went back to digging.

"Could we *please* go inside?" repeated Madeline.

The Professor banged a complex series of taps onto the side of the carrier.

"Oooh, good one!" agreed Alastair, stopping his digging. "We'd like to know: Isn't asking us to go inside the same thing as picking up a jacket, which is against the wishes of your God, the on-high punisher-in-chief?"

Madeline sighed. "Yes, it is. Not quite as bad as picking up a jacket, but very close. You inspire bad habits in those around you."

"Excellent," Alastair chirped happily, and got back to digging.

After another fifteen minutes of shivering in the cold, Madeline braved another sentence. "You know you're the last one, don't you?"

"The last one what?" asked Alastair without losing the shovel's rhythmic stride.

"The last one on Earth resisting the will of God. The last one who cares!"

The Professor spat, tapped, and slapped at the sides of the carrier.

"The Professor says, 'What am I, chopped liver?'"

Madeline didn't dignify the baby with an answer. Alastair once again stopped his digging and looked up at her from the hole. "It's a fair question, Madeline. What about the Professor here?"

"Without you, that child would sink into hopeless despair."

"I don't think so …" he began, but was interrupted by the rapid patter of the Professor. "Really, you would? I don't believe it."

The baby rolled its eyes.

"Believe it," said Madeline, breaking into his conversation. "You're the last man keeping the blessings of oblivion from the human race. Even the Brotherhood is gone."

"Really? The entire Brotherhood of the Damned, even that decent fellow who didn't light us on fire?"

"Yes, even him," she averred. "As each of the hopefuls gave up and went into despair, their Minders—"

"Minders?"

"What those of us who were assigned to the hopefuls were called. We watch and wait till they despair and guide them to acceptance."

"And what exactly do these minders do when they've finished guiding some poor sap to despair?"

"Fully embrace their own despair or find others to guide. I myself," she added with obvious pride, "led four souls from the false path of hope unto the path of damnation. Then," she groused, having fixed an impertinent gaze at her ex, "I was assigned you. The Brotherhood is gone. The rest of the human race is finished but you. You just ... won't ... give ... up! Why?" she demanded.

"I can't, Madeline."

"You mean you *won't*."

Alastair shrugged. "Same difference. I will find that disc. It's the first piece needed to free the human race from this mistake. I believe that with all my heart."

"Find the Mayan disc," she repeated softly. Then repeated it again only this time in unexpurgated rage. "Find the Mayan Disc! Fuck the Mayan Disc, Alastair! It doesn't exist. You've searched all over the world for millennia after millennia of days. You've been digging up this one section of Germany for centuries of days, and what have you found? Nothing!" She fell to the ground on her knees. "Don't you see? I can't stop till you give up. I can't enter *my* final despair until you accept yours!"

"Guess you'll be waiting a long time, then."

Madeline lifted her head slowly and met her ex-boyfriend's penetrating eyes.

He sighed and looked momentarily at his ex with a tenderness he supposed she hated. "I know that I'll find it. It may be with the next shovelful of dirt. It may be in thousand upon a thousand years of days, but it *will* happen. You have a faith in God, Madeline. Well, I guess I do as well—just not in yours. I cannot believe in a god that would put us in a trap without some way out. I'd never have thought I'd be the sort of guy to keep at it, but I guess I am."

Madeline remained silent for some time. All that could be heard was the steady crunch of Alastair's shovel hitting hard dirt and clumps of rock and sand being tossed onto frozen soil.

"I can't do this anymore," she finally murmured. "If you don't despair before I do, I will have failed."

"Then," he said, elbow resting on the tip of his shovel, "you've failed."

But Madeline was no longer listening. She huddled into her robes, clutching her knees tightly to her chest, rocking back and forth. She began to mumble some sort of incantation.

Alastair paused just long enough to look upon her with pity, saw that the Professor concurred, and then went back to work. He drove the shovel back into the ground. But this time it did not sink into the earth. Instead it clanged against something very solid and very metal. Alastair paused in utter shock as the Professor gurgled joyfully. Madeline slowly looked up, her tear-streaked face unable to hide the confused but obvious curiosity etched into every pore of her skin.

"I really, really hate you."

Epilogue

December 21st, 2012
The Last Day

Madeline agreed to fly to Germany, retrieve the disc, and fly it to the Yucatan. Her faith in the Brotherhood had shattered when they'd pulled the ancient artifact from the SS storage box found in the backyard of the young sturbanfurher's parents. The sturbanfurher, records would show, had died on the last day of the war and had obviously told no one about the treasure he'd buried to help offset his future. Madeline didn't care about the details the Professor found so compelling. She did care that her ex-boyfriend had been right, that he was obviously fulfilling the true will of God, who in his infinite and cruel wisdom had gifted the son of bitch with the knowledge to see and the faith to persevere. So she'd agreed to join their team. Every night for a week she'd flown to Bavaria and then to the Yucatan.

Alastair and the Professor met her in Mérida, the capital of the province. In the few hours remaining in the day, they'd fly their appropriated helicopter to the ancient city of Palenque. When they stood atop the Temple of Inscriptions and looked up at the night sky through the Mayan disc, they could see a band of energy crossing its length. The next day, they used a helicopter to rise even higher above the temple. As Alastair suspected, at a certain height it became clear that the band was part of a vast pentagon fifty miles on a side with the Temple of Inscriptions at its center. But Alastair also knew that according to the inscriptions, the disc would need to be placed, like Toltex himself, outside of the center. While Alastair may not have believed in the story itself, he did believe its narrative was a clue as to where the disc should be returned. The only obvious course of action, then, would be to visit each point of the pentagon to see what they would find. At first it was nothing—just acres of thick foliage and large outcroppings of rock. They stood at the first site, scratching their heads, wondering what they'd missed. It took them another week to figure out that the mountain they were standing on was in fact a pyramid—built underground. The disc had led them to the location, but it hadn't told them how to get in. Alastair knew that the Mayans almost always built their cities and temples using astronomy based on an east-to-west alignment, with the major temples forming a perfect isosceles triangle. The Pentagon formation revealed by the disc was a new paradigm but not undecipherable. All Alastair needed to do was figure out what the night sky looked like at the time of the building's existence and then triangulate where, based on that previous night's sky, the entrance would be. With some concerted excavation and spot-on triangulation, they finally found it.

"Movin' on," was the lone phrase Alastair uttered once the hieroglyphic inscriptions around the first temple's entrance were properly excavated.

Madeline stood her ground, hands bunched into fists. "We're not even going in?" she exclaimed. Though she'd already lived tens of thousands of days, the idea of being so close to an answer and then having it summarily yanked away simply got the best of her.

"No point," stated Alastair. "The inscriptions on this doorway don't lie. The only reason to enter now would be to sightsee."

Flustered but conceding the point, Madeline picked up her rucksack and equipment and began marching in the direction of the chopper. "Well, come on," she called after Alastair and the Professor. And then she added with relish, "Time's a-wasting!"

Twenty-one days passed before they finally hit paydirt. Alastair pulled the page from his back pocket and held it up to the inscription on the pyramid's arch. It was Toltex, all right, in all the irascible god's chaotic glory. With a supremely satisfied grin, he folded up the paper and put it back into his pocket.

Madeline studied the hieroglyphics with keen interest. "What do you think *really* happened here?"

"I'm not sure we'll ever know," conceded Alastair. "I mean, we understand the basics. That somehow the Mayans had access to this kickass technology." He patted the bag containing the disc for effect. "Who gave it to them and why, I haven't the foggiest. But they were clearly trying to hide it. I'm guessing the Spaniards got to this temple before it could be fully buried."

The Professor gave a rapid tap on the side of the carrier, followed by slight thump on the chest.

"I agree with the Professor," said Madeline. "What good is kickass technology if it can't be used to repel an invading hoard?"

Both Alastair and the Professor shot her a look of abject surprise.

"Don't be daft," she snorted. "It's not like I wasn't going figure your *super*-secret language eventually. For goodness' sake, it's nothing more than a fancy Morse code with a healthy dose of spittle, burps, and flatulence. It's not like fucking Chinese. Try learning that tonal bastard of a language one day at a time."

"Well," offered Alastair with newfound respect, "It's a good question. I can only hazard a guess and say the technology was used to bring some measure of order to society or perhaps even safeguard against some future disaster. Seemed to work wonders in the Maya's case. At least for a while."

Madeline nodded but said nothing. She was clearly more anxious to step into the pyramid and see what the devil it was that had so upended their universe than get a reasoned answer from an expert on all things Mayan. She was waiting for Alastair to lead them in, but he seemed to be hesitating. In fact, he wasn't moving at all.

"Listen," he finally offered. His voice had grown more serious, and the change in its timbre had raised the eyebrows of both the Professor and Madeline. "The sun will be rising in forty-five minutes. We now know that the second the first rays hit the top of *this* pyramid, the day resets. So I really do need to get going."

"Don't you mean that *we* need to get going?" balked Madeline as the Professor gurgled in agreement.

Alastair shook his head. "The inscription is clear—one person per ticket. Either of you willing to mess with the scariest user's manual in the universe?"

Neither of them said a word.

"Besides," added Alastair, looking pointedly at Madeline, "what do you know about Mayan culture, language, and architecture?"

"Hardly a thing," she admitted, "but give me fifteen or twenty years, and I'll give you a run for your money. In the grand scheme of things, waiting a few more decades won't matter that much."

The Professor squawked and raised a pudgy fist into the air.

"Good point," agreed Madeline, eyes fixed on Alastair. "You *are* too important to risk." At this, the Professor both cried and tapped an emphatic agreement.

Alastair's eyes widened as a slight smile formed on his lips. "We all know I have to be the one to go in. If there is a God, then you've got to admit I'm the *only* one that should be doing this."

Madeline looked about to argue but quickly deflated. The Professor, however, was quite spirited in banging away. It was only after the fart that Alastair was able to get a word in edgewise.

"Yes, Professor, I know that you're an atheist and *almost* as knowledgeable as me on the subject, but we must also acknowledge that you occupy the body of an infant. And bodies count here." The Professor, too, deflated.

"Look," insisted Alastair, "I'm going in. If all goes well, the sun will rise, and this godforsaken day will finally be over. You'll stay right here, I'll come out, and we'll all go into this brand-new day together. If it doesn't work, which between you and me seems to be the most likely scenario, we'll reset and meet back here tonight."

The Professor banged, spit, and tapped out a veritable symphony.

"Your friend is correct, Alastair. The world could finally escape the time loop, but you could remain trapped inside. If things do return to normal, do you have any idea what kind of chaos will follow?"

Alastair said nothing.

"I do," offered Madeline. "Total collapse. We'd need your leadership, Alastair. You've led us this far; how could you not lead us further?"

"And what happens if we wait?" challenged Alastair.

"We can warn people. Get them ready for the resumption."

"Who will listen, Madeline? Who would even care? The rest of the world is too far gone. The only chance some of them have for breaking out of this cycle is to *break out of this cycle*. I don't see how adding a couple of years to the nightmare will help." Alastair's face grew more rigid. "It's time to end this."

"I wasn't really tired that first night, you know," spurted Madeline.

"Excuse me?"

"I said I wasn't really tired that first night. That long, long ago night. I told you I was tired after you picked me up at the airport. I wasn't. I … I was cheating on you."

Alastair's head tilted slightly as he watched Madeline intently.

"He showed up maybe ten minutes after you left. I thought you should know." Madeline watched Alastair's mannerisms closely but saw in them not so much surprise as curiosity. And then it hit her.

"You already knew," she accused. "How? I never told *anyone*."

"Well, you're forgetting the guy you slept with," offered Alastair. "He was there too."

"You … you met him?" gasped Madeline, suddenly laughing at the absurdity of it all.

"Oh, gods, yes; early on, actually. In the first three or four thousand days. Nice guy, really."

The night was slowly receding, giving way to the encroaching light on the horizon. There was no more fight left in any of them, and they all knew what had to be done—more important, who'd been called upon to do it. Alastair gave each of them a hug, looked into their eyes and said nothing. With a smile and a nod he took out the Mayan disc and walked slowly forward into the narrow passageway, its shimmering light playing on the walls, revealing in snippets the story of a god run amuck and a world gone mad.

* * *

All Madeline and the Professor could do was wait, Madeline standing and the Professor in the baby carrier facing toward the opening. Slowly, the jungle grew lighter, and in the elision of dusk to dawn, it was almost as if one had struggled for dominance over the other rather than naturally faded away. Madeline had set her cell phone to go off at exactly the moment the new day would arrive, never once believing she'd actually get to hear it. However, the jungle answered to its own rhythm and exploded in a cacophony of sound concomitant with Madeline's alarm suddenly shrieking to life. With her heart racing, she looked down. An ecstatic scream escaped from her trembling lips as she picked up the professor's carrier and began spinning with it in joyous circles.

"It's here! It's here!" she whooped. "We're still here! It's … it's tomorrow!"

The professor tapped in ferocious bursts of joy.

"Yes," gushed Madeline, "you're going to grow! You're going to grow! What?" she asked as the baby tapped out something she'd never heard before. At the realization of the phrase, she broke into a hysterical fit of laughter. "Screw you! Blue Fairy, indeed!"

It was only after the sun of a brand-new day was shining on their faces and they'd collapsed into utter exhaustion on the jungle floor that they realized Alastair M. Ignacio was nowhere to be found.

An End

CONFESSIONS OF A VAMPIRE KNIGHT IN THE ZOMBIE WARS

First things first—no matter how much you wish to applaud my actions, know this, my precious plasmaccinos—I didn't do it for you. In fact, I don't get why you humans feel the need to anthropomorphize your monsters. Hell, I've *never* understood it, even when I *was* human. Don't get me wrong here; I'm not complaining. If you'd treated us with the same calculation and cruel efficiency as we've always treated you, I sincerely doubt whether I'd have survived even this long—no vampire or werewolf would've. Not that any werewolves made it out of the Zombie wars. Good riddance. Fucking furballs. And even if one of those throat-ripping howlers *had* managed to survive, you probably would've found a way to make it cuddly. Think I'm kidding? Well, when the pitiful few of you who have made it manage to spare a moment from bare survival to look through the records of the old days, you tell me if I'm wrong. Almost all your villains get turned into heroes, whether it's Darth Vader or Captain Barbossa (loved the movie, but trust me—it was nothing like that). Even your real-life villains, like the terrorists you spent as much time trying to understand as fight, you turn into T-shirts.

Che Guevara? Are you fucking kidding me? That monster shed more blood than even me (and that's saying a lot). Get this straight: those maniacs were never trying to understand *you*; they were trying to *kill you*.

But *vampires*—my God, we make you all wet and stupid. And in turn, you somehow find a way to make us … make *me* seem noble. Fuck that. I may have acted in a way that *seemed* heroic, but it was only because I had no choice. It wasn't heroism, blood bags—it was hunger. I *had* to save you.

I suppose I should start at the beginning, which for me means Glasgow, Scotland, late in the winter of 1616. I won't bore you with the details, but it's sufficient to say that I'd gleefully spent a good four-plus centuries drinking, draining, and fucking to my heart's content. In all that time I'd never made any human into a vampire (contrary to your misguided belief that we vampires choose the "special" among you—point of fact, it's largely due to randomness or, more often than not, carelessness). And I haven't exactly been "up" for all that time—too dangerous. A guy like me can leave a bloody trail no matter how careful I am. So I disappear, or, more to the point, do what we vampires like to call "going to ground." It's not that hard. You just have to bury yourself for twenty-five or so years, and by the time you re-emerge, the intervening years have will erased your past. That tactic worked great for hundreds of years, or at least it *did*—before the goddamned information age. Though I went to ground in the late 90s, the problem was that any trace I'd left behind wouldn't disappear. It would be input, cold-cased, obsessed about, blogged about, and conspiracy-theorized about ad infinitum! It wouldn't go away in twenty-five years; it wouldn't go away in a hundred! My only ace in the hole was numbers: yours. The population of the Earth had greatly increased, and I was never greedy enough to make a dent in the neighborhoods in which I hunted. I could get by on a body a week and always made damn sure to pick a loser—and let me just say, you humans have 'em in droves. You're practically a Wal-Mart of 'em. Lonely and desperate—aisle fucking four.

So what went wrong (besides the obvious)? I can laugh at the stupidity of it now, but it comes down to a very "human" condition (yeah, there's still a little bit of it left—even in monsters like me). And before you get any fanciful notions, no, it wasn't an intrepid vampire hunter whose loved one I'd drained (losers rarely inspire vengeful retribution). Nor was it for the love of a woman whose humanity I valiantly chose to protect from my 'curse' (I've already told you that you're food, and rule number one for us vampires: don't fall in love with food). And screwing doesn't count (see "human condition" above). In fact, the whole sex thing is a bit too much like bestiality for my taste. Vampires are, and have always been, seekers of the extreme, sex being no exception. No, the real reason I went to ground when I should have stuck it out was simple: I was bored—bored out of my skull. You try doing the same thing night after night for four fucking centuries and see how "engaged" you stay. (Hell, I should probably thank the zombies for giving my boredom a dose of some serious whoop-ass.)

But boredom drove me under, and the desire to challenge myself to the twenty-first century's brave new world woke me up—networked computers and multiple ID checks notwithstanding. I had to struggle all right, but it wasn't with no computer networks. Goddamn zombies.

It could've been worse. If I'd woken up even one year later, I doubt there would've been a human left for me to feed on (outside of those hiding in bunkers—most of whom didn't make it. And even then ... they were mostly filled with "important" people, i.e.: either old, Caucasian, or both). "Beggars can't be choosers," you say? Well, yeah ... sure. If the world was my oyster and I had billions of you to choose from. I didn't. I woke up to hell. Worse—I woke up hungry.

You might find New York's famed Cloisters museum a funny place for a vampire to sack out for a number of decades, but if you think about it, the decision makes sense. The venerable museum is separated from the city by its high elevation on four acres of protected land, the Medieval French quadrangles are enclosed by a vaulted passageway, and there's a culturally imposed austerity so severe that even the sound of a hardened heel echoing off the pristine stone floors bring the finest of the city's upturned noses whipping around towards you like the guns of an English man-o'-war. And the pièce de résistance—within the museum there's a small, separated room that contains two limestone coffins, one with an effigy gisant of Jean d'Alluye, a French knight of the thirteenth century. Though it would've made more sense to bury myself in the ground, I just couldn't—the carved figure on top of the coffin depicts our brave knight, hands pressed together in prayer, epitomizing his credo of piety, loyalty, and honor. Such delicious irony proved impossible to resist. Another plus of the location: in the event of nuclear strike, I was fairly certain that my crypt would've remained intact. There's a reason the limestone churches and forts of the twelfth and thirteenth centuries are still in existence today—limestone is one tough mother. And finally, fast food. I knew that when I awoke I'd be absolutely famished and New York City would have millions of late-night snacks just waiting for me to sink my teeth into.

But then I did awake. And Jesus, had things gone truly, horribly awry. Normally my craving lets me know where the fresh blood is. Point of fact, I can smell a human (if I'm hungry enough) two miles away. But there was *no* scent; there were *no* humans—not for a hundred miles (but I didn't know that yet). I shifted the heavy stone lid off the crypt and was rewarded to the (at first limited) sight and sound of tens of bodies shambling about the room. The first thought that came to mind was in the form of a question: *How hadn't I smelled them?* The second thought was that now, regrettably, I had. There was, about the creatures, the fetid stench of rotting flesh. Understand that in my centuries of living I'd seen any number of werewolves and I'm pretty sure I got my ass kicked by what must have been a witch. But zombies? Never. They were a myth—at least in vampire lore, and trust me on this, our lore goes *way* back. I was so crazed with hunger I even tried to drain one.

If I live for another thousand years, I will *never* do that again. It was like trying to suck curdled milk through the straw of a juice box. I didn't think it possible for a vampire—especially one deprived of food for over thirty years—to vomit, but damn if I didn't give it my all. Worse still was that first night's interminable search through the empty streets of New York City. There was not a single light, fire, or candle burning anywhere. A full moon bathed the city's sea of paned glass and stone in its unearthly glow, and the lifeless skyscrapers cast the blackest shadows imaginable. At that point I would've drained anything—rat, dog, cat, you name it. Even cow worked well if given no other choice. I'll admit that draining bovine was a lot like eating unseasoned tofu (for a human), but it always sufficed in a pinch. And dear God, did I suddenly find myself in one—for there was nothing living to be had. The monsters had devoured the humans first and then turned to anything living they could catch. Given time and numbers, both of which they had in droves, those bastards damn near caught everything.

All I knew was that for the first time in my existence, I woke and *could not feed*. I was driven by the sun into the sewers (it was too late to return to the Cloisters) and had a sleep as horrible as any I'd ever experienced. You have no idea how terrible our need to feed is. The nightmares I had that first night made the zombies' swarming and subsequent slaughter of New York City seem like the Disneyland electric light parade on a beautiful summer's eve.

I needed to know how many of you blood bags were still sloshing around—if not for slaking my unbearable thirst, then certainly for slaking it well into the future. And so I remained ungrounded.

Now, hunger does two things to a vampire. It turns him into a frightfully emaciated corpselike being far removed from the pathetically romantic vision of your literature. It also greatly increases his sense of smell—the gifted hunter now par excellence. As soon as the sun was past the horizon, I leapt into the twilight. My skin was savaged by the retreating light and stung with the intensity of a third-degree burn, but I didn't care. It would heel quickly, and better yet—*I had a scent*. It was so faint I was convinced that it must have been imagined—the mad hallucinations of a desert wanderer. But still I had to seek it out, had to *taste* it. It came from across the river, but all the bridges, I quickly learned, had been destroyed in an effort (I supposed) to separate the fleeing human population from the advancing inhuman hoard. I, of course, looked for any boats moored along the channel but found not a one. They'd either been scuttled or impressed into service in the mass exodus. Which left the tunnels—twenty-four of which linked the city to the outside world. But once again my plans had been thwarted; every underground channel had been destroyed and was now filled with roiling water and massive piles of rubble. That is, every tunnel but one: the Holland Tunnel (guess you ran out of time, explosives, or fell prey to the ineluctable law of Murphy). When I finally arrived at the landmark's venerable entrance, I was forced to a stop. So odious was the vision that for the briefest moment I actually began considering what it would take to build my own fucking boat. But the thinking part wasn't in charge of your Valiant Vampire Knight (yeah, I know what you've been calling me); the hunger was. I briefly entertained swimming across the Hudson but realized that the river's notoriously strong current combined with my rapidly weakening state would make such a crossing improbable (if not impossible) and that I'd probably be swept out to sea. I wasn't worried about drowning—Vampires can't be drowned. We can, however, be fried alive.

So this is what I saw (and I can scarcely reconcile that vision even to this day): A tunnel mouth filled from top to bottom with writhing, moaning bodies clawing at and climbing atop one another to get in. It looked as if the tunnel itself was a great maw feeding on the bulbous mass of undulating bodies. The zombies tore at each other's flesh, pulling apart appendages and limbs. Not one of them screamed or even bothered to protest. They just moaned and clawed in a desperate attempt to get to the other side of the river, to get to *my* food. Clearly it would've been impossible for anyone (or anything for that matter) to force its way through; anything except for a starved, determined, and now very demented vampire. The journey of a thousand miles begins with the flinging of a single zombie, and so it did. Even in my weakened state I could toss those limbless stench bombs like rucksacks. I had to temper my strength, though. In those first few minutes I managed to fling far more arms, legs, and heads than actual people. I quickly learned to grab for their torsos, the ribcages of which would inevitably crack in my all-too-efficient hands. At the entrance of the tunnel, this method seemed to work just fine, and within a half hour I'd worked my way to the foot of the grand archway. It was when I'd flung my way *into* the tunnel that things got very bad indeed. My zeal was momentarily halted as a hot wind carrying the malodorous stench of decaying flesh hit me with the blast of an open furnace on a hot summer's night. Undeterred, I dove back to the task at hand, clawing my way through the darkened passage, through the crush of bodies pressed even more tightly together. It got so bad that at one point there was simply no room left to fling; no room to even shove the creatures aside. And so I began to tear *through* the innards of the pinioned beasts in complete and utter darkness. I later learned that the tunnel is 1.6 miles long. I began this ghastly routine not one hundred feet from the entrance. No matter; I was a crazed, thrashing machine; the scent of true blood growing stronger with each zombie torn through, pushing me on with every foot advanced. I don't recall how long it took. Maybe I did it in one night; maybe I did it in twenty. All I know is that when I finally did emerge, it was nighttime, for which I suppose I should give thanks. But even if I'd been vomited out of the rathole during high noon, I very much doubt I would've or even could have remained inside—the sheer momentum of that many bodies forcing their way out would've made my return impossible. Guess I'll never know what I would've done. Ask me if I give a shit.

If I thought that first night of hunger was bad, that I wasn't really myself, then the thing that emerged from the tunnel was worse. And that's all I'll say of it.

But hey, what you *really* want to hear about is how your heroic vampire found his first humans, right? About how I came to the rescue of those retched and defenseless humans being besieged by the evil zombie horde. You poor bastards. Zombies aren't evil. Zombies just are. *I'm* evil. Remember those you call the "first ones" because they were supposedly the first humans I brought under my protection? Well, guess what, my pathetic little digestifs? They were in fact my seconds. And the water tower you've immortalized in your stories? I didn't actually create it; I found it.

As soon as I'd cleared that tunnel, I locked on to their scent like white on rice. I didn't even bother cleaning off the entrails. And trust me on this: I'm a stickler for dining etiquette. I like to dress up before I eat; it's all part of the seduction. Hell, I'm not even sure I was wearing clothes. But I do know this: I was on a mission that had already had me rip through the torsos of tens of thousands of zombies; the last thing I was going to do was stop.

So I arrived at the water tower a disheveled mess, drenched in sweat (yes, vampires sweat) and covered in entrails and whatever other detritus I'd managed to pick up in my mad dash towards the beckoning blood. I was up and into that tower in seconds. As I dropped down from above, twenty sets of eyes fixed on me at once; twenty faces playing a visual symphony of sheer and unimaginable horror at the lupine creature now standing in their midst. These people had survived for months in that tiny space. And they'd done so with an ingenuity and courage to be applauded—against a plague of demons that had crushed an entire metropolis, no less! That they'd managed to stay both safe and hidden for all this time ... genius! But all their brains and courage didn't help them—*couldn't* help them—against what I was ... what I'd become. I took the nearest one to me—a small child—drained her in seconds flat; a delectable hors d'oeuvre. The rest were upon me instantly. The strongest attacked first, and I made quick work of them. Their blood is richer; their hearts beat more powerfully, and as such, it was their blood scent that drew me to the rest. It was to the cacophonous rhythm of the survivors' rapidly beating and terrified hearts that I drew life and completed my handiwork. I not only reveled in the deed, I fed off the howls of the humans as they watched the lives of those they loved being taken. When the women and children were done, I moved on and finished off those I'd only crippled. Their fear was even more intoxicating, their hot, surging blood, liberating. By the time the sun rose, I was fast asleep amongst my carnage—a tableau of unspeakable sacrilege. From the body parts left (and by the way, zombies tear apart so much easier) I was able to ascertain that most was from either children or young adults, but from memory all I can truly recall is the bliss of feeding—endless, glorious feeding.

If you want the moment when I started to become that which your literature insists on labeling me, it would have to be from that second night. That first evening after the massacre, I emerged whole and fit but dreadfully unpresentable. The water tower, as I'm sure you can well imagine, reeked of death and was filled with the vivisected remains of the previous evening's meal. The walls were covered in broad and surprisingly graceful arches of auburn spatter. It was impressively awful even by my standards. Remember, it's the rare vampire that finds himself in a situation such as mine. We're insular beings and prefer our food in neat, tidy packets of one. And even then, we'll mostly work quietly in the dark. It took me a few moments to realize that indeed it had been me and only me who'd been responsible for the surrounding mess. I exhaled deeply, brushed off what bits of flesh and bone were still stuck to my body, and then stood up. Thus comported, I leapt to the top of the tower, slid open a hatch, and then peered outward. A warm wind brushed up against my face as a rustle of leaves played across the field. I breathed in the pleasant night air in large, exclamatory gulps. The slow and steady sound of shuffling feet momentarily distracted me, and I peered downwards. The large zombie horde that had gathered beneath the tower (in my hunger of the night before, I'd barely noticed them) was now dispersing like a group of disgruntled children. It was then I realized just how horribly I'd screwed up. You see, twenty humans can keep a vampire going indefinitely if he takes a little from each one. I'd had the perfect set up *and killed it*. But I also knew that there was nothing I could've done—the hunger had overwhelmed me, discharging my regrettably baser instincts (not to mention any modicum of common sense and decency). I realized then and there that if I wanted to survive, I could never allow a similar predicament to occur, never permit hunger to so thoroughly dictate my actions. I'd need more humans, and I'd need them fast.

The first thing I did was to throw what was left of my victims over the edge of the tower. Anybody watching would naturally assume the tossed cadavers to be offed zombies (an oxymoron if ever there was one). Once the bodies had been removed a safe distance from the tower, I jacked a car, hit a local Wal-Mart, and stocked up on bleach and cleaning supplies. It was critical that I remove all traces of the tower's previous occupants. And I'm not just talking about corporeal matter; I'm talking about *chachkas*. If I found anything, *anything*, of a personal nature, I tossed it. Thank your uncaring God that I did. Remember, I'd only been awake for two days after having slept for almost thirty years. Who knew cameras were their own developers *and* slide shows? That cell phones and tablets were veritable bugging devices equipped with camera, audio, and video recording capability? That drove me to my second rule: if I didn't understand what it was, it was gone.

Though my strength and agility are far superior to yours, the task still took a considerable amount of time. One entire night to scrub the place clean and another to haul out all the stuff I'd decided to be rid of. (So much useless crap! What is it with your predilection to collect things?) By the third night, I was finally ready to start creating humanity's new home. I filled it with an ample number of beds, food and water, guns and ammo, medical supplies, clothes, and, of course, books (a passion shared equally by both my species and yours). Then I went hunting.

One of the best advantages I have against the zombies is their abject disinterest in me. I'm not meat—well, mostly not. They're attracted to fresh blood, which is why they stuck around the tower even after I'd beaten them to their lunch. Though I have noticed that they will, compass-like, turn in my direction after I've fed. Guess they can smell *your* blood in *my* veins.

My biggest initial problem was one of dearth. There were so few of you left I was pretty sure I'd have to starve once more just to sniff you out (and we all know how successful *that* method proved to be). Yet even with my heightened senses, I had no clue where the rest of you were. So I despaired. Despaired that I'd killed my one chance to live a "normal" life. Despaired that perhaps I'd killed off my *only* chance to live a normal life. To make matters worse the beautiful home I'd just built seemed to stand, if not in quiet condemnation, then certainly in mock repudiation of my recent efforts. I had come to the sad realization that soon I would once again be ravenous and that therefore the next humans I found would undoubtedly end up like the first—a prospect I could ill afford.

It was during this malaise that my luck finally changed, and I have the murderers of your families to thank for it. Remember what I told you about how zombies can sense humans? Well, here's where we're different. My range is limited. I have to keep moving in different directions until I can pick up a scent. A vampire could go crazy looking for a scent, running in ever-widening arcs, praying he'll eventually pick up something somewhere. But a zombie? Fucking walking compass. Mind you, they're not fast at all, but they will eventually—we're talking weeks if not months here—will *eventually* move towards humans. They simply know. I don't know *how* they know (nor do I give a rat's ass); I just know *that* they know. Once I felt confident that enough of them were moving in a statistically meaningful direction, I would leapfrog and then extend their migration path in wide exploratory arches. Worked like a charm. Fear carries farther for us vampires than any other human scent, and you were all so very afraid.

That's how I found the Park family. You all know the Parks. They're the most unique humans left alive on the planet—an honest-to-goodness bona fide family (as opposed the shattered remnants of families trying to fuse into something new). My first time out, and I find the last family left on the face of the Earth—a mom, dad, five kids ages five to thirteen, and their uncle. I don't know what combination of luck, street smarts, or planning got them through the first three years of the zombie plague, but I am certain of one thing—it had run its course the night they met me. And not just because I'd showed up but because almost ten thousand of my least favorite friends had done so as well. That was why the fear I'd smelled that evening had been so pungent. The Parks were dead, and they knew it. The family was huddled around their car by the side of the road. The husband, sitting behind the wheel, was apoplectic as he tried to get the junker to start up. For every one of his undecipherable tirades and hand slapping of the wheel, the car would rebut with the *click, click, click* of a battery gone to the netherworld. The Uncle was sitting on the gravel with his back up against the door, one leg bent at the knee the other sticking straight out, immobilized by a crude splint. The gravity of the situation didn't stop the mom from busying herself with the making of improvised barricades from whatever she could find (which wasn't much) while shouting orders at the kids to keep cleaning their weapons. Such bravery, such dread. Man, I wanted to drain them all. But that wasn't in the cards.

Watching quietly from a distance, I waited for the sounds of the approaching mob to get closer, for the inevitability of the Park family's impending slaughter to weigh on their minds. When I felt certain that *they were certain* all was lost, I decided to make my move. I appeared almost instantaneously, sitting next to their uncle. The gun I was pointing at his head wasn't loaded, but I felt it necessary to grab their attention before they started firing pell-mell in my direction. Time was of the essence, so I needed them to listen and slowly ease their fingers off their triggers. As you all know, I was completely forthright. I told them who I was and even *what* I was. And then I laid out my deal—as if they had much of a choice. Imagine my surprise when Mrs. Park started to bargain with me! God, I love that woman. Ten thousand zombies bearing down on her family, a vampire with a gun at the temple of her brother's head, and she's working a deal (I don't even know what it was she wanted, to be perfectly honest; I think I might have said "yes" just to shut her up). They'll tell you they would have made a deal with Satan himself to get out of the mess they were in. In the end, they did.

I don't think they *really* believed me till they saw me go to work. I killed thousands of zombies that night and did so with two sharpened railway spikes I managed to pull out of nearby track. The Parks could barely keep up with my movements, and not just for lack of light (they had night vision gear, but that can't compensate for vampiric celerity). What I'll assume looked amazing to them was fuck-all boring for me. You want to know what I remember most of the famous "First Battle of the Restoration"? (How do you come up with these idiotic designations?) Not glory, that's for sure. Though no doubt you'll insert some inspirational soundtrack into the background when you get around to making a movie of it (that is, when you start making movies again). No, what I remember is, "spike to the head," "spike to the head," "spike to the head." And you can thank your uncaring God that I found the Parks early enough in the night that I had time to slaughter ourselves a path towards a working car. I shouted for them to get in, which they did without argument (even Mrs. Park). Then, since the warm glow of dawn was beginning to make its presence felt, I shouted for someone to pop the trunk. It flew open and I hopped in, quickly covering my body with a Mylar blanket pulled from an emergency kit. The last vision I had was of Mrs. Park slamming the trunk down on my face. She didn't look happy, but then again, she never looked—to me, at least—anything other than determined. My life now in their hands, I settled into a deep and exhausted sleep for the second time in as many days.

Now, this is the part that I find amazing. You vein glories make such a big deal of my having put my life into the hands of a family of humans after only one night. Yeah, I know that all they had to do to kill me was pull the car over to the side of the road and open the trunk. BOB would've done the rest (as in *Bright Orange Ball*—a nickname we vampires gave to our most successful killer). But how much of a risk was it really? The Parks knew what I could do. I'd just saved their lives and the lives of their children, and they knew they were going to need saving again. I'd told them I would need blood—their blood—to live, but made sure not to ask for any that night. And finally, you must understand that I, too, had no choice but to trust them. If my plan was going to work, I needed cattle I could work with, and if it wasn't going to work, I would rather have died under BOB's fiery glow than eventual death by starvation.

I wasn't at all surprised by what I saw the next night when the trunk suddenly popped open. Staring down at me was the entire Park family—including the uncle who'd somehow managed to prop himself up for the waking ceremony. I looked past their curious faces and saw to my relief the dimly outlined form of the water tower's base reflected in the moon's evanescent light. I wasn't sure if my instructions—shouted during the din of battle— had been all that clear.

Oh, how you bloodiots go on about that first night at the water tower. About how safe I made it. I'm a fucking vampire, you nitwits. Of course it was safe. I was protecting my cattle! Then you made a big deal about how I requested to drink their blood instead of just taking it. Like I had a choice. Like *either of us* had a choice. What you don't like to think about is what would've happened had the Parks said no. Let me spell it out: I would've drained them on the spot and then prayed I'd find some more humans to make a deal with. Simple as that. But they knew the deal. God, I love those Koreans. I hope there are some more of them left.

After that first night, it got a lot easier. Word spread about the "Vampire Knight," and soon humans began trickling in. Before I knew it, I had thirty people in my water tower and soon found myself having to set up another (in the next town over) just to handle the overflow. They all knew the drill, knew that I had to feed, but that I would not kill. I only had to give the "need to feed" speech two or three times after the Parks. Like I said, word spread fast, and people wanted to live even if living meant exposing their veins to my ineluctable thirst. Mrs. Park set up a feeding schedule, and let me tell you, you don't ever want to be late for a feeding when Mrs. Park is doing the organizing. Victims of her acid stare and scornful reproach included not only the squeamish first-timers but also yours truly. She'd just as soon berate me for being late to a "withdrawal" as she would my victims. She was right, of course. Fear is a terrible thing for morale, and to leave a child sitting for longer than necessary—especially one being made ready as a human Slurpee—bordered on cruelty. For the first time in decades, I was finally getting enough to allay my cravings. Alas, the heady peace and tranquility of the two towers phase of my existence soon came to a crashing halt. Fucking zombies.

They just kept on coming. Sure, I'd kill them immediately. And we'd have peace for a short time after. But the times of peace between the killings went from weeks to days and then finally to hours. I had the biggest concentration of humans within three hundred miles, and they knew it. That's the part of all this that makes me wonder if the plague wasn't some sort of demonic plan. Or maybe it was just bad timing that the plague struck with the worldwide release of the movie *Zombie Wars*. It of course didn't help that everyone thought the hordes descending on their towns were just a publicity stunt. But as you well know, by the time everyone did figure it out, the plague had spread too far and too fast. I can chalk most of that up to bad timing or twisted coincidence. But the fact that zombies can hone in on a living human despite the zombie's inability to smell, hear, or even see the human (when not in their immediate vicinity, that is) ... well, that's just freaky. If for some reason you're stupid enough to leave any zombies around for study, see if you can figure that one out. Lord knows it's beyond me.

I figured I could keep a hundred humans alive and mobile pretty easy. That's five times more than I need. Plus, between my eradication of the zombies and their eventual decomposition, they'd cease to be a threat in a few generations. But so too, I quickly realized, would my humans. Remember how I told you how I used to go to ground out of sheer boredom? I was no longer bored. I was scared. I like being a vampire. I like that I've sailed the Caribbean on an honest-to-God pirate ship and was one of the first to ride a train on the Transcontinental Railroad. I wasn't on the *Titanic*, but I was on the maiden voyage of her sister, the *Olympic*, and it was one hell of a great memory. I liked watching the moon landing on TV and even had plans to go there myself. But now that dream wasn't going to happen. If I only got a hundred humans out of this mess, then that would mean in four hundred years the race would be nothing but a useless herd of infertile, inbred idiots no more intelligent than the zombies who were after their flesh. More importantly, instead of the bright, shiny future I'd always dreamed of, I'd instead be saddled with four centuries of brain-numbing boredom and then would end up starving to death anyways! Mrs. Park was a nurse and knew enough about genetics to tell me that I would need, at a minimum, six thousand survivors—though more like ten—if my food supply was to have a real chance at making it. It wasn't just "my" humans I would need to save; it would have to be the whole goddamned human race. Shit.

All I can say is thank God for the Dork Lords—the greatest, smartest, luckiest geek warrior class the human race has ever produced. Those computer dweebs managed to hold out against a phalanx of hundreds of thousands of zombies and couple of idiot vampires at a super-max prison in Illinois. Unfortunately, it was my own breed that had whittled them down to the few I was fortunate enough to save. Yeah, we know I wasn't the only bloodsucker and we know I was the "good" one and that all the others were bad (not that there were many left—by my estimation, maybe thirty to fifty worldwide by the time I'd gone to ground—and don't ask me where they went; I ain't got a clue). Point is, the ones I found weren't bad; they were just stupid, which to my way of thinking is far worse. They were also young, still living within their natural lifespans, and in their short lives had amounted to nothing more than a couple of thugs. Why someone would've bequeathed those morons with vampiric power is beyond me. But the bottom line was that they continued to do what they'd probably been doing even before being gifted with the dark power—take what they wanted, when they wanted. And that's exactly what they were doing when I found them attacking the Dork Lords—feeding from a smaller and smaller pool of humanity without any regard for the consequences.

But their stupidity isn't the point. The Dork Lords' prowess is. Those geeks were being attacked by zombies *and* vampires and had still managed to hold out for an ungodly stretch. Unfortunately, by the time I found them, there were only fourteen left. Fourteen from a pool of over one hundred and fifty of the best your species had to offer. The Dork Lords had planned, escaped, supplied, and secured pretty much every damn cellblock in the place. I'm pretty sure that had it only been zombies they'd had to contend with, those guys might have pulled off the salvation of the human race all by themselves.

First thing I did was kill the two bastard vampricks and toss their bodies over the wall for the Dork Lords to see. That, of course, didn't gain me entrance into their sanctum sanctorum. Can't say that I blamed them. I told you they were smart. So I went to plan B, which entailed spending two months killing the zombies that had massed around the prison walls and then another few weeks disposing of their corpses in order to clear a path safe enough for my chattel to walk through. Seeing me show up with a group of thirty very un-scared humans was what finally convinced them to open the gates (that and Mrs. Park's harangue ... God bless Mrs. Park). I convinced the Dork Lords to keep the prison going. It would be my central US repository. I also set up prison-shelters in five other locations to act as further collecting points. Since I couldn't possibly be in every place at once, I ... well, truthfully, Mrs. Park decided that I'd need to make a few more vampires. There would need to be one per prison, and that one must be chosen from among the group of humans.

It was the Dork Lords who finally led me to the silos. That they'd withheld that information even after all I'd done for them was testament to their lack of trust. Love those guys! We had one plane, a DHC-3 Otter. Just after sunset, a couple of the guys flew me over to the silo sites, both of which were crawling with zombies. We flew over acres of open, arid land covered in a macabre, undulating carpet of the undead. Ever see a zombie try to claw his way into reinforced concrete? Not gonna happen. That, of course, didn't stop the zombies from clawing into each other to get to the concrete. What a mess that was.

The Dork Lords knew some back ways into the silos (they'd hacked the US defense grid and worked the blueprints). The plan required our having to land the Otter some distance away, but it seemed worth it at the time. So in the dead of night, I carried the pilot and copilot the fifteen or so miles to site of entry and then began the arduous task of digging out the survivors while the pilot and copilot kept watch. At the first two sites, all we managed to find were a smattering of humans who'd denigrated into a tribe of cannibals. They were too far gone to be of any use to us. I was prepared to leave them to their own devices, but the Dork Lords insisted—*insisted*—that I drain the bastards right then and there in order to put them out of their misery. Great humanitarian that I am, I complied.

The third silo was jackpot city. It was being run by a staff sergeant who'd taken over when the commanding officer had upped and shot himself. Sergeant Caine—Dominique to all of you—had arranged runs to get all the supplies and people she could salvage. That woman had kept over two hundred souls alive for almost two years on the false promise of an impending rescue. Imagine her surprise when one actually showed up. After a brief but intense sidebar conversation between Dominique and the two Dork Lords (with lots of furtive glances over towards me), Dominique nodded solemnly, and I was brought into the fold. The planning then began in earnest. The silo crew, it turned out, had the skills and knowledge base we desperately needed. On top of that, they knew where a lot of the good shit was being stored. That was the day we got ourselves an air force. We were only able to find one other silo after Jackpot City, and with it another twenty-five hearty souls.

A half a year's work in the States, and all I'd managed to save and preserve was twenty-five hundred humans—including the silos. Not even a quarter of the way to my safety margin. It was at that point I realized that if we were really going to make the plan work, we'd have to go international. Luckily, there were a crap load of durable transports all over the place, and the Dork Lords had these wondrous plastic books that seemed to contain thousands of books within them. All of human knowledge stored in an eight-and-a-half-ounce marvel. *That's* the shit I wanted to live for! It was through one of those books plucked from the air that we learned how to salvage aviation fuel. Did I mention my love for the Dork Lords?

Our first forays were to Canada and Mexico. We got a thousand out of Canada. That might not seem like a lot, but it ended up being more than we got out of any other country. It was cold up in Canada. Zombies move a lot slower in colder temps, and so the Canucks got to take the winter off. Only got a hundred out of Alaska. Yeah, it's cold up there, but unlike in Canada, most of the population was concentrated in two major cities. Zombies took advantage of that. The bears, however, seemed to be holding their own. Other than us, bears might be the only creature larger than a field mouse to survive the zombie apocalypse.

Holy shit, I forgot the cows.

That's when we found Mad Farmer Jeff up in Colorado. By staying constantly on the move, Farmer Jeff had somehow managed to avoid the zombies *and* save a herd of twenty cows and two bulls. How he did that for three years I'll never know, but boy were you guys overjoyed to get fresh milk again.

Mexico was a washout. Apparently the Mexicans had been involved in some sort of civil war when the apocalypse struck. Everyone assumed it was the end of the human race, and so whoever the zombies didn't kill, the population ended up killing for them. Crying shame. We crisscrossed the whole place and found not a damned soul. Truth is, we never had much luck in places that didn't have a real winter. No winter meant no respite because in temperate locales, the zombies could keep moving. For that reason, Hawaii was a bust. Fortunately, it made a great gas station for our trips over to Asia. I suppose this is where I should mention how much I hate flying. I never did much of it before the zombie apocalypse, and I'd hoped I wouldn't have to do much after. See, airplanes are way too confined—and private jets way too conspicuous. Add to that the prospect of any sort of an emergency that could irrevocably screw up a schedule, and I'd be at risk of having to land during daylight hours. But the simple fact of the matter is the damned things terrify me, especially the big ones. It didn't help that they came about while I'd gone to ground for a thirty-year stretch. You see, I went down in 1890 to clear blue skies and woke up to the constant buzz of oversized mechanical hornets. Plus, I could never figure out how the damn things flew. No matter how much it was explained to me—and the Dork Lords loved to explain things—I never did quite buy it. But I didn't have a choice. If humanity was going to be saved, I was going to need the airplane to do it. And so I flew.

I had no idea how bad the apocalypse was till I realized the only way to find people would be to once again starve myself in order to pick up their scent. The Dork Lords kept a big-ass thermos of warm blood in the back of the plane for when my eyes would start to roll back in my head. I'd failed to mention my little escapade at the tower (you, my little blood banks, are the first to be told), but it didn't take a rocket scientist to see the effects of starvation on my body. We used this "starve the vampire" honing method to our advantage, but the troopers knew, via my caveats as well as the telltale signs, when the line had been crossed between my being effective and my being dangerous.

So exactly how bad was it out there? The numbers speak for themselves. Fifteen hundred in China, 250 in India, over a thousand in Nepal/Tibet, four hundred in both the Korea, twenty-seven in all of Japan. Damn, I liked the Japanese—so sweet and salty all at the same time. In all of Russia, nine hundred. They were cursed with the same bad luck as the Alaskans—concentrated cities. We did get some signals from the Siberian wasteland, but there were too few and it would've proven too difficult to extricate them. We didn't even bother with the island nations after we saw what had happened in the Philippines. From what we gathered, it turned out that zombies will even walk *under* water to get to human flesh. I would have thought islands would be the perfect place to defend against those things. Turns out they got overrun from all sides. The islands were the perfect death traps.

We'd hoped that perhaps the unmoored ships would offer up some survivors, but those hopes had also been quickly dashed. Apparently, even fish could act as carriers (if they'd been bit or had eaten from those that had). As a result, a lot of ships that thought they were safe had instead been hauling in huge nets of zombie-infected catch. All in all, we managed to salvage three thousand from the seas. Those that had survived—mostly military vessels—had done so either through dumb luck or because they had been fortunate enough to not only know what was happening to the other ships but to also be carrying enough rations not to have to rely on what was in the water for sustenance.

Got three thousand out of Europe. The Middle East and Africa,were total busts. I had hopes for Israel. That country was *always* waiting, *always* preparing for something to go wrong. If anyone would've been prepared for a zombie apocalypse, who better than the Israelis? But one flyover of the region confirmed our worst fears—radioactive craters from Jerusalem to Tehran … and a plethora of zombies. What is it with you people? Even when your very existence is in jeopardy, you launch nukes at one another? At moments like that, if I could've lived off hamsters for the rest of my life, I might have called it a day and let you all fuck yourselves.

Then there was Africa. African culture was rife with legends about zombies, so I thought maybe there'd be a chance some of the wives' tales would be true and that perhaps we'd find a smattering of survivors. Too damned hot. Zombies turn fast in that kind of heat. Everyone was overrun. We managed to save 270 from the entire continent; that's Alexandria to Cape Town. You want horror stories? Just watch the interviews with those poor fucks. I'll do you all a favor and not talk about Australia.

At the end of these cattle calls, I'd managed to gather thirteen thousand genetically diverse blood donors. Now all I had to do was keep them safe from the six billion or so zombies that wanted to finish the job.

I called a council meeting of all the human and vampire representatives and explained the situation: Given the zombies' ability to sense the presence of humanity, our burgeoning success now had the potential to kill us. Yes, one vampire can take out tens of thousands of zombies, but eventually the sun will come up, which would've left billions more of the fuckers for my precious little blood banks to contend with. And now that the human population had begun to coalesce, the potential of being swarmed and then picked off one prison at a time was even greater. After a few days of rancorous debate, we all decided the best thing to do would be to find a town high in some mountain range, damn near impossible to get to, and where it would be cold most of the year. We found it in Europe. Norway, to be exact. I don't remember what the town was called originally. Some of you wanted to call it New Zion—again with the inane romanticism. I renamed it what it was: Last Stand. To be honest, I thought we'd be fine. I mean, the town was so high up it stayed below freezing most of the year and even when it wasn't, the place was completely unapproachable from three sides and for all intents and purposes cut off from the fourth (the placement of an amazingly high amount of explosives saw to that). Last Stand also had a small airport that we'd spent months readying while more and more zombies began their inevitable congregation around the five prisons. We lost one of prisons, but not before utilizing hot air balloons to get the last of our people out. Suffice to say, when you need a bunch of rainbow balloons to save your ass, it's time to move.

At the beginning, Last Stand was perfect. Zombies were few and far between, and we got good at clearing out those that somehow made it to our perimeter. It was so damned cold that first year that the zombies simply froze in place and could be easily picked off during the first thaw. By this time there were nine vampire knights including myself. All of us were very well fed and, I still laugh at this, *loved*. For the first two years, it went exactly as planned. The town ran smoothly, the population began to grow, and it looked as if our cozy little haven would be a benchmark in how to continue a successfully realized mountaintop evolution. I have no idea how many zombies we took out during those first few years, but then again, we never really counted. Had we, we might have understood exactly what kind of threat we were facing. Even when you take into account the number of zombies that fell down ravines, got crushed by the ocean depths, smashed against rocks, or taken out by countless other means (man, what an America's Funniest Home Videos episode that would have made), there were still well over five billion of the motherfuckers headed our way. And at the beginning of that third year, it seemed like every one of them arrived our doorstep (in retrospect, I probably should've chosen a different name). Yes, our ravines were miles deep. But billions of bodies will eventually overflow even the Grand Canyon if you shove them in all at once.

We waited for winter to save us, and it seemed that it came in the nick of time. However, what we'd failed to realize is exactly what would happen when billions of bodies decompose all at once—and all in one place. Fuckers should've frozen, but we forgot—decomposing bodies produce heat. Now, zombies decompose slowly—insanely, unnaturally slowly—but they do decompose. And when you place billions of them together, they will produce just enough heat to keep themselves mobile, even if it's fifty degrees below—and it *was* fifty fucking below!

I know you attribute your eventual victory to me, but the truth is it was the lovely Dominique. I know the stories you made up about her. How she was the last vampire I made. How she was my "true love" and all that bullshit. Oh, I'll give you she was pretty amazing in the sack, but I made her a vampire because everyone loved and listened to her as much … hell, even *more* than me. I figured the best way to keep her from eventually conspiring against me would be to make her part of my growing coven (which just goes to show we vampires are not nearly as smart as you bloodiots make us out to be). I didn't have any reason to suspect foul play when she suggested a near-perfect escape plan for our city. If your entire enemy is in one place, the solution, it turns out, is rather simple—get all Middle East on them.

It didn't take us long to locate the nukes. And they were actually pretty easy to move because there weren't many zombies left in the US to offer resistance. And this is where the Dork Lords really, really came through for us. Nukes are designed *not* to go off. And the stuff we needed, the inordinately powerful five-megaton hydrogen mothers, are almost impossible to blow up unless you have the proper codes. And until you have those codes, those warheads are nothing more than huge, military-grade paperweights. Sadly, all the people who had the passkeys were either dead or in sealed-off bunkers that wouldn't open up for decades. I don't know how the Dork Lords did it, but all it took was one week for those magnificent bastards to get all five of those hellfire-on-Earth nukes ready to rumble.

That's when my "True Love" tried to fuck me. I know why she did it. She felt humanity needed a chance to survive on its own (can't say I blame her). The werewolves were gone. If any witches had survived, they were long gone to whatever dimension would take them. Which left us vampires and the zombies, and after what we were planning, there wouldn't be enough zombies left to worry about. The humans were about to eliminate them all from the face of the earth, and even if a few did manage to survive, humanity wouldn't be caught by surprise like that again. Which then left only one group of monsters for humanity to deal with—mine. And my kind, Dominique realized, were far worse because, like I said before, there's something about us that makes you all stupid and wet.

Dominique's plan was simple. We vampires would stay behind and make sure all the nukes went off without a hitch (we had one in Last Stand as well as four others strategically placed in a fifteen-mile radius around the town). Since the countdown sequence required a manual start, our superior speed and agility meant that we could wait till the last possible moment, set the bombs a–ticking, and still make it back to the airport in time for a last-minute escape via a waiting jet. We primed our Gulfstream for the getaway and used our dear Otter for insertion for the simple reason that it was easier to jump from a prop plane than a jet. We set our bombs in motion at a predetermined hour and then made our way back to Last Stand through precisely calculated routes. Our ability to scale walls and negotiate seemingly impassable terrain made our selection for the mission a no-brainer. Phase one went off without a hitch. Phase two—not so much. Dominique and the other vampires turned on me just as we gathered in the hangar to celebrate our success. Strong as I am, I was no match for those I'd not only birthed but had also personally trained. Plus, I'd never once flown the jet and so, in my captors' minds, escape would have been pointless—even a centuries-old vampire couldn't outrun a hydrogen bomb, much less five.

My darling Dominique was smart, charismatic, and careful. But there's a reason I'm the oldest vampire left alive. She knew I hated flying, knew I didn't understand how the damned things worked. And to an Air Force sergeant, that meant I was not as smart as she. But just because I never flew our planes didn't mean I couldn't. I learned how to fly from the best: Amelia Earhart. Tasty woman. Either way, Amelia's lessons gave me the basics; the Dork Lords' manuals for our Gulfstream G650 gave me the rest. I was fairly confident (after studiously watching our pilots for years) that I could manage. I also took the further precaution of poisoning the conspirators' celebratory blood packs with zombie sludge.

There wasn't enough sludge to kill them, just to leave them all bent over and retching while I calmly strolled over to the Gulfstream, entered, and began the preflight regimen. I'll admit, as I powered up the jet, I was tempted to take the treacherous bitch with me, but I knew she would've just tried to kill me again. By the uncaring God, I will miss her.

I slowly pulled out of the hangar, taxied onto the runway, hit the throttle, and lifted off into the star-strewn sky. I'm pretty sure I saw the first of the zombies pouring over the wall, but it's possible I was mistaken. There was a lot on my mind that night.

As far as the pitiful remnants of the human race are concerned, most of the zombies are now gone, as are we vampires who died with them—martyrs for the cause. How unbelievably gullible can you be? Didn't the zombie apocalypse teach you anything?

So I'm about to go back into the ground, my lovely plasmaccinos. As I write this, you should be setting up your new home in Texas. Nice, warm, and *flat*. You'll see the few zombies that do manage to find you miles before they can even get into groaning distance. My glorious Dork Lords will have that place rigged with radar motion detectors and whatever else they can think of. I wish I could see it, but my job is done. Humanity is safe, and I've drunk enough that I may be able to stay in the ground for a century or more. What sort of world will it be? Hopefully one created by the smartest, luckiest, and toughest humans who've ever lived. I just need to finish this letter, placed in the Gulfstream, which now sits in an empty, hardened hanger in an insanely big American airbase somewhere in Germany.

You may be wondering why I wrote this at all. Wouldn't it be better if I just destroyed the plane and disappeared? There are certainly good reasons why that would be true. But there are better reasons why it wouldn't. First off, I don't know if anyone will find this confession or, if they do, even believe it. But by my leaving it here for you to find, I'll know that when next I come into your world, I'll have to be more careful and move with greater caution. This confession makes me nervous, and a nervous vampire is not prone to the overconfidence that has been the main cause of most of our deaths over the centuries.

But the main reason I'm writing this is for *you*, my darling bloodstock. I want you to grow and I want you to prosper and I never, *ever* want you so complacent that you almost check out again. The world is finally yours—for now. But there is one monster left, bloodbags. And I'll be back. And when I am, I'll be very, very hungry.

To be continued.

STREET LEVEL WITH A MADMAN

March 1944

The passenger's eyes flitted across the words with a snort of contempt. An avid collector of books, he couldn't imagine putting anything published by this ... fool into his library.

"Recent events have amply demonstrated that the regeneration of the Jewish race through the Reich's generous support of the Zionist element was yet another brilliant example of the Führer's genius. Our heroic leader's stunning success at turning what should have been a committed racial foe into a worthwhile ally will surely go down in history as one of the greatest feats of applying the science of eugenics with the art of politics."

—Dr. Hans F.K. Günter, Professor of Racial Studies,
University of Jena

Does the professor actually believe the drivel he writes? thought the passenger. *Sadly ... probably.* He closed the book and shoved it into the back of the seat. *Better to believe ... than to think—a very dangerous proposition in the Reich.* The passenger, who'd been nervously rubbing his index finger back and forth across a mustache that didn't exist, looked down at his nails, all bitten to their stubs. Disgusted, he lifted himself out of the seat with an exasperated sigh and began pacing the aisle. He walked stiffly, hands clasped firmly behind his back. He occasionally jerked his right shoulder nervously, which, oddly enough, made his left leg lift slightly off the floor. His eyes were sallow and brooding, and his demeanor seemed to indicate a man one pin-pull away from detonation. The crew of the Lufthansa trimotor restrained their normal inclination to tell him to remain seated. He could sit, stand, or walk—on the wings if he so desired—by order of the Führer himself. The passenger noticed the steward staring at him. It was a look with which he'd grown familiar. Normally, the solidly Teutonic steward would've had little use for a Jew, no matter how useful this particular Jew's people had been in getting the Iraqi oil fields working or in having made the Eastern provinces productive. *"Ein Scheisse Jude ist ein Scheisse Jude,"* went the popular phrase—no matter what the party line said about Zionism having remade the supposedly incorrigible race. The passenger's lips curled up into a taciturn grin. The steward's opinion had no bearing whatsoever because the man now walking the aisle knew what every other steward, pilot, or employee knew: that he was *the* Jew, and named as such by the German people themselves. Being rather short, middle–aged, and with a shock of white hair that seemed to resist all attempts to control it—like a Russian fighting the occupation—this Jew was far from the Führer's idealized vision of a true Aryan. To add insult to visual injury, the passenger's suit was wrinkled, and one corner of his unkempt shirt had already made its escape from the front of his creased trousers.

The Jew leaned over some seats and stared out a small window. *A Zeppelin would have been nice*, he thought. Though rare, the Germans had flown a number of the dirigibles back and forth from Tel Aviv—there was even talk of starting a dedicated route after the war. *That would've been grand*, he thought with a dour grin. *But this is faster.* He got down on his knees and sniffed at the carpet and then suddenly stood on his head. He remained that way for a few minutes before being interrupted by the clearing of a throat.

"Chancellor Ben Gurion," said the steward, "we're making our final approach to Tel Aviv. If you would please ..."

Ben Gurion's already reddening face went a shade deeper, swelling up like an overly ripe tomato. "You don't think I know we're descending!" he screamed. "Do you think this is easy? Have *you* tried standing on your head in a descending airplane?"

"I'm sorry, Chancellor, I meant—"

"You *will* be sorry!" shouted Ben Gurion, unfolding himself and standing back up. "You'll *all* be sorry!" He shot a look at the steward, who shrunk under his withering glare. "Do you know who you're talking to?" The steward said nothing, head bowed.

Ben Gurion made a swatting motion with his hand. "Get out of my sight."

The steward backed away, then quickly disappeared into the galley.

Serves the bastard right, thought Ben Gurion. *Let him know fear for once.*

As Ben Gurion sat down, he turned his head towards the window, staring out at his people's now fully secured homeland. Tears began to well up, eventually finding purchase on the dark bags that had formed beneath his eyes. He started whispering to himself one question, over and over again. It had been same one he'd been asking since the improbable rescue of the Jews had begun: *How has it come to this?*

June 16, 1933

Lodz, Poland

"Haim Arlosoroff has been shot."

David Ben Gurion looked up from his stack of papers to find Berl Katznelson, one of the leaders of the Labor Zionist movement, standing in front of his desk. Berl's hair was unkempt, and though he was short and physically unimpressive, his outward appearance said nothing of the tigerish resolve within.

"Is he alive?" asked Ben Gurion, lowering the papers.

"Yes."

Ben Gurion let out a palpable sigh of relief.

"I talked to his wife," continued Berl. "She was with him. Says his foot slipped on the clutch, which jerked the car forward. The bullet meant for his chest hit his shoulder instead."

"He always was a lousy driver."

Berl allowed a brief smile.

Ben Gurion's eyes met his friend's. "Any ideas as to whom?"

"We don't know, David, but Haim seems to think it may have been the British."

"Because of his negotiation with the Nazis?"

"Presumably."

Ben Gurion absorbed the nugget for brief second. "I would think that Jabotinsky's Revisionists would be a more likely suspect. They see these negotiations as nothing short of a deal with the devil."

"I agree with you, David, but Haim's insistent."

"If we could blame the Revisionists, it would cost Jabotinsky many votes."

"Enough to gain control of The World Zionist Conference?" asked Berl.

"Indeed," laughed Ben Gurion, picking up his stack of papers, "but if Haim won't blame them, than neither can we."

January 1934

Tel Aviv, Palestine

The election had been close. Chaim Weitzman had been thrust from power, but Jabotinsky's Revisionists had done almost as well as Ben Gurion's Mapai party. And so it was now that Zev Jabotinsky and David Ben Gurion sat at a table, eyeing each other warily, each convinced that the other was the far greater danger to Zionism and therefore to the Jewish people. The Revisionists were capitalists at heart, though with a grudging admiration for the strong-arm tactics, but not necessarily the politics, of Mussolini. Ben Gurion's Mapai was a labor socialist party to the core. Even with their vast ideological differences, there was one thing Ben Gurion and Jabotinsky could both agree on: Palestine should be turned into a Jewish homeland. Though Ben Gurion's party had won, the victory hadn't been decisive. In order to rule the World Zionist Movement, he'd need the Revisionists, and if he allowed the negotiations to take their natural course, the fledgling Zionist movement would crumble—and just when a Jewish state was needed most.

Jabotinsky hardly looked the experienced, battle-tested commander Ben Gurion knew him to be. The man doffed a simple shirt, pants, suspenders, and a billed cap. It wasn't the firebrand's normal attire. He preferred his clothing, like his upbringing, a little more refined, but the British were determined to exile him from Palestine, and the Revisionist Party leader was determined to stay put. The outfit was purely functional, allowing him to blend into crowds and disappear quickly

"Well?" Jabotinsky finally asked with studied intemperance.

Ben Gurion remained silent, mulling his response, fighting the urge—despite his pacifist tendencies—to reach across the table and slap the brash bastard across the face.

"Well," repeated Ben-Gurion evenly, a bare smile twitching at the corners of his mouth, "you may be a fascist pig, but I can't do anything without your help."

"And you, a communist bastard," countered Jabotinsky, eyes narrowed but lacking any real malice, "still believing the farce of a socialist utopia." Jabotinsky exhaled. "But you and I face a problem far more grave."

"Hitler," uttered Ben-Gurion through stiffened lips. "Have you read it?"

"*Mein Kampf*? Insane drivel."

"But well timed."

Jabotinsky nodded solemnly.

"What does it mean?"

Jabotinsky's eyes were drawn into a hawklike glare. "It means, my misguided friend, what I've been saying all along—that the man is absolutely capable of killing every Jew in Germany."

"Marr, von Schönerer, Lueger," said Ben Gurion, reciting from a litany of German hate mongers. "Hitler's not said anything others haven't said before. He's no different."

"Ah, but he is, Mr. President."

Ben Gurion noted the complete lack of deference in the salutation and laughed inwardly. He indicated with a slight nod of his head that Jabotinsky continue.

"Those others' hatred of us was merely visceral—screeds, really. But Hitler has upped the ante. He doesn't hate us so much as what it is we represent."

"Which is?"

"A moral revolution. We had the audacity to introduce the sixth commandment, an idea that is antithetical to the man's worldview."

"Thou shalt not murder," said Ben Gurion, his nod slow and sad. "And the price for having introduced it lo those thousands of years ago is murder—of our entire people." A nervous laugh followed, then a quick exhalation. "Ironic, actually."

"Don't look at me," groused Jabotinsky. "I've been warning you all for years."

"A state is our only solution."

"Clearly," answered Jabotinsky. "Why don't I just ring up the High Commissioner now and ask him to have Whitehall draw one up for us?"

Ben Gurion ignored the sarcasm and rifled through the stack of papers on his desk. He picked one up and waved it into the air, shaking his head. "You do know that he's reducing our immigration numbers again."

"To make nice with our Arab neighbors," added Jabotinsky with barely contained derision. "The British close the gates on us as Hitler's crusade ramps up. My reports from Betar speak of beatings, robbery, imprisonment … murder."

"I know," answered Ben Gurion, mussing some more papers about. "I read the reports … in here somewhere."

"Never mind those, old man. Now that you're president, what do you plan to do about it?"

"What can I do?"

"Exactly," said Jabotinsky, finally deeming to pull up a chair in front of Ben Gurion's desk.

The two men sat in silence for a few moments before Ben Gurion finally let out a strained laugh.

"I'm glad you find this humorous," said Jabotinsky.

The president's eyes twinkled with mischief. "Oh, I don't. Though what I'm about to propose, I'm quite sure you will."

Jabotinsky was suddenly all ears. "*Nu?*" he asked, using the common Yiddish word that best expressed impatience.

"I suppose we could just talk to him."

"Good luck with that. The high commissioner's no friend of ours. You yourself said …"

"Not him," interrupted Ben Gurion, sliding a newspaper over to the other side of his desk. He put his index finger solidly down on the picture of Adolph Hitler. "Him."

January 1934
Two days later

Tel Aviv, Palestine

Jabotinsky stood outside the drab prefab building so typical of Tel Aviv. People skirted by, lost in the day's errands, pulling at toddlers, clutching valises, and generally carrying on as if oblivious to slow and steady tank tread of Nazi Germany rolling ineluctably toward their doom. The Revisionist Party leader spat in disgust. It went unnoticed by any passersby, and if noticed, certainly not made much of. To them, Jabotinsky was just another Jew wronged, another Jew angry at something. Get in line. But on this day, Jabotinsky's disgust was reserved more for himself than for the man he was about to meet. Where Ben Gurion had abhorred violence as a means to an end, Jabotinsky had venerated it. Harsh enemies called for harsher tactics. That mantra had been proven in blood and realpolitik time and again. But the Jews, most of whom were weak and servile from too many years under the boot of host nations, were simply too daft too realize it. That diffidence, combined with Hitler's charismatic venom, had set up a perfect storm. Hitler was the madman at the rudder, steering his angry nation straight for the Jews. And now, this cretin Ben Gurion, a man Jabotinsky had for so long held in disdain because of Ben Gurion's illogical revulsion to violence, seemed to be offering a way out of the morass that was contrary to everything Jabotinsky believed in. The revolutionary shook his head, took a deep breath, and entered the building. Moments later, he stood before the President of the Zionists, rendered mute by the unexpected elision of long-held contempt and unfamiliar hope.

* * *

Ben Gurion looked up from his pile of papers as Jabotinsky entered the sparse office. The president didn't bother with pleasantries; there simply weren't any. The gravity of the situation merely sealed the protocol's demise.

"Arlosoroff's been in Germany since he recovered from his attack."

Jabotinsky took a seat in front of the president's desk, grunting his acknowledgment of the news.

"He and Ruppin," continued Ben Gurion, "have been making the rounds in Berlin. The Nazis think the British tried to assassinate Arlosoroff, and if the Brits don't want the Zionists talking to the Nazis, that means the Nazis suddenly want to talk to the Zionists. At least, that's what Arlosoroff has them thinking."

Jabotinsky cracked a doubting smile. "Why don't I like where this is going?"

"We need a stronger agreement with the Nazis, Zev. If the world will not help us with this lunatic, we must deal with him ourselves."

"You can't possibly hope to …"

Ben Gurion held up his hand. "Ruppin and Arlosoroff have arranged a meeting for me with Adolph Hitler."

Jabotinsky's mouth hung slack. "Oh." A moment later, he regained his composure. "I see why you needed to meet me."

"We both agree this man can kill every Jew in the Reich and the only thing stopping him is him. I need to go and make some sort of deal, convince him—strange as it sounds—that we have the same goals, maybe even …" The president paused, knowing full well that what he was about to say would sound preposterous, "… the same enemies."

Jabotinsky's face grew taught. If he thought the president's suggestion ludicrous, nothing in his demeanor gave it away. "So what do you need from me?"

"I can't take that meeting," admitted Ben Gurion, "without Revisionist support ... without *your* support."

Jabotinsky had his enemy right where he'd always dreamed, but for naught. Hitler's threat made their mutual hatred seem like a lover's spat.

"It'll cost you."

Ben Gurion's brow creased upward; even rows of flesh pressed together in consternation. "But I thought you agreed th ..." The President saw the look in his adversary's eyes and shrugged. Gamesmanship till the end. "Fine," he groused. "What do you want?"

They spent the next three days arguing the details.

June 1934

Hotel Buchwald, Berlin

David Ben Gurion and Haim Arlosoroff sat at a small, round table sipping coffee, barely touching the Baumkuchen cake Arlosoroff had ordered up to the suite. It was already a warm day, and the large, double-paned window had been thrown open to let in some air and lessen the pungent smell of old furniture and musty curtains. A light summer's rain fell, typical of June, and the soft hum of foot traffic and the intermittent bleating of a car horn could be heard from a distance. Those sounds competed with the occasional creak of footsteps meandering along the hallway's parquet floor just outside the tiny room.

"How did it go?" asked Arlosoroff with obvious concern.

Ben-Gurion's eyes swept the room.

Arlosoroff gave the president a reassuring pat on the shoulder. "My man checked. He found one but moved it into the bathroom. We'll put it back when this meeting's over."

Ben Gurion nodded.

"Well?" asked Arlosoroff, brow raised expectedly.

"It went better than I would have thought."

"*How* much better?"

"He seems to think I'm some sort of Josselman of Rosheim."

"Josselman." Arlosoroff twisted the name around in his mouth. "Josselman ... that name is very familiar."

"He was a Rabbi who was a favorite of Maximilian and Charles, the Holy Roman Emperors. They made him protector of all the Jews in the Empire, and he helped the Emperors with fundraising and information."

"So you're a Josselman now?"

"Not quite, but someone's been plying the Nazis pretty well, somehow managing to convince them that I run a unified world Jewish power structure."

"Really?" asked Arlosoroff with a lopsided grin.

"You wouldn't happen to know who could have given them such a crazy idea."

Arlosoroff shrugged his shoulders in mock innocence. "I still don't know how that party could've managed to take over a country as advanced as Germany. Bulgaria, maybe ..."

Ben Gurion nodded, eyes glimmering intently. "No, it does not surprise me at all. The same twisted mind that believes there is somehow a human decency virus that can only be destroyed by wiping us from the face of the Earth can just as easily be fooled into thinking we have some sort of persuasive power that might be used towards more nefarious ends. What really worries me is what happens when the Nazis want us to deliver on that supposed power."

Arlosoroff's mouth crooked into a sly grin, and there did not appear to be the least bit of concern in the smooth, unperturbed lines of his face. "Leave that to Ruppin and me," he assured. "The Nazis believe all our power is hidden, that we somehow have a supernatural ability to communicate with one another. It's no wonder they want us dead—what they can't comprehend, they kill. But that superstitious ignorance can work to our advantage as well."

Ben Gurion motioned for him to continue.

"When something bad happens to them," explained Arlosoroff, "I'll drop some hints that it would've been much worse without the Jewish Cabal's intervention. When something goes well, I'll wink at Himmler or Eichmann knowingly, and they'll spread tales far and wide about how they got the Jews' dark magic working for them."

"And you really think they'll buy that?" asked Ben Gurion. "Hitler I can see, but Himmler? Eichmann?" Ben Gurion shook his head. "They're not so much idealists as pragmatists."

"That's the beauty of it," answered Arlosoroff, "They don't have to buy it. What they *must* do is follow Hitler's whims—if they want to stay alive, that is. This Jewish Cabal nonsense allows them to do just that *and* gives them something to sell to their subordinates ... most of whom *do* believe in that anti-Semitic tripe."

Though Ben Gurion's eyes were rapt and curious, his expression left no doubt as to his true feelings.

"Yes, David," agreed Arlosoroff, "it's crazy, I know. But do you doubt for even a second Hitler's fear of us, his belief that we are *vermin*? Not my word, his!" Arlosoroff's voice was filled with contempt. "Do you doubt, sir, that he'll use that false belief to harm us—to murder us? Yes, my plan is audacious, but this man *is* going to war." Arlosoroff had the look of someone defiantly staring down his shooters in a firing squad. "If Hitler ... *when* Hitler conquers Poland, how many Jews will be left at his mercy? How many of us will have to die before my crazy idea starts to make sense? No, David—we cannot wait. We must act now if our people are to have any chance of getting out of this thing alive." Arlosoroff's face remained cold and impassive. Finished, he took a small bite of the cake, but there appeared to be no joy in its consumption. It was simply something to do while awaiting the president's response.

Ben Gurion's smile was forced, his hands pressed tightly over one another. By his acquiescence, he knew he'd be agreeing to give credence to every blood libel and anti-Semitic trope that had, leechlike, clung for centuries to the backs of his perennially victimized nation. And that his first act as the new Jewish President would be to spit on the million-plus graves of every innocent Jew who'd died as a result of history's most heinous and vile lie.

"All right," he finally agreed, exhaling deeply. "If it saves my people and gets us all safely to Palestine, then I will play the cabal's leader."

* * *

... any individual of the Jewish race who accepts the authority of the World Zionist Congress shall no longer be considered a Jew under German law but shall henceforth be identified as a Zionist. This shall be stamped on all their papers. They shall be resident aliens under the direct authority of the WZC until such time as immigration can be arranged.

—Excerpts from the *Zionist Protocols* as amended to the Nuremberg Laws.

The end result being that just about every Jew in Germany is now a Zionist. As resident aliens, they can work, earn money, and pay taxes in any number of jobs they could not have as Jews. It is true that they must send their children to Betar (a Jewish version of the Hitler Youth) and live in ghettos run by the WZC. This however, is an improvement over living as a Jew under German law. In this way, the German economy is aided, as German companies can still use Jewish lawyers, engineers, architects, etc., as long as they are Zionist lawyers, engineers, architects, etc.

—Excerpt from the *Saturday Evening Post*
September 4, 1936

1936

Vienna

It was the last place Ben Gurion wanted to be seen—to be, even. He stared up at the sign and confirmed it on the crumpled paper he held in his hand: Berggasse 19. The cobblestone streets and simple storefront signs gave the neighborhood an airy provincialism that suggested that though time marched on for the rest of the world, those living in Vienna's ninth district were somehow immune. Their little shops, quaint cafés, and corner markets seemed to have always been there, and the history-soaked stones Ben Gurion stood on seemed to indicate that they always would. He was the odd duck in this pond of swans.

Ben Gurion rang the bell and was soon greeted by Vienna's most regarded citizen. Doctor Sigmund Freud was still rather spry at eighty years of age, his bald head and crisp white goatee were instantly recognizable, as were the three-piece suit and gold pocket watch dangling from the middle button of his vest. Freud's crinkled eyes sparkled in tandem with his bright, inquisitive smile. After a warm handshake, Ben Gurion was led into a comfortably sized room whose walls were partially illuminated by three large, drape-covered windows. The place, noted Ben Gurion, smelled like a humidor—a testament to the doctor's twenty-cigar–a-day habit. A few black-and-white etchings of various sizes announced themselves along the walls, hung in odd groupings. Though Freud's desk was sparse, containing a writing pad and a few small sculptures, the rest of the room was not. Antiquity was strewn about by way of busts on pedestals and an odd assortment of small statues, vases, precious stones, and a few phallic amulets lining the well-stocked, dark mahogany bookshelves. A large Persian carpet covered the polished wood floor, and directly in front of the desk rested the doctor's famous couch. It was not how Ben Gurion had imagined it. His vision of an austere leather divan was smothered by the warm embrace of a plush, afghan-laden chaise longue topped with a pile of bright, ornately stitched pillows. There was even a Persian prayer rug hung at the back of the couch, giving the whole ensemble the feel of a place that might be settled into with a good book and a hot cup of tea rather than a place to confess one's deepest, darkest secrets.

Freud noticed the object of Ben Gurion's gaze.

"Perhaps you'd like to try it out?"

Ben Gurion lifted a bushy eyebrow to the doctor. "You have got to be kidding."

"Forgive my little joke, Herr Ben Gurion. It's just that everyone seems to want to."

"I can rest when I'm dead, thank you very much."

Freud graced the president with a half smile, inviting him to take a seat in front of the desk. "What brings you to see an old retiree like myself?" asked the psychiatrist, easing himself into a chair.

"The Nazis in general, but Hitler in particular."

"I see," mused Freud, pulling a cigar from his pocket and neatly clipping its end into an ashtray.

Ben Gurion's lips pursed accusingly. "I thought you were ordered to give those things up."

Freud nodded. "Many times." He struck a match and brought the pirouetting flame to the cigar's tip and then drew in. "The cancer's killing me. Half my jaw's been replaced by surgery, and no amount of medication can reduce my heart palpitations nor reduce the constant agony I've been living with."

"So?"

"I can no more quit smoking than you can give up fighting for the Jews—it's part of our makeup." Then, "How may I be of assistance?"

Ben Gurion nodded, understanding all too well. "On the face of it, the Nazis seem to be insane and, I fear, making me that way as well. Who better to help me figure this out if not the great Sigmund Freud?"

"Figure what out, exactly?" asked Freud.

"The Nazis, of course. Terrifying bunch."

Freud exhaled a plume of cigar smoke. "Interesting."

"What is?"

There was slyness in corners of Freud's upturned mouth. "This fear of losing control."

"Ha!" laughed Ben Gurion.

"More, in fact," continued Freud, "than your fear of the Nazis themselves."

Ben Gurion's brow cinched, a poor levy to restrain the flood of emotion he was feeling inside. "What in Zion's name are you prattling on about?"

"You, I presumed," answered Freud good-naturedly. "Why else would you be here?"

"I've already told you: to help me understand *Nazi* mentality."

"That is not what you said. Or," he added quickly, seeing Ben Gurion's irritability, "not the totality of what you said."

Ben Gurion grumbled his acquiescence. It was hard to argue with Freud when it came to matters of the mind.

"What do you fear so much," continued Freud, tapping the end of his cigar into the ashtray, "that it drove you to Vienna to talk to a dying old man in a small, smoke-filled room?"

Ben Gurion sighed, resigned. "And how long will this psychoanalysis take, Herr Doctor? My schedule seems to be pretty busy,"—he paused to check his stopwatch—"for the next decade or so ... that is, if I make it that long."

"I'm glad you think *I* have that long," laughed Freud through a small fit of coughing. "No need for years of therapy. When you called for the appointment, I took the liberty of looking into your biography ..."

Ben Gurion laughed. "Which one?"

"Please. The German one is complete rubbish. Though the Americans didn't seem all that happy with you either."

Ben Gurion considered the backhanded compliment. "Had the Americans not closed off their country to us, I might've felt inclined to listen to their opinions. As such, their sensibilities are not my highest priority—those of our impending executioners are. Now," he repeated with more stridency in his voice, "will you help me?"

Freud viewed his prospective patient with studied impassivity. He drew again from his cigar. As he exhaled, the smoke swirled upwards, filling the shafts of light with a series of beautiful, undulating patterns. "How may I be of assistance?" he finally asked.

"This Hitler fellow."

"Yes?"

"Every time I talk to him, I can't ever be sure if something I say will be misconstrued—something that could very well get every Jew in Germany murdered. Do you have any idea what that's like?"

Freud mumbled in acknowledgment as he busily began jotting notes into a small pad.

"Talking to a man who is insane," continued Ben Gurion, "powerful, *and* intelligent, and that that insanity can be directed at you like a thousand Cossacks looking for a synagogue to burn on Easter. What do I say? What do I do with such a man? I've been working on instinct up until now. But the stakes have become far too high to gamble on instincts."

Freud stopped writing, placed his fountain pen neatly on the table, and then opened a small drawer. He removed a blank pad of paper. "Take this," he said, handing over the journal, "and fill out everything that Herr Hitler has said in your presence. Do you need a writing instrument?"

Ben Gurion shook his head and removed a fountain pen from his inner breast pocket.

"Please try to separate what you *think* he meant from what you actually heard. Every meeting, phone call, or personal communication of any kind. These recollections are of the utmost significance. When you're done, leave the journal with me. I'll have some sort of answer for you by tomorrow."

Ben Gurion nodded, his eyes now less probing, his demeanor more relaxed.

"You must realize," cautioned Freud, "that this is not the way I prefer to work, but given the extraordinary nature of the events in question ..." The psychiatrist did not finish his sentence, merely stared at the president encouragingly.

"Which language do you wish me to write this in?" asked Ben Gurion.

"German, if you please."

Without another word, David Ben Gurion began scribbling into the pad. He'd look up occasionally—nowhere specific—pulling snippets of memories from the air. It took him the rest of the afternoon and on into the evening to finish the task.

* * *

"There was only one Jew in the world that Adolph Hitler was friendly with. It is, of course, very lucky for us that the Jew in Question was Ben Gurion."

—Excerpts from *The Two Chancellors*
Tel Aviv: Tel Aviv Press, 1966

Ben Gurion was back the very next day at the very same hour, sitting in the chair across from Freud. The father of modern psychiatry looked at the President of the Jews with unguarded bemusement.

"Out with it," groused Ben Gurion.

"You have no idea what a tight rope you're walking, do you?" offered Freud.

Ben Gurion nodded. "That it *is* a tightrope, certainly. The height from which I might fall, no idea whatsoever."

"Well, I'm pretty sure that I do … *Papa*."

Ben Gurion stared blankly. "Papa? What sort of *meshugena* talk is that?"

"Forgive me my little joke. You are not *my* father, you are—strange as this may sound—Herr Hitler's."

Ben Gurion's lower lip dropped, his mouth twisting into a rictus of dismay. "What?" he finally sputtered.

"I only meant in a psychological sense, of course. In a way, the Jews have always been something of a father figure to the German people."

"In that case, they sure have a funny way of treating their parents."

"No," corrected Freud, "they are acting in the expected manner. You love your father. Then you want to be free of him. Then you want to kill him. But you *always* want his approval. Most of us never escape the bonds that form in early childhood. The German nation is just a larger example of this."

"So they're not insane?"

"I never said that."

"But you just …"

"… said they're acting in a predictable manner," continued Freud. "I know. But this is no normal child, Herr Ben Gurion. Our behavior and actions are typically inculcated from birth, usually via society, family, religious culture, or some combination of those three. We do not go out and indiscriminately kill and rape and destroy and take. Civilization would not survive if we did. Occasionally, a member of society does go insane, and we're forced to take action. But this is the first time that an entire country has done so. If Germany decides to kill every Jew, they will. And most likely they *will* decide to kill every Jew."

Ben Gurion absorbed the news, slack jawed. "Is there nothing we can do?"

"There is," he answered authoritatively, "but it contains the very real prospect of driving the patient mad."

"Patient?"

Freud looked at Ben Gurion. The initial bemusement that had greeted the President of the Jews was no longer there, replaced instead by unremitting pity.

May 1938

Berlin

Ben Gurion couldn't understand what Hitler saw in Hermann Goering. The commander in chief of the Luftwaffe seemed to do nothing that didn't involve some sort of glutinous extravagance. He was rumored to have mistresses, though Ben-Gurion cleared those thoughts from his mind—the images conjured were too grotesque to entertain. To make matters worse, the Jewish president had to contend with the fact that the calculating bon vivant actually seemed to like him. Of course, Ben Gurion realized that Goering's relationship with him might be a pretense, but that in itself was not surprising. Many in the Nazi top hierarchy had recently befriended him in order to please their Fuhrer, who'd of late seemed taken with the strange little Jew. But most, if not all of them, were clearly pretending—evidenced by their stentorian smiles and all-too-polite mannerisms. Of course, the Reich's Minister of Propaganda, Joseph Goebbels, made no such pretensions—he hated Hitler's Jew with a fathomless passion. *That*, at least, Ben-Gurion could get behind. He'd actually found such forthright honesty refreshing.

It's because he still can't accept that his pure Aryan wife used to sleep with Arlosoroff, decided Ben-Gurion. *It also doesn't help that Hitler continues to rib the sanctimonious bastard about it.* The head of the Luftwaffe, however, was not pretending. Ben Gurion thought that maybe Goebbels just wanted *everyone* to like him. Whatever the reason, the Jewish president just wished the huge man would like him a little less. The problem was, if Goering liked you, he'd treat you the way *he* wanted to be treated. He'd try to drown you in alcohol and smother you in food—with plenty of women thrown in on the side. Ben Gurion had to be polite with this powerful member of Hitler's hierarchy, especially when stuck, as he was now, at yet another of Goering's overindulgent dinner parties. All things being equal, he actually preferred dining with the Fuhrer. Ben Gurion didn't mind the vegetarian fare, seeing food as a necessary evil anyway, and, like Hitler, wasn't much of a drinker. It was true that the mad German could talk about anything, but then again, so could Ben Gurion, and while the conversations were often erratic, occasionally bordering on deranged (rainfall in Bavaria could lead to a discussion on Custer's last stand), they were never, *ever* boring.

"My dear Jewish friend," urged Goering, bits of masticated pig flesh pitching through his still-gnawing teeth, "you must, you simply *must*, try the swine brauten!"

Ben Gurion resisted shaking his head in flat-out refusal. If Herman Goering loved pork sausage, then everyone must love pork sausage—Jewish heritage notwithstanding.

"I am sure that they are as delectable as you say, my dear friend and air marshal." *When did I start sounding like them?* thought Ben Gurion, not for the first time. "But after much discussion with the Fuhrer, I have stopped eating the flesh of all animals."

Goering looked crestfallen but quickly sized up the situation. If he criticized Ben Gurion for being a vegetarian, he'd be criticizing Adolf Hitler, and that was something none of the Nazi leadership would ever do.

After a moment, the rotund mass of coruscating medals smiled and shrugged. "Well, then," he laughed, "that just means more for me!" Goering took leave, and his booming voice could soon be heard trailing down a cavernous hall of the resplendent mansion.

Thank you, Dr. Freud, mused Ben Gurion as once again Freud's psychological insights and perfectly hewn answers proved sufficient to avert another crisis.

The rest of the evening would have been dreadfully dull but for the presence of Dr. Hugo Eckener, the Director of the Graff Zeppelin company. Even in his late seventies, Dr. Eckener cut a powerful figure. He had the sharp, crow-lined eyes of a survivor. A tuft of white mane held firm on his forehead against a receding hairline that dropped back onto close-cropped silver hair. A small white goatee protruded just beneath his lower lip. Though his ears were small and pressed tightly against his head, there was nothing the man did not hear. Eckener was particularly pleased to be sitting next to the leader of world Jewry. He seemed to want to thank Ben Gurion personally for a device one of his Zionist engineers had invented to dissipate the static electric buildup plaguing Eckener's Zeppelins. The first device had been installed in the *Hindenburg*, Germany's flagship dirigible. The ship, insisted a beaming Eckener, had a stellar safety record thanks to the invention. Not wishing Eckener's gratitude to go to waste, Ben Gurion used the opportunity to pitch an airship line from Germany to Palestine. Grateful as he was, Eckener remained unconvinced. Gratitude was one thing, execution quite another. But Ben Gurion was persistent and promised to bring it before Robert Ley, Head of the German Labor Front, who also had Hitler's ear. That Ley was yet another drunk lout and shameless embezzler sucking from the golden Nazi teat was beside the point.

"If it could be turned into a Strength through Joy program," conceded Eckener, "maybe German tourists could use it to visit the Holy Land."

And we Jews could use it to finally get to Palestine, thought Ben Gurion.

* * *

Ben Gurion left the palatial home of the air marshal and quickly spotted his Mercedes four-door sedan parked just outside. The 260D was large and spacious enough to accommodate the Jewish president and, if need be, one or two others, but it was modest compared to the hefty amounts of polished chrome, dimpled leather upholstery, and oversized grills of the other waiting limousines. Before his limo could even pull up, Ben Gurion strode over and hopped into the passenger seat, paying no notice to the upturned noses of the appalled chauffeurs. As the car sped off, Ben Gurion turned to face the driver. Most who looked at the young man averted their eyes. It wasn't that he was ugly; it was that his obscenely large ears—flayed out at almost ninety degrees from his head, demanded to be noticed. It was simply easier not to notice the man at all than attempt to avert one's eyes from the two demanding protuberances. That, of course, suited the driver just fine. He was, after all, a spy.

Isser Harel seemed absurdly young to Ben Gurion. Though only in his midtwenties, Isser carried with him a bag of tricks one would expect from a more experienced operative. The very fact that he'd been waiting inside the car as opposed to outside already let the Jewish President know that something urgent was afoot.

"What now, Isser?"

"The Americans will be cutting off *all* our funds."

Ben Gurion's eyes flickered anger for a moment but then quickly waned to resignation. As the Zionist movement had grown closer to the Nazi Party, American funds had naturally begun to dwindle. But the truth was that the new German Zionist donations had more than made up for the loss. Plus, the operating budget Ben Gurion now had to work with as a result of the ever-increasing pool of donors was far larger than any he'd ever had before. The downside, knew the president, was that it made the Jews even more dependent on the Nazi regime.

"Not unexpected," grunted Ben Gurion. "In some ways, it may even help."

On Isser's raised eyebrow, the President continued, "Hitler hates the Americans even more than he does the Russians ... maybe even the French."

"The enemy of my enemy," said Isser, grinning, eyes focused like a hawk on the road ahead.

Ben Gurion found it difficult to think of the Americans as the enemy. But the Jews in America were safe. So safe, in fact, they really didn't act like Jews at all—at least, not as far as he could tell. The Jews of Europe, the Jews of Germany—not safe. And until they had their own land, protected by their own soldiers, they never would be. If the Americans couldn't understand that, indeed, choosing only to send moralizing words from behind the protection of their vast ocean walls while allowing no one to enter, then to hell with them. The car drove on into the dark night towards a meeting the Jewish president in many ways desired to attend even less than his fraught-filled talks with the Fuhrer. The Reichsführer of the SS waited for him in much the same way, mused Ben Gurion, that a jackal awaits its prey—hungry, determined, and so very patient. Yes, Heinrich Himmler was another matter entirely.

* * *

Himmler chose to entertain Ben Gurion at No. 8 Prinz Albrecht Strasse, Berlin—the former art museum and now infamous Gestapo headquarters. As the limousine pulled up in front of the building, it was immediately besieged by the black-clad guards of the SS. Fortunately, though, Ben Gurion's face was widely known and the scanning of his documents, perfunctory. He was waived through to the building's grand entryway, where a wide stairway, thick with balusters, led up to a vaulted entry hall. There, two large swastika flags clung stiffly to the wall. Beneath each flag sat a bust, one of Goring and one of Hitler, both separated by two twenty-meter-tall, multipaned arched windows. Why there was no bust of Himmler, Ben Gurion could only imagine. Perhaps it was because the building's interior had been made in Himmler's image—cold, grandiose, and ominous—rendering a bust unnecessary. Or perhaps it was because it would've been almost impossible to portray the thinly mustachioed, delicately framed man with the Prussian haircut in anything approaching the heroic miens of the Luftwaffe's air marshal and Germany's Fuhrer. It was of little relevance to Ben Gurion. He'd once again been pulled into the Reichsführer's web, and he'd once again have to carefully and painstakingly find a way to get himself out.

Like most of the high command, Himmler enjoyed entertaining his officers with lavish dinner parties. It seemed that most business in Germany got done not in offices during the day but via the parties at night. For the sake of efficiency, Himmler had constructed both an opulent dining room and a fully stocked kitchen within the same building where everyone worked.

When Ben Gurion was finally ushered into the dining room, he was presented with a lavish feast—a table piled high with a veritable cornucopia of kosher meat delicacies from knishes and schnitzel to brisket and chulent—the Eastern European meat porridge Ben

Gurion loved and so desperately longed for. *How could Himmler have even gotten that information?* he wondered. Unlike the boorish Goring, Himmler knew that Ben Gurion was a vegetarian of convenience only who'd snookered an overjoyed Hitler into believing Ben Gurion had followed his example. But unlike Goering, Himmler knew how to make his Jewish dignitary pay for the deceit.

The second most powerful man in Germany was busily chowing down on a plate piled high with all sorts of meat. His round glasses reflected the opulence of the table's finery. "We have news," he offered while his delicate hands fastidiously carved off slices of succulent brisket, "that you might find interesting, *Zionist Leader*." It was a moniker of which the Reichsführer had of late become enamored.

"Does this have anything to do with the Americans cutting off our funds?"

Himmler stopped cutting and looked up, vaguely annoyed.

"You have excellent sources of information."

"What sort of leader of the international Jewish conspiracy would I be if I did not?"

"You do not seem upset about this," Himmler noted in his usual bloodless tone, placing his knife and fork ever so delicately on his plate in an inverted V shape.

"The value of America in Jewish affairs, though great, is no longer—how can I put this?" Ben Gurion paused.

"Vital to your well-being," finished Himmler.

Ben Gurion nodded. "We hate to lose those assets, but they can be ..."

"... sacrificed," Himmler finished.

Ben Gurion understood the game. The Reichsführer was always looking for a psychological edge, always seeking a way to get the Jew's goat—even if with something as slight as constant interruptions. If he saw it worked, he'd file it away for later use—for the interrogation Ben Gurion was sure Himmler must have been dreaming about. But the Reichsführer wouldn't succeed—not this time, and not until Herr Freud felt it pertinent that he should.

"That is what our intelligence unit had determined as well," continued Himmler, unperturbed. "Your interests are now firmly aligned with the success of the Reich."

Ben Gurion, not trusting himself to speak, gave a small nod.

Seemingly satisfied, Himmler picked up his knife and fork, and once again the sound of utensils on fine china filled the large room as he sliced through the fine meats. But the Reichsführer wasn't quite through. "The international Jewish conspiracy is no longer a threat to the Third Reich," he said, never once looking up at his guest. "But you seem to have some internal dissent."

The feeling Ben Gurion most feared quickly moved its way into his gut. There would be a sacrifice, and it was absolutely critical that he remain calm, no matter who or what that sacrifice would be. "Not everyone understands our actions, Reichsführer. We have generally found it is best to ignore them."

Himmler lifted a crystal goblet filled with red wine, swirled it once, tipped his nose into the glass and inhaled deeply. He took a sip, and then a moment later, a small, satisfied smile broached his lips. "That is your prerogative *outside* the Reich," he answered, once again gazing up at Ben Gurion. "But inside, we have no such luxuries of time. By order of the Fuhrer, those especially critical of your leadership have been detained and are no longer your concern."

Ben Gurion knew what that meant—knew, in fact, to whom the Reichsführer had been referring to. He'd warned the men in question, and in the case of the Rabbi in Berlin, he'd done so personally. Both men had felt that they could not in good conscience support the Zionization of Germany's Jews and had spoken out not only against Ben Gurion but Hitler. And now they were probably dead. For the sake of the Jews Himmler could kill now and for the Jews who, by dint of the Reich's machinations, he'd soon be able to, Ben Gurion said nothing, revealed nothing. Instead, he offered a tepid smile.

"In that case, I must thank you and the Fuhrer personally. It would have been politically difficult to deal with this myself."

Himmler acknowledged the remark with an appreciative nod. "That is what we understood. All must be constantly reminded that there is a price to be paid for threatening the Nazi-Zionist alliance."

"Of course, Herr Himmler," answered Ben Gurion, feeling oddly claustrophobic in the oversized room—thinking that perhaps he would be the next bit flesh waiting to be skewered and added to the Reichsführer's meal. "Though," he pretended to add as an afterthought, "it might be more effective if I could have one of the dissidents back."

Himmler pushed his plate aside and then peered down his spectacles at the Jewish President. "Really?"

"Yes," answered Ben Gurion. "The power to make people disappear and then have them reappear would have quite an unnerving effect, I imagine. And I want my enemies within the Zionist movement, especially the ones I don't know about, to be nervous."

"You have enemies you don't know about?"

The spirit of Freud then took over with a phrase purposely designed to elicit an empathetic response. Ben Gurion heard the old man's words leaving his own mouth as he said them, "There are always enemies you don't know about, Reichsführer, *especially* in your own organizations."

The smile Himmler gave was now chillingly genuine. "You are correct, of course, Zionist Leader. I am afraid that the men in question are … how shall I put this? Beyond retrieval. But we will keep that in mind for the future."

May 1939

The Fuhrer was unusually apoplectic. "It's simply too dangerous for you to go back to Palestine; that is final!"

After five years of Freud's painstaking psychological manipulation, Hitler's friendship with Ben Gurion had finally cultivated itself into a very real need. So much so that the Fuhrer's own staff would ensure Ben Gurion's presence whenever matters of great urgency needed to be discussed with their volatile leader. While Hitler's addiction to Ben Gurion had managed to work wonders for the Zionist cause in Europe, it had roused a long dormant anti-Semitism within the United Kingdom. In an irony lost on no one, the safest place in the world for Jews was in Nazi Germany—so long as they called themselves Zionists.

"I must return, Adolph. The Arab Revolt is over, and it's rumored that the British are going to outlaw the Haganah."

"The treachery of the British knows no bounds," scoffed Hitler. "The Arab *untermenchin* rebel, and it is the Zionists who are punished? You who've been loyal to the British cause from the beginning, whose men have died alongside their soldiers!" Hitler's face grew flush with rage. "And this is your reward?"

Ben Gurion's face remained placid, his manner calm. "Nothing has happened yet, Adolph, and if I return, I should be able to calm things down. After all, I have your backing and the British, while antagonistic towards us, are manifestly political creatures. They can be reasoned with."

"I have my doubts."

"As well you should, and so do I, but Palestine must be secured if we're to arrange for the emigration of the Jews out of Europe. For the Reich's sake, this must happen. Nothing must get in the way of their exodus. Jabotinsky will remain here in Germany and continue organizing the Zionists."

"I don't like him," Hitler said flatly. "He's like Mussolini ... only with hair."

Ben Gurion chuckled. He continued to be amazed not only at Hitler's rapier wit but also the fact that someone as unbalanced as the Fuhrer could actually have one. "That may be," Ben Gurion said with assuredness, "but he's the only one able to keep a lid on things until I return."

Hitler sighed, then ran his fingers through his thick brown hair. "Nobody here knows a good vegetarian dish from bad. And they all drink and smoke."

"Adolph, *I* still smoke."

"Yes, but you're down to what—half a pack a week? Soon you'll give that up as well." The tone of his voice, the sheer conviction, momentarily caught Ben Gurion by surprise. It was Hitler's way, his gift. And it didn't matter whether he was speaking to a single man or to a crowded stadium of acolytes, the result was almost always the same—momentary stupefaction. It was always then that he inserted his divination.

Ben Gurion recovered quickly. "I'll tell you what, Adolph: I'll give up *all* smoking while I'm gone. That way, if I'm away long enough, I'll *have* to quit."

Hitler's piercing blue eyes cut holes through his friend. "Not a single cigarette?

Ben Gurion nodded.

"Not a pipe, nor cigar?"

"Nothing," confirmed Ben Gurion. "But it's an easy vow, Adolph. How long will I really be gone—two, three months at the most?"

* * *

David Ben Gurion Arrested!

By order of the British Mandate Authority for Palestine, World Zionist President David Ben Gurion was arrested upon his arrival in Tel Aviv yesterday, May 28, 1939. The British authorities gave no reason for the arrest other than to say it was to calm tensions.

— ***The** New York Times*

* * *

1) The prisoner is to be allowed no visitors.

2) The prisoner is allowed no books, newspapers, or reading material of any kind.

3) The prisoner is not to be talked with or communicated with in any way except as is strictly required by the nature of his confinement.

4) The prisoner will not be alone with anyone at any time. There must be a minimum of two prison personnel in sight of each other when the prisoner is interacted with.

5) If there is the slightest chance the prisoner can escape, he is to be executed immediately.

—Orders found in a Tegart Fort in Ness Ziona
Office of the Commandant
From the Appendix of *My Cell, My Hope, My Victory*
By David Ben Gurion

* * *

The Government of the Third Reich protests in the strongest possible terms the confinement of the President of the World Zionist Congress and demands his immediate release. If he is harmed in any way, the consequences for relations between our two nations will be most unfortunate.

—Telegram from
the Reich's Foreign Minister Von Ribbentrop
To His Majesty's Government of Great Britain

* * *

May 1941

David Ben Gurion woke up in the middle of the night to a tiny cell that had not changed one bit in the two years he'd been forced to call it home. Even the blankets hadn't been changed. This he knew because he'd been forced to do his own laundry in a tub provided by a cadre of ever-silent guards. In fact, the cell and corridor were the only things he'd seen during his confinement. He was more familiar with every sound, smell, stone, and crevice of the dank prison than he'd ever been with anything else in his life. Which is why, when his eyes sprang open as if preternaturally aware, he knew something was different.

Before he could apply reason to the sensation, the sound of footsteps filled the outer corridor, keys worked the tumbler, and a moment later, his cell door swung open. Though it was the middle of the night, it was no lowly guard that had come to roust him but rather the prison commandant. The short, boyish-looking man was the first and only individual who'd ever spoken with him—as opposed to at him—over the course of Ben Gurion's two-year stay. And it had only been on that first day, when the hood had been yanked from his head, that the conversation took place. Ben Gurion still remembered the Commandant's words.

"You're going to die here, Nazi lover. The only way out of this cell will be via a crate." The man had uttered the words as if a proclamation—

delivered with both certitude and enmity.

And now, as if to put the final stamp on that earlier proclamation, the Commandant removed the service revolver from his holster. Ben Gurion got up slowly from his bed and stood in front of his executioner without flinching.

"Why now?" he asked in a voice that hadn't used speech in months.

"You cannot be allowed to escape," answered the Commandant, snapping open and then checking the chamber of his Webley revolver. "The harm you can cause to the war effort is too great."

One of the President's bushy eyebrows arched upwards. "There's a war?"

"Not for you," answered the Commandant with a half smile. He snapped the gun shut and pointed it at Ben Gurion's chest. Instead of the pop-pop sound Ben Gurion had been expecting, the pistol roared to life as if it were an automatic machine gun. Why such a small revolver would make such a big sound was, to say the least, rather odd. The fact that the Commandant had missed him from such short range was odder still. That is, until the man keeled over—a lifeless, bloody pile on the cold cell floor. Just as suddenly, two men appeared—both wearing British field officer uniforms. One was a complete stranger to Ben Gurion. He was sporting what appeared to be a fencer's gash that started from the middle of his right cheek and went all the way down to his chin. But the other, even with the bloody bandage taped over his right eye, was familiar.

"Moshe?" Ben Gurion exclaimed.

The man nodded.

"What happened to your eye?"

"This little thing?" scoffed Moshe. He then leaned over the dead man's body and began rifling through his pockets. "I must have poked it with a pencil. It's nothing."

"Bullshit, Moshe," said the stranger in perfect German. He then looked over to Ben Gurion. "Your fucking kike friend was almost killed by a sniper who hit his field glasses instead of his stupid kike head!"

"Fuck you too, Otto," replied Moshe, now holding up a set of keys. He smiled proudly. Although the language was crude, Ben Gurion recognized that it was not true vitriol but rather banter—the two men were friends. Moshe tossed Otto the keys with such force that Otto was forced to duck before snatching them midair with his gnarled fist. The German smiled ruefully at having been caught off guard. Then he glared at Ben Gurion.

"Move your ass, Jew. I'll be damned if I can't keep my promise to the Fuhrer because you dawdled." And with that, David Ben Gurion stepped out from the room that had been his prison and once more stepped into the annals of history.

* * *

Ben Gurion had been both horrified and amazed to learn of what had transpired in the two years he'd been gone. The world was at war. Poland had been conquered and the Jews liberated under Zionist control. France had been toppled and its skilled Jewish labor force, wanting very much to stay alive, had readily acceded to being brought into the Zionist fold. There'd been the failed Battle of Britain and the denunciation of Zionism by both the British and the American governments. Both eventually disavowed the Balfour Declaration and promised that *all* of Palestine would be an Arab state. This was followed by the mass arrests of many leaders of the Zionist movement in Palestine, Britain, and eventually America.

Ben Gurion had been saddened to learn that Albert Einstein, his hero, felt it necessary to flee to the German embassy in New Jersey and plead for asylum. The Nobel Prize–winner had been roundly denounced as a traitor but was safely transported back to Germany despite British efforts to intercept him. Einstein had been given a hero's welcome upon his return, and Ben Gurion had stared, awestruck, at a photo of Hitler, Einstein, and Heisenberg all shaking hands. In the photograph, Einstein looked very confused, *But*, thought Ben Gurion, *who could blame him when he lived in a world that had been turned upside down?*

Hitler had signed a nonaggression pact with, of all people, Stalin, but had to invade the Balkans because they were supporting the British and had begun murderous pogroms against the Jews in Yugoslavia, Albania, and Greece. But it was not until information secured by Orde Wingate, a British officer, ardent Zionist—despite being a non-Jew—and friend of Moshe Dayan, that things really got going for the Jewish nation. Orde had discovered and then managed to leak Ben Gurion's secret whereabouts. With that information, Hitler was finally able to launch the rescue mission that had had him chomping at the bit for two long years. Of the ten German paratroopers who parachuted in and the ten Haganah soldiers who met them, only Otto Skorzeny and Moshe Dayan had survived. Through Moshe's connections, they'd managed to find a safe house, and over the course of that first week of freedom, Ben Gurion had learned a lot from the SS *Untersturmführer.*

"I was the fucking junior officer," Skorzeny had barked over his Slivovitz, a plum brandy he seemed to favor. "Nine assholes who outranked me, and I survive. Well, me and that crazy kike," he'd said, pointing to the door where Moshe was busy "entertaining" the woman whose home they'd been hiding in. "There were only two of us left by the time we got to you with only three good eyes between us, but did that maniac even think about quitting? I don't have much use for you Jews, but if the ones who live here are like him, the Fuhrer's right—we need to get *all* of you people over here."

Ben Gurion had listened carefully to what Skorzeny had said all that night and through many others. He listened, he learned, and when he had all the facts, he decided. A few weeks after Ben Gurion's rescue, The SS *Untersturmführer* received a coded messaged from the German High Command. He handed the paper over to the Jewish leader. Ben Gurion nodded gravely and immediately set about getting to a broadcasting station.

* * *

"Jews of Palestine," he began. "Jews of the world, I speak to you from hiding, in the land that was promised to us. A land Jews must hide in and be afraid in like all the other lands of the Earth because of a promise broken. A solemn promise was made by a nation that was supposedly our friend—when they needed us. But when we needed them, we were scorned and betrayed. Well, my brothers and my sisters, maybe we have to be afraid in all the *other* lands of the Earth. But we will no longer be afraid in *this* land. On this night of May 29th, 1941, paratroop forces of the Third Reich are landing all over Palestine to liberate us from oppression and fear as they have liberated our brothers and sisters in Poland, France, and the Balkans. These brave German forces are landing on fields even as I speak and are joining members of our outlawed Haganah— outlawed for the crime of wanting to defend Jewish lives with Jewish fighters. But these brave soldiers are outlawed no more.

"From this moment forward, I declare the State of Israel reborn." Ben Gurion paused to taste those words as a smile crept up his face. "But if Israel is to survive this night, we must rise up. We must rise and join our German liberators in throwing off the yoke of British oppression. We must fight from every Kibbutz and every Moshav. We must fight from our cities and towns and fields. We must fight till we've earned the right to be called Israelis and once again call this ancient holy land ours—our Israel."

As Ben Gurion stepped away from the microphone, a young woman took his place.

"You have just heard the words of Chancellor Ben Gurion," she said in a voice thick with pride, "of the newly declared State of Israel. All units of the Haganah, Palmach, and Irgun are to muster and begin Operation Liberation. I repeat: all units are to muster and begin Operation Liberation ..."

Ben Gurion was no longer listening. He left the cellar and slowly climbed the stairs up to the apartment's first floor. Through a partially opened window, he could hear the sound of cheering and gunfire. Both sounds would continue to echo long into the night.

* * *

Suez Canal Falls to Combined Nazi/Israeli Force.

German forces are reporting another stunning success on top of their already impressive gains in the Soviet Union. British forces, already starved from the German submarines based in the port of Haifa, were overrun by a two-pronged attack on the Suez Canal from Libya, under the leadership of Erwin Rommel, and from the Sinai, by combined German/Israeli forces under the command of Moshe Dayan. Although the Sinai operation was small in scale, the overwhelmed, poorly supplied, and demoralized British and Egyptian armies offered little resistance. The meeting of the Israeli and German advancing forces was a cause of joyous celebration throughout the Reich and amongst the Zionist populations protected by the might of German arms. Zionists throughout Europe were seen dancing in the streets, toasting the names of Ben Gurion, Hitler, Dayan, and Rommel as the days of their millennia-long exile were finally coming to an end.

—Der Spiegal

* * *

Turkey and Spain Join War on Behalf of the Axis Powers!

The treacherous though not entirely unanticipated entry into the war of Spain and Turkey have completed the transformation of the Mediterranean into an Axis lake. Malta, besieged with a starving population, is expected to surrender shortly. It is reported that Turkish forces are already advancing into the Southern Soviet Union and if not stopped could end up in the oil-rich Caucuses before winter. Military leaders in Washington are unable to comment on whether the loss of the Caucuses or the imminent capture of the capital city of Moscow will be the worse blow for the Soviet Union. Either would be a calamity, sufficient to effectively knock the Soviet Union out of the war.

It was rumored that President Roosevelt had made a personal appeal, backed by a significant financial aid package, to President Inounou and Generalisimo Franco requesting they not enter the war. However, with the loss of Egypt and the Suez Canal to German/Israeli might, the Turkish and Spanish entry on the side of The Axis was considered by almost all experts to be regrettable but inevitable.

—The New York Times

* * *

March 1942

Berlin

David Ben Gurion was bathed in a sea of flashbulbs. He wished he could have worn sunglasses as he advanced across the field at Templhoff to greet his "friend" Adolph Hitler. With the dizzying array of lights, he could barely make out the Fuhrer, but the Fuhrer could clearly see him. Hitler seemed to be bouncing with joy.

Could he have actually missed me that much? wondered the new Chancellor of Israel.

Hitler grasped Ben Gurion's outstretched hand with both of his own. The look of joy on the Reich Chancellor's face was both obvious and now, fittingly, preserved for all time.

Ben Gurion was prepared for this moment. He'd been briefed by Arlosoroff and had reread the old reports from Freud, now deceased. Even after two years of separation, Hitler still considered Ben Gurion his closest friend and had equated the Israeli Chancellor's imprisonment with his own brief sojourn at Landsberg jail—a fallacy Ben Gurion had no intention of disabusing him of. Ben Gurion learned how frantic Hitler had been over his incarceration. But none of it seemed real until his hand was in Hitler's and he saw … love—deep and abiding love. Ben Gurion did not know if he wanted to laugh or cry. Wisely, he did neither.

Once in the limousine, Hitler's countenance changed yet again. He was no longer the Chancellor of the Reich and undisputed ruler of its ever-widening territories but rather a young, effervescent child who'd gotten exactly what he wanted for Christmas. It was in these few moments of silence that Ben Gurion was finally able to speak to his and his people's savior. Of all the things he'd been prepped to say, what emerged from his mouth was not one of them.

"I haven't smoked a single cigarette since I last saw you, Adolph. But the British mamzers made sure that meat was in my rations."

"That's all right, my friend," said Hitler, leaning across the limousine and giving Ben Gurion a warm pat on the knee. "They've paid for their treachery and will, I assure you,"—the Fuhrer's eyes suddenly grew cold—"pay even more."

* * *

The secretary peered up from her stack of papers as the doors to the antechamber swung open. Two stern-looking Wehrmacht soldiers entered, perfunctorily scanning the room. They glanced over at the secretary as if she, too, were just another piece of furniture, nodded to each other, and then held the double doors open wide. As the dignitary entered, the woman's mouth dropped slightly, but she sprung to her feet, recovering quickly.

"Welcome to the Israeli Embassy, Office of the Chancellor, *Reichsmarschall.*"

Goering bowed politely but smiled impatiently.

The secretary punched the intercom. "Goering to see you, sir."

There was a brief pause followed by a barely perceptible sigh. "Send him in, Golda," squawked the voice and then clicked off.

* * *

Ben Gurion stood up from behind his wide, expansive desk— gift of the Fuhrer. Unlike the Fuhrer's desk, however, Ben Gurion's wasn't swallowed up by a warehouse-sized room. In fact, it took a good-sized portion of it. Hermann Goering strode in, his polished leather boots squeaking slightly as he crossed the short distance to Israel's Chancellor. As usual, Goering was bedecked in a sea of medals that adorned a well-tailored uniform. The man, noted Ben Gurion, had grown even larger and, judging by the cheek-to-jowl grin he was currently sporting, was even more jovial than usual. Ben Gurion returned the smile and extended his hand to the newly promoted *Reichsmarschall.* Goering took it and began pumping Ben Gurion's arm as if it were a car jack. Goering then wrapped his ungainly arms around the Israeli Chancellor in a bear hug.

"You did it, you amazing Jew, you did it!" exclaimed Goering, stepping back to reveal his still-beaming face. "I wasn't sure anyone could—we all tried—I didn't think you could either, but what else could we do? And you," said Goering, grabbing Ben Gurion by the shoulders, "you convinced him!"

"Do you mean that jet thing?" gasped Ben Gurion, finally extricating himself from the Reichsmarschall's burly grasp.

"That 'jet thing,' you call it. Hah!" chortled Goering. "The Fuhrer insisted that we turn the ME-262 into a fighter-bomber. Do you know what sort of delay that would've caused? We are ready to begin production of an interceptor now. It could've set us back two years. Everyone tried to talk him out of it; everyone but you failed—only you. In six months we'll have a test squadron; in a year we'll have a thousand jets patrolling the skies of the Fatherland. Then the Brits and Americans can go fuck themselves."

"Why did he declare war on the Americans?" asked Ben Gurion, realizing his slip-up too late. One never questioned the decisions of the Fuhrer—at least, not openly. Private conversation with Hitler was another matter entirely—there, intellectual sparring was a necessity used to build trust. But in public—never. Freud had drilled that into Ben Gurion repeatedly, but Ben Gurion had been tired and distraught. With Hitler's pronouncement, the Americans had declared war on the fledgling state of Israel—an obvious German ally. And now, in one fell swoop, the Jews of America had been torn asunder from their promised land with little hope—at least for the foreseeable future—of reconnecting to their lost heritage or, God forbid, finding refuge when the world turned against them. Though the American decision had been more of an afterthought, it was yet another reminder of how precarious Israel's situation had become, and of how it had fallen on Ben Gurion's tired shoulders to lead his people to the promised land on nothing more than a tightrope.

"After Pearl Harbor," answered Goering, seemingly unconcerned by Ben Gurion's breach of protocol, "it seemed like the right thing to do. Plus, he hates the Americans. In some ways, he hates them now more than ever."

Ben Gurion not only agreed with the Reichsmarschall's assessment but understood it as well. Hitler needed to hate. He needed to hate the way some men needed to make love or to drink or to play with their children. It was primal and undeniable. And thanks to Freud and Ben Gurion's masterful manipulation, the Fuhrer had, bit by bit, stopped hating Jews. As that hatred ebbed, he'd found a replacement in the Anglo-Americans.

Better them than us, thought Ben Gurion.

"But what does it matter, David? We have this war practically won. All of Europe except for Britain is ours. It is true we were thrown back from Moscow—damn the Russian winter—but we're only twenty-five miles from the Kremlin, and the Caucus oil fields are a ruined no-man's land between our Turkish Allies and the Bolshevik dogs. In the spring we'll take that, and there's nothing the Americans can do. We owe much of this to you and your brave Haganah soldiers."

No longer trusting his words, Ben Gurion acknowledged the compliment with grunt.

"If there's anything," continued Goering, "*anything* I can personally do to repay you, do not hesitate to ask!"

Ben Gurion laughed inwardly. He'd just a moment ago determined to remain tight-lipped, but now Goering had given him an opening—one he'd be a fool not to exploit. "Well, Reichsmarschall ..."

"Herman. You must call me Herman," insisted Goering.

"Herman, then."

Goering became uncharacteristically quiet, looking at the Israeli Chancellor expectantly.

"It's just that we finally have a state of Israel, and, well ... so few people to put in it."

"Yes?"

"I mean, we have people; it's just that I keep getting the runaround."

Goering's eyes remained wide and attentive. "Go on."

"Thanks to the Reich's generous support, we control everything from the Suez Canal to the Jordan River and beyond. But that's a lot of land, and we have less than a million Jews to oversee it. Except for some token transports, we've sent hardly anyone over. For nine years, the Zionists and Nazis have been working, struggling, and fighting to create a Jewish state so the Jews of Europe could leave and settle there."

"And what a glorious partnership it's been, David!"

Ben Gurion nodded. "One I owe my life to, and that of my people. But they're ready to leave, Herman, and now, oddly enough, are being delayed in doing so."

Goering stared at Ben Gurion for a brief moment, and it soon became obvious he was doing his level best not to laugh. "David Ben Gurion, you are a funny man. You're so smart in so many ways—and strong. Two years in solitary under such harsh conditions would've broken most men. Though now I'm beginning to wonder if perhaps the desert heat didn't get to you."

"How so?"

"We need Jews, you silly Chancellor." When he saw Ben Gurion's blank look, Goering sighed. "I will explain. We're in the middle of the greatest war in history. Our occupation of Europe is not universally popular. Exploiting the resources of Europe efficiently is not easy. But Jews make all of this easier. Everywhere we go in Europe, we find some Jews, and God Bless them, they're almost all highly educated and speak some form of German you insist on calling Yiddish. They can be used in everything from factory management to railway work. We've placed them in our universities, hospitals, and engineering firms. I can't begin to tell you how many we have working on the ME-262 and V-1 programs alone."

"But if Israel—a country *both* our nations worked so hard to create—is to survive, then those Jews are exactly the sorts of people we'll need." Ben Gurion could see that his plea was falling on deaf ears—despite the Reichsmarschall's previous promise. If Ben Gurion had ever thought the one force keeping Jews *in* Europe would be the Nazis ...

"And you will get them. You will," assured Goering. "Just not till the war is over." A mischievous smile sprang from the corners of his mouth—"Or maybe a little while afterward."

* * *

Moscow Has Fallen!

Proof of Soviet Atrocities Against Helpless Jews Enrages Reich!

—*Der Spiegel*

* * *

May 1943

Haifa, Israeli Reich

David Ben Gurion was not used to making house calls. Hospitals, military bases, and factories, yes. Countries? Absolutely. And of course there were those who continued to call on him—politicians, dignitaries, businessmen, and the like. When he reflected on it, Ben Gurion realized it had been ages since he'd felt the need for a personal visit. But circumstances had changed, and the need had arisen like so many others, as if via a *hamsin*—the scorching desert wind that would occasionally blow through the Middle East, sending both temperatures and temperaments to the boiling point.

Ben Gurion stood before the entrance and briefly looked over his shoulder at the security detail that had accompanied him to the home. He smiled gamely at the unflinching men, then turned around and knocked. An eye peered at the Chancellor though a small peephole. The door swung open immediately, and a short, round woman holding a duster and a tray greeted him as if the Chancellor of Israel showed up at the door every day.

"The Professor is expecting you in the study," she said, head pointing down a cramped hallway overflowing with books. "I will bring tea."

As he passed by and briefly perused the shelves, Ben Gurion thought about how wonderful it would be to grab six or seven to take home and read but then banished the thought from his mind—he simply didn't have the time. He wondered if he ever would again.

When he got to the library, he laughed. The outside shelves were a mere adornment to the cavalcade of books fighting one another for space in every square corner of the professor's study. Ben Gurion noted two open books on a paper-covered desk and somewhat alarmingly, a lit pipe plopped in an ashtray—but no professor. Ben Gurion peered into the open books but saw they were written in one of the few languages he could not understand: advanced mathematics. There was a rumbling from another room, followed by the sound of flushing water. A moment later, a stooped man with hair as wild as Ben Gurion's entered. When he saw the Israeli Chancellor, his face brightened.

"Chancellor Ben Gurion!"

"Professor Einstein," greeted Ben Gurion, equally as warm.

"Welcome to my house, and please forgive the mess. I'm just moving in."

"What mess, Professor?" asked Ben Gurion with an impish smile.

Einstein nodded, satisfied. "It is an honor to finally meet the leader of the Jews."

"The honor, Professor, is all mine." For Ben Gurion, it wasn't simply a platitude. He'd been with so many men wanting to be great and pretending to be great and needing to be great that it was wonderful to finally meet one who truly was. They were briefly interrupted by the housekeeper, who brought in a tray with some thick tea glasses, an old kettle, and plate of biscuits. It was only after she poured the tea and arranged the biscuits that Ben Gurion, who'd been beckoned by the professor over to a pair of worn leather armchairs, got down to business.

"I received your letter, Herr Einstein," Ben Gurion said, purposely reverting to German. Einstein's broken Hebrew could not be trusted for so auspicious a conversation.

"I thought that may get your attention," Einstein said with a half smile.

"Is it true?"

"Is it true?" repeated Einstein, and then seemed to roll the question around his mouth. "I don't know. But it sounds true; it feels true. The man who communicated with me included letters and notes from others. Ferme, Oppenheimer—before the Americans shot him, that is."

"Shot him?"

Einstein nodded, his shoulders slumping. "It would be foolish to assume it is not true and go from there."

"I agree," said Ben Gurion. "What could this super bomb do?"

"Have you seen pictures of Moscow lately?"

"Yes, including those that have been censored."

"How many men, how many bombs and artillery shells, do you think it took to cause the damage you saw in those pictures?"

"I couldn't fathom."

"No need to. Hundreds of tons of explosives, over a million men, and months of unremitting assault," answered Einstein. "If my calculations are correct, and I will have to check them again"—Ben-Gurion snorted in disbelief—"one super bomb could do equal or greater damage in an instant."

"One bomb?" exclaimed Ben Gurion.

Einstein nodded.

"And the Americans are working on it."

"It is what I'm forced to conclude."

"Can they do it?" Ben Gurion heard the pleading in his own voice and hated himself for it. Overcoming the madman had been hard enough, the trenchant anti-Semitism of the Reich, equally difficult, but this—this wasn't something you could reason with or manipulate. This American weapon wasn't interested in currying favors. It would do one thing and do it unequivocally— destroy in an instant everything in its path. Not even Freud could have talked his way out of that.

Einstein took a few more pulls on the pipe and answered. "Yes, they can. But because they've imprisoned or will not use many of their best physicists and mathematicians, it will necessarily take them longer than it should have."

"How much longer?"

"It's a big country, Chancellor, and they have a huge number of adequate physicists and mathematicians who'll get there eventually."

"What if I gave you everything—and I mean everything—I could? You'd have at your disposal all the resources of the Israeli Reich. Could you build one then?"

Einstein chuckled. "Given another twenty years, perhaps. But I'm not sure I'd even want to build it, and even if I was sure, I am sure we lack the resources necessary to do it in a timely manner— your Israeli Reich notwithstanding. Oh, sure, we have enough scientists, I think, and maybe close to enough engineers, but there's no industrial base here to speak of—no machine tools nor skilled workers to operate them, no uranium or the means to refine and form it. No," he said, banging his pipe into an ashtray, "it can't be done in any useful time frame. I'm afraid we'll have to make peace with the Americans."

Ben Gurion's lips pressed together. "The Americans will not make peace with us, Dr. Einstein. Even if they were willing, it could only be done at the price of betraying the one nation that stood by us, protected us, freed us, and, if honor is not enough of a motive, still has millions of our clansmen under their direct control." Ben Gurion watched as his words penetrated Einstein's thoughts. Clearly the scientist hadn't taken every factor into account. "Even if we make some sort of peace with the Americans," continued Ben Gurion, "and once again turned our brothers and sisters in Europe into targets of Nazi vengeance, it would still do no good. The Americans would turn us over to the British the first chance they got, and the British would arm the Arabs to destroy us. The Brits hate us more than anyone. In their eyes, we made them suffer the worst loss in their empire's history. That they betrayed us is not even a consideration in their minds. After all, they've betrayed almost everyone. But mark my words, Professor: they will destroy us if given the chance."

"Then we are doomed," answered Einstein, looking forlorn. His frame seemed to sink even deeper into the armchair.

Ben Gurion put his hands on the armrests and leaned forward. His back was rigid and his eyes cold and ruthless. "For the survival of the State of Israel and the seven to nine million Jews in Europe, I will ask you this question once again: Are we able to build a super bomb?"

Einstein's brow furrowed. He didn't answer right away but rather began mumbling to himself. Ben Gurion, normally a very impatient man when it came to this sort of thing, did not say a word.

"It is possible," Einstein finally admitted.

Ben Gurion exhaled and nodded, motioning for the professor to continue.

"But not us."

"Then who?"

"Our wardens, that's who. They have the industrial base and enough skilled workers to spare. They also control the uranium mines of Bohemia. Still," he said, doubt edging his words, "they're surprisingly weak in the basic physics. Heisenberg is brilliant—smarter than I am, I think—just not in the right way."

"We could help them with that," said Ben Gurion softly.

"They may already be working on it," offered Einstein. "If they are, perhaps we don't need to get involved."

Ben Gurion slowly moved his fingertip around the edge of the teacup. "No," he finally said, "I don't think so. If they were working on something of this magnitude, I would've found out. That sort of effort involves Jews and lots of them. They may have a small program—that I wouldn't notice—but that doesn't help us. Not with the Americans apparently devoting all of their vast resources to this super bomb. If it's the Germans we need, it's the Germans we shall have."

"Not the Germans, Chancellor, the *Nazis*." The manner in which Einstein had said the name left no doubt as to his feelings.

"What choice do we have, Professor?"

"To not give this bomb to a madman," answered Einstein, "to the murderer of children—that's our choice!"

Ben Gurion's voice was calm and his answer measured. "We don't have such luxuries."

"But history …" pleaded Einstein.

Ben Gurion's face tensed. "What of it?"

"It will never forgive us."

"Forgive us? Forgive *us*?!" yelled Ben Gurion in a voice suddenly thick with rage. He slammed his fist on the small table, rattling the china. "History has recorded our shame, our exile, our pain, and our loss. How *dare* history judge us! If anything, Professor, it is history that should be asking us for *our* forgiveness!"

Einstein remained mute, either too afraid or too disturbed to talk. Ben Gurion softened his tone, but the steel in his voice did not falter. "We're talking about our very survival. If we don't give Hitler this bomb, we Jews will finally end up as the footnote of history that countless generations of anti-Semites have dreamed about. There have always been 'troubles,' Herr Professor, and we've managed to survive them all, but this ... this super bomb will be the end of us. I know it, and now you know it as well. The question is, are you prepared to let that happen?"

Einstein leaned forward, placing his elbows on his knees. His hands slid into his garrulous mane. He remained hunched over like that for a few minutes and then finally looked up. His eyes were wide and pleading, their corners pricked with tears.

"I will do it," he mumbled.

Ben Gurion offered little in the way of thanks or encouragement. "Good," he said. "Maybe if you do, we can write our own history. But first we must survive it."

"Have you any idea," asked Einstein, "what Hitler will do with such power ... of what will become of the world?" It was more a warning than question.

"Professor," answered Ben Gurion coolly, "when the world shows any sign of truly caring about us, then maybe ... *maybe* we can start caring about the world."

"They will, Chancellor. One day. You'll see."

"Tell you what, Professor: you let me know the next time that happens, because as far as I'm concerned, it will be the first time that that happens."

Einstein slowly nodded his agreement. "We'll have one major hurdle to get over first."

"I told you," offered Ben Gurion, "resources will not be a—"

"I'm not talking about resources, Chancellor. I'm talking about ego. How can we get the Germans to even listen to us? They think they know everything. Heisenberg's a perfect case in point."

Ben Gurion reflected on that for a moment and finally nodded. "I'll need you to write a letter. You'll have to explain things very simply and give lots of credit to the German physicist, emphasize what the Americans are doing."

"The world," repeated Einstein, this time in a barely audible whisper, "will never be the same."

"Yes, Professor," agreed Ben Gurion, "but that is no longer our problem. We cannot be expected to repair a world that would see us to an early grave. The world will just have to save itself."

Einstein shook his head in despair, took a deep breath, and with pen in hand, began to write: *From the desk of Dr. Albert Einstein. To: Adolf Hitler, Fuhrer of the Greater German Reich ...*

* * *

March 1944

Berlin

David Ben Gurion peered out from the back seat of the *Kommandeurwagen*, a luxurious four-door coach-built convertible used by high-ranking officers in the field. That he'd been accorded a vehicle of such status was a testament to just how far he'd risen within the ranks of the German High Command. But Ben Gurion had little interest in the car's appointments or even the crowds who'd thronged the sides of the road to cheer him on; it was Berlin that now drew his attention. The city, he noted in awe, was almost completely undamaged. The once ever-present sound of air-raid sirens had disappeared with the Reich's ascendancy in the air. As if on cue, a thunderous roar cracked open the sky and a squadron of ten ME-262s flew in tight formation overhead. These swept-wing airplanes with the unearthly howl were far faster and menacing than the prop planes they'd so recently made obsolete. *I'm surprised the Reichsmarschall didn't hug me to death*, mused the Israeli Chancellor.

Thousands of handheld flags bearing the Star of David undulated alongside those bearing the swastika, all to the cacophonous cheers of an energized throng. For the first time, realized Ben Gurion, the adulation did not seem forced; the appreciation of what his nation had done for theirs was as real as the Messerschmitts roaring overhead. *I am a strange and magical figure.* He laughed inwardly. *Perhaps even Wurdiz, their Norse god of fate.* But Ben Gurion also remained aware of the precariousness of his situation. If Hitler decided, he could kill the Jews outright with not a finger in the world lifted to save them. Certainly not the USA, currently rampaging through the Pacific. All they'd do is cheer. The fact of the matter was that there was no one left who would or even could stand up to the Reich. The Chosen People were now at the mercy of a lunatic.

Ben Gurion nodded to the bystanders and waved gamely. His face creased into a smile he did not feel. Hitler had ordered—no, *commanded*—him to come to Berlin. That didn't bode well. The Fuhrer hadn't done that in years—not since Ben Gurion's rescue from the Brits. The car finally pulled up in front of the Reich Chancellery, the nerve center of the government. Hitler's architect, Albert Speer, had built a smooth-stoned behemoth designed to impress and intimidate. The entrance's four high columns were topped by a large eagle and framed a set of massive doors. To the left and right of the entrance, all Ben Gurion could see was row after row of evenly aligned windows with slightly protruding ledges that disappeared into a multitude of horizontal lines. Speer had created the epitome of the Nazi ideal: absolute order—cold, calculated, and impenetrable.

An honor guard saluted Ben Gurion as he emerged from the vehicle. Hundreds were on hand to cheer him into the building's great maw. He couldn't wait to escape the crowd, even with the growing discomfort of not knowing what waited inside.

As he entered, Ben Gurion tried to think of what it was that had gotten Hitler so worked up. Everything seemed to be going so well. His Zionists had achieved smashing success in the Gotterdammerung Project, the Nazis' version of the Manhattan Project. They'd created a working prototype of the flying wing—a plane that in theory could carry bombs all the way to New York. They'd helped Werner Von Braun with his V-3 rockets, and thanks to them, the first intercontinental ballistic missile was going to be operational within a year. Zionists were keeping the Suez Canal running and had been found to be excellent managers of the forced labor factories in all the captured countries. Their command of German-related Yiddish as well as that of their native countries made them invaluable go-betweens. Plus, not being nearly as harsh as the Germans had almost always resulted in better production.

Ben Gurion considered but quickly dismissed the notion that his many requests for Jewish immigration to Israel may have been the culprit. True, he'd been a bit insistent, but the Nazis were still racist bastards, and no matter how happy they were to have the Zionist brain trust, they still dreamed of a Europe and Fatherland free of Jews and any of the other "impure" races—though apparently not anytime in the near future.

Ben Gurion followed his escort through the grand foyer of the building, but instead of heading towards the rebuilt offices, he was led to the underground levels—hardly ever used now that Germany owned the skies of Europe. But when he was shown to the big conference room, he finally began to relax.

He wants to show me another model.

Hitler and Speer had been designing the new Berlin even before the beginning of the war. It was rumored that Hitler was even a little annoyed that the Allied bombing hadn't been more effective because it would make tearing down and rebuilding more cumbersome. Still, Speer continued to make scale models of all his potential buildings, whether the space for them was ready or not. Often, when one was ready to show, Hitler would bring Mussolini or Ben Gurion over to view it. As far as Ben Gurion knew, he and Benito were the only ones invited to these show and tells, much to the jealousy, he was sure, of Hitler's inner circle.

It was always the same. They'd be escorted down to the conference room to find a large table covered with a huge white cloth, beneath which waited another Speer "masterpiece." Speer was never present. All the other attendants and hangers-on would be peremptorily dismissed. Then the game would begin. Ben Gurion learned early how to play it, as it was one of Hitler's favorites. After the unveiling, which was a game in itself, they would crouch down and put their eyes on the edge of the table to see what it would be like if they were standing on the actual street. Then Ben Gurion would ask the technical questions that showed he cared. Where would the subway stations go? Would the power lines be above ground or buried? He would try to guess where the secret passages were, and Hitler would delight in telling him if he got it right or wrong. Then they would have an argument about where would be the best place to live in order to get the best view of the new building. Ben Gurion would always lose that argument, but he always argued hard and would always end up saying, "Well, Adolph, what do you expect? You're the one who lives here," and Hitler would laugh and be in a damn good mood for weeks afterwards. But it was the part before the unveiling that Hitler seemed to really enjoy, and Ben Gurion was going to let him.

The Israeli Chancellor stared at the outline of the building hidden beneath the cloth. He knew the rules. He'd take off his jacket and fold it over a chair. Then, very formally, he'd walk around the model. Hitler would follow closely behind, studying his every reaction with a gleeful grin, practically drooling in anticipation of the big reveal. Ben Gurion would reach for a corner of the covering making as if to lift if up for a peek. Like always, Hitler would stand in his way and say the exact same words in the exact same way: "No, no, no … peeking," and make as if to slap his hand, but he never would. Ben Gurion would walk around some more and start to hazard a few guesses. Had Ben Gurion really been honest with himself, he would've admitted to also enjoying the game. It was fun to guess. But part of the fun was getting to be annoyed.

"Well, it's too flat to be a new dome or arch," he began, looking at Hitler for clues. None were forthcoming. Just the Fuhrer's same "bet you can't guess" grin. "At first," continued Ben Gurion, "I thought it might be that new stadium you never finished—a redesign, if you will."

"Is that what you think it is?" asked Hitler, radiating excitement.

"No, I can just make out that the building is rectangular, not oval or circular. It is not a stadium."

"That was easy. I'll give that one to you. Correct, Chancellor, it is not a stadium."

"Hmm," Ben Gurion said, continuing his walk around the model. "It could be anything rectangular. An office building, a museum and mausoleum for the war dead … but the ground is not flat." He stopped, realizing that that was important. "The ground is not flat like most of Berlin. Whatever this is, it is built on a bit of a hill. That means it does not have to be Berlin." He saw from the look on Hitler's face that he'd guessed right. "It's not Berlin; I knew it!" Ben Gurion shouted, getting into the spirit of the game.

"Alright, alright, it is not Berlin," admitted Hitler, "but you will not guess it, even knowing that."

"We'll see, we'll see," Ben Gurion said, now looking intently at the cloth, trying to pick up any little clue. "There are clusters of buildings around this one. I know what it is," he shouted in triumph. "This is going to be that University complex you talked about building near Munich. That's what it is; I know it!"

Hitler's lips curled up triumphantly. "Wrong, wrong, wrong. But don't feel bad, David; you never would've guessed this in a million years or, to be more precise, one thousand eight hundred and seventy-four."

On Ben Gurion's blank stare, Hitler continued, "Really, David, that's the last hint I can give you!"

"Well, don't keep me waiting, Adolph. What is it?"

Hitler went to the table and flung off the cloth sheet with the pirouetting grace of a matador.

Ben Gurion froze at the visage. *We're going to have to kill forty million Muslims,* was his first horrified thought. The word "no" ricocheted through his head like a bullet in a bomb shelter. Hitler was droning on about all the facts involved in the building—where the marble would come from, how much quartz would be used, how they would demolish the old building on the site and the fact that the Third Reich would foot the entire bill as a token of gratitude for all that the Zionists had done for the German Volk—all prater in Ben Gurion's ears.

It was the Temple of Jerusalem.

Only it wasn't. This building was at least twice the size of the last one destroyed by the Romans in 70 AD. More ominously, there was no sign of the Dome of the Rock—Islam's third holiest site—nor, Ben Gurion noticed, the Western Wall—Judaism's holiest site. Huge retaining walls of imported marble surrounded the holy of holies, now a veritable cathedral thick with swastika-laden columns each topped off with stylized Eagles intricately carved into the stone. A monstrously large Star of David, apparently made of gold, hung atop the building's entrance. Hitler had, of course, positioned the conference room's overhead lighting for maximum effect.

Himmler did this, thought Ben Gurion frantically. *He knows Hitler's mystical side and planted this seed knowing I'd be cursed no matter what I did. Himmler fucked me—fucked all Jews—good with this.*

"You are silent, David," Hitler said, an edge of concern creeping into his voice. A concern, Ben Gurion knew, that could quickly spill over into anger. "What do you think?" pressed the Fuhrer.

What do I say? thought the most powerful Jew in history. Nothing came to him. In a desperate flash of inspiration, he knelt at the edge of the model and peered into the street leading up to the holy of holies, where the *Kohanim* used to offer the sacrifices. But when Ben Gurion looked down, what he saw at the other end of the table was anything but holy. It was a monstrously huge face, blue eyed and fever bright with a saliva-flecked grin. Hitler stared across at him, and Ben Gurion, dumbfounded, stared back—street level with a madman.

The End

Teach Your Children Well is the continuation of a side story that takes place in our Unincorporated series of books. Although you can enjoy it without knowing that universe, a little background is in order. Keep in mind, however, it will contain spoilers from our first two books.

The Unincorporated novels comprise a near-future story that takes place in our solar system roughly three hundred years from present day. It's a world in which the problem of classic capitalism, apathy, is solved by a system known as Personal Incorporation. This system posited that each person be incorporated at birth, with part of their earning potential sold to investors. The investors, in turn, made sure their "stock" stayed happy and healthy, thereby guaranteeing all a profit on human potential and productivity—a positive feedback loop. In a relatively short period of time, everyone in the world, and soon the solar system, owned shares of each other. Soon, the scourges of hunger, no healthcare, joblessness, and illiteracy disappeared. They were simply not profitable. Eventually, a majority of the human race ended up as minority owners of themselves. Because of the popularity and success of Incorporation, no one gave this fundamental loss of liberty a second thought.

That is, until a man named Justin Cord was found in a cryopreservation unit and awoken. Because Justin came from a time before the Incorporation movement, he owns no one and is owned by no one. He is *The Unincorporated Man.* Justin's initial resistance and eventual refusal to incorporate begins a process whereby people start to ask questions no one in control wants asked. Questions like, "Are we free?" "Are we really better off?" "Have we paid too high a price?" And the clincher: "Is it too late?" Some see Justin as a hero; others, as a villain. Eventually, Justin's questions turn to protest and, in the outer planets, outright revolt. In *The Unincorporated War* that ensues, the core worlds of Earth/Luna and Mars have the overwhelming bulk of the population and most of the industry while the outer orbits of the Asteroid Belt and everything beyond have a rugged, resourceful, and determined population with a vast amount of territory in which to operate.

It is within the chaos and freneticism of *The Unincorporated War* that *Teach Your Children Well* takes place.

TEACH YOUR CHILDREN WELL

An Unincorporated War Story

Year 4 of 7 of the Unincorporated War

Fourth Battle of Anderson's Farm

The assault transport was flying through a debris field of sister ships from three battles past—unfortunate victims of questionable tactics, shoddy armor, and a determined enemy. If the heavily armed occupants of the current transport had any reservations about returning to this floating war memorial, they gave no indication. And if any glimmer of hope existed at all, it would be that if the third time hadn't been the charm (which clearly it hadn't), then perhaps this, the fourth battle of Anderson's farm, would do the trick. The only other advantages they could be said to have was that they were soldiers, very well trained, and motivated by an almost unparalleled hatred of the enemy as opposed to a once inestimable fear.

Inside, most of the UHF assault marines were quietly checking their gear, and more than one was sound asleep despite attempts by the Alliance missiles, lasers, mines, and directed rocks to jolt them awake one last time before tossing them into space. It was the advantage of a veteran crew. The only marine up and moving was the sergeant. Her ancestry was mostly Southeast Asian, which was not a branch of the human race known for its giants. It was, however, known for its share of implacable warriors, and the good sergeant, tiny though she may have been, had no intention of letting her ancestors down. She was absurdly young for the rank but had earned it by dint of not dying in the two years she'd served the UHF. The sergeant was now walking up and down the length of the transport, stopping by every trooper, checking to see if they were ready, looking into their eyes for the emptiness that told her they would kill without mercy. She hadn't bothered performing the ritual with "Daddy" or "Baby Girl," the team's two latest additions. They were only with her unit temporarily, and she already knew there was nothing she could teach them.

Baby Girl's Story

Year 2 of 7 of the Unincorporated War

At key moments in her life, Sally Meadows would look up from washing her face, see herself in the mirror, and realize that she'd changed. Her face was not really any different than the one that had been staring back at her for the past few months, but the person peering out from within it was no longer the same. Death did that to a person.

Her older sister, Emily, had been one of the first to volunteer for the war and had been one of the first to die. Sally's need to avenge her sister, who would never live to get a majority of her own shares, never marry, and never have children, was greater than the oath Sally had once made to Emily not to follow her into the navy.

Someone in the Outer Alliance would be made to feel Sally's loss and understand what it was like to have a sister and best friend's future snuffed out.

* * *

With over a million residents, the Highland Living Complex was in effect a city unto itself, even if only as one small part of all the other living complexes that made up the almost 70 million residents of New York City. As Sally looked around the city's main auditorium, she was amazed at just how many of the thousands present she knew—if not by name then at least by sight. These were not only her friends and classmates; they were her neighbors and the older and younger siblings of her older and younger siblings—faces she'd seen her entire life. Yet even with all the comfort and familiarity of home, she couldn't wait to leave.

"Hey, Sal."

Sally turned to follow the voice.

"Hey, Gemmy," she answered, remembering the young woman's nickname.

"It's just 'Gem' now."

"Decided to be more grown-up, then?"

Gem paused for a moment, smiling. "Something like that. My uncle was the first one to call me that name, and now that he's gone ..." She let the sentence hang.

She and Gem had, for a time, been good friends during their two-month sexuality program—mandated by law at the onset of puberty—but had drifted soon after it had finished. At the time, it was all very exciting stuff. In retrospect, though, it had been a bit of a snoozer. They'd all had extensive testing and had all been summarily informed what sexual orientation the tests had revealed. They were then introduced to others of the same orientation, and the facts of life where explained in a matter that precluded any need for awkward guessing or confusion.

"Here with anyone?" asked Gem.

Sally shook her head.

Gem's tepid smile suddenly brightened. "Well," she said, taking Sally's arm in hers, "you are now!"

Together they made their way to a pair of open seats. The din of thousands of conversations carried to every corner of the filled-to-capacity auditorium. Sally decided to splurge and ordered some soda and popcorn cubes from the seat's concession stand (though she often wondered why it was called that since it didn't concede anything unless you paid it first). A bottle blank was summarily produced from the seat back.

"Mr. Pibb, cold level seven, carbonation nine," she said, pulling the bottle from the tray. It began to transform and assume the coloration and wording of the respective brand.

"That's right," Gem said. "You always used to amp your carb." She then picked up her blank. "Coke Zero, cold six, carb six."

With their bottle tops now melted over into smooth rims, the girls bit into their popcorn cubes. Sally stopped after a few bites.

"Why do you eat it like that?" she asked.

"Like what?"

"Everyone I know starts with a corner. Then usually bites off the other three. You started between two corners."

"Oh, that," she said, shrugging. "It's just the way my uncle used to eat it."

"Used to?"

Gem shared an all-too-common look of those who'd lost a loved one in the war.

Sally nodded empathetically. "Guess you guys were pretty tight."

"Me and Uncle Mel? Yeah. Especially since my dad was hardly ever around."

"I feel you," answered Sally. "Mine neither … as in ever. What was the deal with yours?"

"Well," answered Gem, "he was always taking any contract that came his way—especially in the outer orbits. The credits were good, and he never skimped on sending most of it home."

"But he was never around to help you spend it, right?" asked Sally.

"Not 'never,' just hardly ever. Thankfully, Uncle Mel was."

"What did he do?"

"Teacher. Fifth grade. In our building, actually. L-27. Ever have him?"

Sally racked her memory and came up blank. "Don't think so—unless your uncle is a woman. I had Ms. Tellesburg. She wasn't so great."

"Definitely not a woman," laughed Gem. "Nor was he ever interested in becoming one. Anyways, when the war broke out, my dad decided to stay in the outer orbits. Last I heard, he'd joined the OA's Navy."

"Wait," said Sally. "Your dad's fighting for the Outer Alliance?"

Gem nodded. "Pissed off my uncle so much that he went and joined our navy to even things out ... they never did get along that great," she added with a half smile. "They made him an officer in marines."

"Good leader, I guess."

"He was," agreed Gem, "but never wanted to be. Uncle Mel was happiest teaching kids. I still can't believe he's gone."

Sally's expression suddenly changed from one of sympathy to one of concern.

Gem looked at her askance. "What?"

"Nothin'."

"C'mon, Sally, I remember that look. It's not a 'nothing' look."

Sally, outed, smiled awkwardly. "If you join the navy, you risk fighting your dad."

Gem stopped nibbling on her popcorn cube and sighed. "Yeah. The thought had crossed my mind. But he made his choice, and now I'm making mine. What about yours?"

Sally's voice was laden with contempt. "I'm sure that wherever dear old dad is, it will be as far from any battle as he can manage. He was never exactly good at commitment, and volunteering for war is about as big a commitment as you can make."

Gem reached over and squeezed Sally's hand.

At that moment, the lights dimmed and Hektor Sambianco, president of the UHF, appeared.

The crowd was riveted. The president was as compelling in his current VR manifestation as he was in real life.

"We were told," he began without the usual pleasantries, "that this war was going to be quick and easy. Well, I'm here to tell you that that's a lie. As you're undoubtedly aware, we're in the second year of a conflict that, according to the experts,"—he said the last word with such disdain that Sally felt a surge of hatred for all experts everywhere—"should have lasted three months at most.

Well, *I* won't lie to you," he added before he began to lie. "This war will take many years and cost countless lives. And yes, I'm talking *permanent* deaths. Many of you are here because you've already lost loved ones. They can never be replaced. And even though I'm only a minority shareholder of my own stock, I am the majority shareholder of the trust and future of every human being in this room, this city, this planet, this solar system." He paused as a wave of applause swept through the room.

"Under new leadership, we've revamped the war effort. No longer will we underestimate the guile and cunning of our enemy. We know the depths they're willing to sink to in order to destroy our beloved incorporated system." Hektor paused, waiting for the booing and catcalls to die down. "A system that has brought undreamed of levels of prosperity and happiness to untold billions is now under attack by an evil from the past. An evil that calls itself ... Justin Cord."

The enmity towards the father of the Unincorporated Revolt was visceral, immediate, and bellicose.

"This monster," sneered Hektor, "claims to bring the 'gift' of freedom with him from his properly forgotten and, until recently, dead past. But what he really brings is discontent, anarchy, and despair!"

The crowd rose to its feet, screaming its hatred at the interloper from three centuries past. Sally was surprised to find herself up and shouting with the rest. She wasn't usually so free with her emotions.

"But incorporation is not so easily defeated," continued Hektor. "As long as young men and women are willing to fight for the greatest system of justice and prosperity the human race has ever known, we ... will ... not ... fail!"

The President smiled, encouraged by the cheers and support.

"As you know, we're a market system that rewards what's most valuable, and you," he said, pointing his finger in a cadence that led many to assume the President was talking directly at them, "are now more valuable than ever. The UHF will not skimp on rewarding you for what you're worth." At the smattering of applause, his eyes looked downward and his mouth quivered slightly. "But before I list how we'll compensate our heroes, I want to share something." He inhaled, then exhaled deeply. "I've lost friends to this war—men and women so precious to me as to be more important than family. They gave their lives, and because of that, I'll continue to risk mine. So let me say, 'thank you.' Maybe your families won't understand."

Sally joined a chorus of nodding heads.

"Maybe some of your friends will ridicule you. Maybe the planets at large will not pay attention to what you're about to do here. But" said Hektor, pointing his thumb inward, "*I* will. I know how extraordinary you are. I know the losses you've borne and the risks you're about to take, and for that,"—he now bowed his head in humble submission—"I thank you." The president basked in the adulation as the hall echoed in deafening applause. He gave one final wave and then faded from view. Moments later, Hektor's visage was replaced by that of a hardened marine in military dress, sporting a panoply of medals that glittered like stars on a moonless night.

The virtual marine went on to list the benefits of signing up for the war against the Outer Alliance. They'd all get two-tiered salaries. The larger one would be paid directly to them regardless of how much stock they owned. This was a more recent addition as it was found that soldiers could get easily disheartened if every two weeks 75 percent of their earnings went to stockholders safely on planet while the soldiers risked life and limb out in the depths of space. Now, only the smaller salary was subject to normal stock payments. Further, everyone sitting in that auditorium would get the right to sign up and go through basic training with anyone they wished. This meant that apartments, schools, or companies could and would have hundreds of friends, coworkers, and families join, train, and be assigned to units together. Sally felt Gem squeeze her hand and looked over at her. Sally, understanding the request, gave a brief nod and was rewarded with smile of such warmth and beauty it took her by surprise.

"I was going to ask you anyways," admitted Sally as they both giggled at the prospect of their new adventure together.

But what Sally was truly interested in was the stock buyback plan. From how she understood it, if she completed her tour of duty with an honorable discharge, the government of the UHF would match her credit for credit the amount she'd put into a special stock buyback program up to 5 percent of her salary. And she knew she was going to put in the maximum percentage. With any luck, Sally Meadows could finish out war with a majority interest in herself.

* * *

It was on the second day of her three-day leave that Sally received a message from the UHF High Command. Her orders had been changed. Instead of training in Camp Pendleton, California, she'd been reassigned to Camp Adam Smith in Russia. Sally looked it up. CAS was less than a month old. She wasn't too upset. It was the government, after all. A certain level of ineptitude was to be expected. If only the war could've been contracted out to a private bidder. But making war was apparently a sovereign power that even the incorporated system still respected.

Unlike the rest of her family, Sally didn't really have many close friends. She was much more of a loner. Sure, she had plenty of acquaintances, but Gem was turning out to be different. In the past few days, Sally had found it easier to talk to her than to anyone else. Sally knew the world had shifted in strange and terrible ways when her mom was actually eager for her to talk to "that man, your father," which was the phrase Augustine Meadows always seemed to use when talking about her ex to her children.

Sally placed a call to Gem. The line connected, but all Sally could see was her friend looking frazzled and all she could hear was the sound of a woman yelling in background.

"And how," challenged the woman, "can you expect to fight the rebels if you can't even clean your own room?!"

Gem rolled her eyes. "Mom," she barked, looking over her shoulder, "I'm on the holo!"

"Room! Now!" said her mom.

"I'll get to it, sheesh!"

"Don't you speak to your mother like that!" another woman's voice commanded.

"She's not listening to a word I say," complained the first woman.

"Hey," Sally began.

"Sorry," said Gem. "Parents."

Sally laughed. "At least you have both."

Gem nodded, eyes flecked with appreciation.

"Say," offered Sally, "would you like to come with me to—"

"Yes," interrupted Gem. "In fact, let's go *now*."

* * *

They met fifteen minutes later, and Sally explained her dilemma. It did not improve Gem's already surly mood.

"But they promised we could train together!"

"I know," agreed Sally, surprised at her friend's vehemence.

Gem marched up the street with Sally following close behind. Within moments, the automated taxi they'd summoned arrived. "Let's go!"

* * *

The large man behind the desk actually seemed taller sitting down than the diminutive Gem did standing up. Even so, he shrank ever so slightly from the righteous indignation blazing in his direction. More annoying to Sally was the fact that she couldn't even blame him for the mess. The government had contracted out the training of all recruits to Mudder Inc., a newly merged company of the three former competitors who'd decided the only way to meet the new work orders was to make a larger firm. Gem was not arguing with a hapless government flunky but rather a hapless corporate one.

"It was," Sally said, joining in, "a factor in our signing up and could be considered a breach of contract, which could give us legal grounds to get our enlistments canceled." The combination of Gem's tirade and Sally's calm, legalistic tone eventually struck a nerve. The man behind the desk blinked.

"Let me see if I can figure out what's going on."

He quickly called up three different holographic interfaces and began a mad scramble to track down the relevant information.

"Ah," he said, finally deigning to smile. "I see what happened. Because Camp Adam Smith just opened, they needed additional recruits to round out the next training cycle. Since you didn't put any specific preferences, you were transferred automatically." He smiled as if that explained everything, which it did, and thought he'd actually solved the problem, which he hadn't.

"Well," answered Sally with cool resolve, "you can just transfer me back."

"Um," answered the man, looking unhappily at his holo display, "I'm afraid that's not possible. Pendleton is full up for this and the next two cycles."

"Fine. Then delay our enlistment for two additional cycles."

The man blanched. "Uh ... delay?"

The women stared him down, arms crossed. Truthfully, the last thing either Gem or Sally wanted was to spend four more months at their respective homes, but the recruiter didn't need to know that.

"Yes, delay," answered Sally. "It's the only fair way to honor the part of the contract that states I can train with family or friends. Clearly, I cannot—certainly not in this situation. I'm sure your superiors will understand you had no choice but accede to my very reasonable demands."

Sally knew that the exact opposite was true. That once the bureaucratic wheels had been set in motion it was almost impossible to grind them to a halt, much less get them to reverse. But she also knew the last thing this guy wanted was to let her and Gem continue to complain up the chain of command with his name dragged through each layer of it as the guy who should've prevented the headache from starting in the first place.

He first looked over to Gem. "Would Ms. Suttikul be willing to accommodate a small change?"

Gem's eyebrow arched a tad. "How small?"

"Well, Camp Adam Smith is not yet full. If you were to request a transfer, I could have it authorized before you left the office. Then the two of you could train together."

Sally saw that Gem was about to say "yes" and broke in. "Unacceptable!" she bellowed.

Gem silently glowered at her, but Sally pressed on. "So," she said to the recruiter, "your solution is that Ms. Suttikul, like me, will have to give up going to war without the support of her family and friends?"

"But ... but you're her friend," the man stammered.

"Are you implying she only has one?" asked Sally, indignant.

"I never said—"

"So she should do this transfer to correct an error *your* corporation made just to make *your* problem go away. There's nothing in this for her, is there?"

"Well, I ..." He consulted his holo-display. "Perhaps some form of compensation?"

"Now we're talking," said Gem, teeth glinting in a calculated grin.

"Um ... ," he said, scanning the holodisplays for any way out, "I believe I can authorize a payment to the two of you for ... let's see here ... five hundred credits? For the inconvenience, of course."

"A thousand," Sally said flatly. Then added, "Each," for good measure.

"Each!" repeated Gem, winking at Sally.

"And not any of your brand-new corporate script either," insisted Sally. "GCI credits, thank you very much."

"I'm not authorized to ..."

"Then get me someone who is," demanded Gem, leaning over the big man's tiny desk.

Within two hours, Gem's transfer to Camp Adam Smith and Mudder Inc.'s transfer of one thousand credits to both Gem and Sally was complete. All they needed to figure out now was how to spend it all in the twenty-four hours they had left before being carted off to war.

* * *

"Off the transport, maggots!"

The drill instructor's order seemed a perfect fit to the dark and miserable day that greeted Sally and Gem at Camp Adam Smith. When the thirty recruits had finally gotten off the hover transport and were standing in what was close to two lines, the head instructor took her baton from a subordinate and walked up and down the line, shaking her head in disgust.

"It depresses me to think that these plains were once occupied by the fiercest warriors in the history of all the human race. On this very ground rode the Mongols, led by the greatest general of all time, Subodai. He defeated the Russians, the Ukrainians, the Poles, the Hungarians, and others too numerous to mention. To think that you're what I have to work with, that a race that could produce the Mongol horse archers is reduced to"—she eyed the motley crew warily—"this. To realize that the UHF must defeat the treason and rebellion of the Outer Alliance with"—she spat on the ground—"you."

She then picked her first victim.

"Well, what have we here?"

The recruit remained stone faced.

"Ladies and gentlemen, may I present"—she looked at the insignia on the recruit's shoulder patch—"Recruit Cody Foster. Looks like all hope ain't lost. This here's a genuine hero from Mars."

The drill sergeant was now toe-to-toe with Private Foster, who stood almost a full head taller than her. She pushed her baton up under his nose.

"Maybe that should be your call sign."

"Uh, I-I-I'm n-n-no hero."

She pushed the baton up a little higher.

"No hero, what?" The sergeant's tone was dangerously gentle.

"Uh, no hero, sir?"

The baton dropped swiftly from under Foster's nose to the side of his body, where it found its mark across the bare knuckles of his outstretched hand. He yelped.

"No hero, ma'am?" he whimpered.

She raised the baton to strike his face.

His eyes suddenly widened. "No hero, Sergeant!"

The sergeant rewarded him with an icy glare, as if deciding whether she'd wallop him anyways. Another recruit down the line made the mistake grunting a laugh.

The sergeant was in the other recruit's face in a flash.

"Something funny, Recruit?"

"No, Sergeant!"

"But you laughed."

"Yes, Sergeant!"

"So either you're a liar or a fool. Which is it, Private"—she read the patch on his uniform—"Jensen?"

"Neither, Sergeant!"

In the absence of an answer, he stumbled through an explanation.

"He doesn't seem like a hero. He ... he ... seems like a goofball."

The sergeant nodded appreciatively, then stopped.

"I don't think so." She then turned to the rest of the recruits and began pacing the line. "Over the next two months, I will have the impossible task of training you from worthless civvies to something that may fool the enemy into thinking you're actual soldiers. I will probably fail. There is, however, one silver lining—I get to give you your call signs, which will follow you in the UHF Navy for the rest of your career—short as it'll probably be."

She then turned her attention back to Jensen as a smile crept up the corners of her mouth. "You ..."

"Sergeant!"

"... are hereby known as Recruit Goofball." She did not take her eyes off him. "What do you say, Recruit Goofball?"

Jensen stood there in confusion until Gem whispered at his side, "Say, 'Thank you, Sergeant,' Goofball."

This brought a smattering of laughter from the other recruits, though Foster and Sally's faces remained placid.

"Thank you, Sergeant!" repeated Jensen.

But the sergeant was no longer paying attention to Goofball. She was now focused on Gem. "Well, what do we have here? Mama's little helper?" And so it went.

* * *

What the recruits soon came to realize was that they weren't going to get cool-sounding call signs, like T-Bone or Razor or Demon Dick. They would only get a call sign after they'd messed something up. Besides Goofball and Mother's Little Helper, the group had gotten to know Farty, Suck Up, Chuckles, Twinkle Toes, Fish Breath, Taco Tony, Dumbass, and Cutie Pie.

The recruits were eventually issued uniforms and gear and soon thereafter began to form some group cohesion. The team gelled more quickly by virtue of the fact that they'd mostly come from the same corporation. Sally, Gem, and Foster were the only ones who didn't know anyone and so ended up spending most of their downtime together. Hanging out with the old man, decided the girls, wasn't so bad. How old he was, though, was anyone's best guess, especially since there were so many who pretended to be older than they were in order to appear more sophisticated. If Sally had a credit for every thirty-year-old who tried to pass him- or herself off as a seventy-year-old, she would've had majority years ago. Cody was different, however. When asked his age, he'd invariably say he was in his thirties, but both Sally and Gem suspected he was older … much older. It was the way he moved and what he said—which wasn't much. Most thirty-something-year-old boys couldn't wait to tell the universe and every creature in it how they'd figured it all out—*all* of it. But Cody mainly listened. Boys didn't listen; men did. On top of that was the strange fact that Cody had yet to make a pass at Sally. At first she thought he might have been gay, asexual, or questioning, but after a couple of days it became obvious that he noticed women in ways that he didn't notice men. Sally was also pretty sure Cody was more attracted to their drill sergeant, inconceivable as that might seem. In a flash, she realized why. Older women tended to be attracted to older men. Especially older, confident men, and Cody Foster was stacking up to be a lot more confident and brazen than his surface stammering would suggest.

For instance, the base's entertainment complex showed patriotic vids. They were expertly conceived, shot, and edited. They were able to sway emotions with the precision that centuries of increasingly skillful marketing had begotten. Every once in a while, though, Cody would add a word or a phrase to the propaganda, and it would suddenly become very obvious that what the recruits were experiencing was nothing more than agitprop. Cody was never loud or overt about it, but the effect was just the same. At the thrice-weekly holo-vid events, Cody, Sally, and Gem were the only ones who were not truly hooting and calling for the destruction of the "vile" and "heartless" enemy—though most looking on would be none the wiser.

In those initial few weeks, Sally began to wonder if Cody wasn't perhaps a covert antiwar activist. But she quickly ruled that out—antiwar activists didn't usually sign up for the wars they protested. So, then, why his targeted sedition? Sally got the feeling that the only reason she and Gem heard his clever rebuttals was because he wanted them to. It was more than just to make them laugh, which they did often, but rather to make them think.

Their training went about as well as could be expected. But it seemed to Sally as if it was a very hurried affair. They'd start each day being woken up from their bioelectric-induced sleep. The troops had aptly nicknamed the beds go-dozers. With a go-dozer, recruits got the optimal amount of REM-state sleep required to maximize their effectiveness. Go-dozers also ensured that the recruits didn't get into any midnight mischief (effectively putting a halt to thousands of years of proud tradition). Once a marine was in bed and hooked up, they'd be down for the exact amount of time the base commander ordered. The go-dozers also had the advantage of stage one electro-muscle sleep generation. Or, as the grunts liked to call it, "Night Gym." Sure, go-dozer could build muscles while you slept (and you slept great), but Sally still found, along with everyone else, that she'd wake up very sore, achy, and grumpy—REM sleep be damned. Of course, they still had to do a full range of daily calisthenics and general exercise as well. Some of the larger, more heavily muscled recruits grumbled that the new regimen was turning their bigger, chiseled physiques into the lithe (some would say scrawny) musculature of a swimmer. But in space combat, Cody had personally related, speed and stamina were far more important than brute force and strength. Eventually those who'd grumbled most came around. Nothing focuses the mind like getting to live another day.

It was, thought Sally, amazing that Cody could command so much attention given what an absolute klutz he seemed to be. It didn't matter if training involved the proper use of an airlock or the operation of marine battle armor—Cody never, ever got it right on the first try. And he asked more clarifying questions than the rest of the training squad combined.

As a result, Cody was often ordered to stay late and help with the cleanup and storage of whatever weapons or ordinance they happened to be training on that day. He never once complained. Sally found herself sticking around to help because she was genuinely interested in the details, from the inner workings of an airlock panel to the cleaning and putting away of assault rail guns (otherwise known as ARGs) to the maintenance and mastery of the MechAssault body armor. Plus, Cody always offered to buy the rounds when the task was complete, and he never skimped. He must have spent a fortune because he was always served the best scotch, hardest-to-come-by appetizers, and finest cigars. It didn't take long for Sally to get Gem dialed in—she was mostly bored anyways. Though the rest of the team thought the trio nuts for taking on so much additional work, Sally and Gem at least recognized it for what it was—an incalculable edge. Even peeling potatoes had its merits, though they had yet to figure out exactly what that was.

* * *

"This," said the sergeant, firmly gripping her ARG, "is capable of propelling matter at I-shit-you-not speeds. It's why so many of the battles beyond the blue," she said, glancing skywards, "take place within proximity of an asteroid. If our ships just went out there and tried to slug it out, battles would not only be short; they'd also be mostly fatal. The rail guns they use in space are huge motherfuckers on big-ass ships with big-ass launchers and have nearly unlimited power. Ours work on the same principle but with much smaller energy outputs. They're dialed back for a reason. True, they aren't nearly as badass, but'll kill you without prejudice just the same.

A hand shot up.

"What is it, Chuckles? And it better not be stupid, or it'll be reactor laps for you."

Chuckles nodded solemnly. "Sergeant, why we gotta dial down the ARG? Can't some egghead make 'em as powerful as those beyond the blue? I think it would be pretty bonus to go into battle with something like that." He then made the motions and sounds of a gun presumably taking down the side of a mountain.

"Done, Chuckles?"

"Yes, Sergeant," answered the recruit, looking around at his team, clearly proud of himself.

"Five laps … with a shock drone," ordered the sergeant.

Chuckles' eyes widened. Before his lids could even drop, he took off at a dead run, followed by an angry drone dispensing shocks like a bee whose hive had been violated.

"On me!" demanded the sergeant. The team, who'd been watching the poor private disappear towards the reactors with the angry drone on his tail, swung their heads back as one, focusing intently.

"Now," continued the sergeant, "does anyone care to guess why that was such a stupid question?" She had no takers. By this point in their training, most of the recruits had learned to shut up.

"Fine," she groused. "I'll tell you. Even if you could warp the laws of physics to create an ARG that could project matter that quickly, no corporation or government on either side of this war would be stupid enough to make it. Your own troops could do more damage to your side with one accidental on-planet discharge than a barrage of meteors. But don't you worry your little heads. What you have in your hands is plenty destructive enough."

And it was. Their gun could shoot a pellet the size of a grain of rice at nearly 100,000 kilometers an hour. Even more impressive was that it could shoot almost anything that could fit into the magazine. Sally was surprised that the sergeant hadn't transmitted that salient fact to the troops—nor, Sally was to discover, had any of the other sergeants. Sure, there were bound to be a few knuckleheads who'd invariably try to wound their buddies with a booger, but Darwinian stupidity aside, this was war, and the more weapons they had at their disposal, the better—*even if the projectile were a lowly booger*, thought Sally. The only reason Sally knew about the magazine trick was because Cody had casually mentioned it. Plus, she knew better than to ask unformulated questions and risk the sergeant's ire. Really, everything she needed to know came from Cody, so why bother exposing herself to the ridicule or, worse, an embarrassing handle?

After seven long weeks, Sally and Cody had been the only ones left who hadn't been saddled with any nicknames, much less a humiliating one. And with only one week left in their training, Sally was beginning to think that maybe they'd actually get out of basic training stupid-name free.

* * *

By week eight, they'd all done time in the MechAssault body armor—practically a spacecraft in its own right with enough firepower to level a small town. It was fully contained and could even maintain human life in the vacuum of space. It was magnetized for deck adhesion and was capable of short-distance flight beyond the blue, just not on terra firma. Sally could still jump pretty far in one but was disappointed she couldn't leap twenty meters into the air or cross large distances in a single bound. She, Gem, and Cody had had even more practice with the armor, having regularly maintained and serviced the suits. But they were all smart enough to know that familiarity was not the same as experience, being shot at not the same as stemming a hydraulic leak.

And so they approached the day's exercise with extreme caution. They were each given different objectives. Sally's was to target a building sheltering the enemy—in this case, fifty Alliance Assault Miners. Sally first had to incapacitate the miners, then bring the building down around them. She'd made quick work of the first task by having her MechAssault unit jettison five perfectly targeted stun grenades through holes that had been punched into the bunker. She was then given the order to advance close enough to fling a disc-shaped explosive, given to her only moments before by Cody, into any opening she could find. Once launched, she would beat a hasty retreat. If she were really lucky, she'd even be able to watch the whole thing come tumbling down. Sally saw the "go" signal flash in her HUD field. She immediately pivoted her right shoulder back and then just as quickly spun her torso forward, extending her arm in a wide, sweeping arc. At the last possible moment, Sally opened her fingers in order to release the disc along its proper trajectory. Much to everyone's surprise, the now fully armed disc did not budge. It had somehow adhered itself to the suit's armor. Sally was still too confused to be scared. Her heart finally skipped a beat when she noticed the countdown timer hit ten and keep going. Then she saw Cody's panic-stricken face. He burst from the group of trainees as if being chased by a swarm of striker drones.

"Hang on, Cookie!" he shouted over the com, "I'm coming!"

That can't be right, she thought with only seconds left to live. Then Cody was at her side, making quick work of her gauntlet's emergency release bolt. With surprising speed, he managed to detach the disc-adhered gauntlet and fling it into the nearby bunker. With the less than two seconds he had left, Cody threw himself over Sally. The explosion came just as they both hit the ground. Moments later, they were buried beneath the bunker's rubble.

All Sally could think about as the world went dark was that Cody Foster had called her a name that only one person in her life had ever used.

Sally awoke to a view of the sky, the stench of burnt plastic, and the faces of her team looking down at her, concern evident in all their eyes—especially Gem's and Cody's.

"Vitals are fine," she heard the sergeant say. "Get her up."

"Are you alright?" asked Cody as he helped her up off the ground—something only he could do, given the weight of her MechAssault armor. A terror filled his eyes that Sally had never seen before. Or had she? *Completely wrong face*, she thought, *but that look* … Despite the ringing in her ears, the deluge of questions, the waiting-for-the-other-magboot-to-drop look of concern from her teammates, even—albeit briefly—from the sergeant herself, Sally remained focused. Cody's voice, his desperate look, that name he used … *Cookie*. And then it hit her: it was Cody who'd been drawn to her, not she to him. Cody who'd not so much protected her as refused to abandon her.

"Daddy?" she asked, eyes narrowing in disbelief.

Tears pricked the corners of his eyes. "Hey, Baby Girl."

Their brief father-daughter moment was interrupted by the sound of nearby laughter. The sergeant stood astride the pile of twisted metal and stone, arms folded across her chest, her face a rictus of cruel intention.

"Well, it took longer than I would've thought," snickered the sergeant. "Hell, I was even tempted to make something up just to get it over with. But I figured if I just held out long enough, you two would do something that would make it easy. Glad to see you didn't disappoint."

On Sally and Cody's confused look, their commanding officer continued. "Team," said the sergeant, a mischievous glint in her eye, "I'd like to introduce you to our last two call signs." She then flashed the grandest smile any of them had ever seen, much less believed she was even capable of. "I give you 'Daddy' and 'Baby Girl.'"

And that's when Sally Meadows slammed her uncovered fist into her father's unprotected face.

Daddy's Story

In another time and place, Cody Foster had been called Thomas Meadows. And even that wasn't his real name—at least, not the one he'd been born with. But it was the name his four children knew him by. And because of that, it was the one name and face that he actually maintained links to. They were tenuous threads at best with lots of precautions to make sure they couldn't be used to track him down. Not that Thomas Meadows had ever done anything that could be considered in the slightest way illegal. He made sure to pay all his fines and tickets even when he knew he could've easily won in court. Thomas Meadows did not argue or complain or do anything to get noticed. It was the one identity he maintained that was completely clean.

The irony was that he'd planned on maintaining it for no more than a few weeks. It was the simplest of scams. Steal a valuable piece of property from a person or persons who would never report the item missing because they never had the right to possess it in the first place. In this case, it was an actual original of the American Declaration of Independence residing in an apartment in New York City. Not the signed one—that had been vaporized in the destruction of Washington. Thomas was after the one from the same printing press. How the indolent, lazy bastard he'd stolen it from had come across it, Thomas would never discover nor would he care to. Thomas did, however, know that his posing as a harmless, innocent civilian would allow him to turn the valuable document in to the police, wait about a year, then come back to claim the reward with nary a fuss. It was true the remuneration would only be one-tenth of its actual value, but it was one-tenth he could keep and the system would let him have.

And Thomas Meadows had a great deal of respect for the system. In the twenty-second century, crime was not altogether impossible, but it was very risky. If you were caught at criminal behavior once too often, you'd find yourself getting a psyche audit from the state free of charge. Though it was a painless procedure, the very thought of it scared him to death—because anything that could so fundamentally change his nature might as well kill him.

It had been a good plan, and but for the brief dalliance with a woman named Augustine Cooper, Thomas Meadows would have disappeared, never to be heard from again. Augustine was not a particularly attractive or even intriguing woman. In fact, it was her overwhelming averageness that made her so appealing to Thomas. While with her, he became as completely average as she was. Their hookup, he'd reasoned, was completely fortuitous as it played in perfectly with his everyman cover. And so, to the allotted two weeks planning the theft, he looked upon Augustine as his inadvertent bonus. The breakup was easy. He told her that he'd "accepted" a job that would be taking him to the outer planets. What he did in fact do was drop his name and spend the following year running basic tourist cons in the tropical islands of the Pacific. Nothing major, nothing to get him noticed, just suckers on vacation who'd find that their accounts had been dipped into, but never by any amounts large enough to trigger a major investigation. When that well dried up, Thomas took a ship to Mars to run the same scam at the Thousand Canals resort. The once and future Thomas Meadows did have one rule he always adhered to: never, ever run a scam or even a fishing expedition while on a ship. It could be a ferry to an island off the coast of Thailand or a starship heading on a three-month voyage to the outer orbits. His logic was sound; it would be foolish to commit a crime where you had no chance of escape. However, in all his expert planning, he'd missed the one thing there was no escaping from—fatherhood.

When, one year later, Thomas Meadows reappeared in New York City to claim his reward, he discovered that while he'd been gone, Augustine Cooper had given birth to a baby girl. It was the first careless act he could ever remember making in his adult life. But it didn't matter. The first time he held that baby girl in his hands, he knew that something had changed. In one instant, he went from being a man pretending to being an average guy to actually becoming one. Of course, it took an incredible amount of skill, money, and luck to buy a backstory deep enough to survive the scrutiny that inevitably came from domesticity. The biggest problem with being a rube was that you were trapped. Trapped by a job, by family, and, in the case of the suddenly real Thomas Meadows, by a baby named Emily staring longingly into his eyes.

Although the man history would come to know as "Daddy" ultimately failed as a family man, it was not through want of trying. He lasted six years in the role and had a total of four children with the fascinatingly plain Augustine. They were: Emily, Sally, Ashley, and then his son, Lee (Thomas could not get Augustine to relent on "lee" sounding names). He loved all his children and became the best father he could. He had an average job but used his Declaration reward money to buy his family a nice condo in the Highland Towers Living Complex in New York City. It was a three-hundred-story skypiercer typical of the class. Homes and schools and the businesses that catered to them were all maintained within the massive structure. They lived in a unit on the 237th floor with an acceptable view of New Jersey. Thomas could have easily afforded a Manhattan view, but he decided against it as too conspicuous. The meme against New Jersey had survived the collapse of one civilization and the rise of another. No matter how spectacular the view from the home he provided his family, few would envy him—it was perfect.

Thomas's life had stayed perfectly settled until the unexpected arrival of some old cohorts at his door. He didn't bother wondering how they'd gotten past security. After all, it was he who'd taught them. They'd come bearing gifts and an easy-to-follow backstory they fed to him so he could maintain the illusion for his wife and children who, too, were surprised so boring a man could have so obviously edgy acquaintances. Only Thomas knew how real and palpable the threat was. They might as well have burst into his home and put neurolizers to everyone's heads.

Shortly thereafter, he excused himself to go out for drinks with his "friends"—yet another odd request to his still-astonished family. Once at the pub, the gloves came off. Either, threatened the crew, Thomas helped them with a local scam they were running, or they'd out him to his family and the law. Knowing he had no leverage, all Thomas could ask for was assurances that they'd leave him and his family alone if he helped them this one time. They readily agreed. Thomas knew, of course, that the promise was worth what it cost them to make it.

That last week he'd spent with his family was the worst one of his life. He wanted more than anything to stay with the children he'd so grown to love and the aggressively plain wife he'd grown to cherish. But the die had been cast.

And so, for only the second time in five years, he fed Augustine a story—namely, that Thomas's "friends" were actually his spouses and that his marriage to her was a fraud. Naturally, she demanded he leave at once.

As for his comrades, he turned them into GCI corporate security the first chance he got by hacking into and leaving a warning on the database of Kirk Olmstead, head of GCI special operations. They were arrested and psyche audited in far less time than the law should have allowed for. As for Thomas Meadows, he was wanted for questioning but not charged with any specific crime. Kirk was willing to let one bird fly for the ones he had in hand.

But now Thomas Meadows had to disappear again. He may have been able to patch things up with his wife and kids, but it would've been under the scrutiny of GCI, not to mention being even more visible to any of his other past "friends." So Thomas Meadows went from being the greatest father in the world to being a dad who sent holodisplays every once in a while and credit transfers for child support. He could have sent enough to give all four of his children top-level educations and comfortable majorities of their stock. But that would have brought far more scrutiny than was safe. Better for them to think of him as the failed father who sent just enough and occasionally a little more. The one thing he did, though, was make sure to send each of his children a personal message on their life day—a celebration of the moment they were conceived and put into the gestation tank. And that seemed to be that—until the war.

He wasn't even on Earth when it broke out. He was on Mars with a new identity and found, much to his surprise, that he'd become caught up in the anti-corporate revolt that had swept that planet. It had been folly to stand up to the Incorporated system, costing him a year of his life as he was forced to go underground in an effort to escape the inevitable witch hunt for Alliance sympathizers. To add insult to injury, when the Unincorporated Man, Justin Cord himself, took over the planet with an Outer Alliance fleet, Thomas almost got himself killed because his new cover—Cody Foster, patriotic Core Worlds supporter—was just a bit too good. Easily disarming two heavily armed Alliance Assault Miners in front of a crowd of gawkers only added to the subterfuge. On the plus side, he was able to escape back to Earth with a new backstory and newly minted anti-Alliance bona fides.

It was only on Earth that he discovered his eldest daughter, Emily, planned on enlisting as an assault marine in the UHF fleet. She had this fantasy that she'd join, single handedly defeat the Outer Alliance and end up with enough credits to earn a majority of herself. Plus, she'd explained to him in their brief, terse conversation, all her friends were doing it. Thomas had even revealed his monetary hand by offering to pay for her majority outright, but she'd just scoffed—either out of disbelief or obstinacy. Absentee fathers do not get a say in their children's lives, especially after years of holo-vid parenting. He did manage to exact a promise from her that she wouldn't encourage her siblings to sign up. It was an easy one to make. Lee and Sally were young, and the war would have to go on for years before they could even think of volunteering.

After that, Thomas Meadows made sure to keep in regular contact with his family, hoping that more time invested would translate into more influence, or at least more than he'd had with Emily. Though he'd never be stupid enough to reveal his original Outer Alliance sympathies, he did keep his fingers on the pulse of UHF politics—especially anything having to do with the military. Unfortunately, the more he learned, the more disturbed he became. It seemed to him that if there was an idiotic corporate executive who had *not* been given the rank of admiral or colonel and allowed to kill untold numbers of hapless underlings, it hadn't been for lack of trying. And then one of those idiotic executives had gotten Emily killed. Even worse, it had been a permanent death. There would be no reanimation because there was nothing left to reanimate. She'd died at the first battle of Anderson's Farm in the Asteroid Belt's infamous 180. The number had been designated because the location was exactly opposite Ceres, the unofficial capital of Outer Alliance. The battle was the first thrust of the UHF's attempt to limit the enemy's economic viability. If the Core Worlds managed to cut off the Belt at the 180, the Outer Alliance would lose half its population and two-thirds of its industry. Which was why they were defending it with everything they had. Anderson's Farm had turned into a meat-grinder, and Thomas's daughter had been ground to bits.

When his second daughter, Sally, came of age, the war was still on. Much like her older sister, the fire raged in Sally's belly but with the added impetus of revenge. Thomas tried to convince her not to enlist and failed just as he had with Emily, and mainly for the same reasons. So this time, Thomas would be more proactive. He found out what training camp Sally was being assigned to and, using some of his ill-gotten if hard-earned credits, managed to have his daughter transferred to a brand-new camp that was filled with lots of brand-new people in brand-new jobs who had no idea what they were doing. Then, as Cody Foster, the man who disabled two Alliance assault miners on Mars, he volunteered in such a time and place as to get sent to the same camp as his daughter. After that, it was child's play to buy himself a new face and then get assigned to the same unit.

Baby Girl and Daddy's Story

The problem with the stockade was not that it was uncomfortable. Any other age would have called it luxurious beyond compare. The bed was body temp adjustable; the bathroom and shower facilities were pampering to a degree that any Roman emperor worth his toga would have sacrificed fifty thousand slaves to possess. It had excellent exercise facilities and was supremely comfortable by the standards of any age and quite nice by the standards of Sally Meadows. The problem was boredom. Prisoners were not allowed any entertainment options. The only stations Sally could watch or listen to played agitprop, and the only thing she could access in the library were regulation, maintenance, and tech manuals. On the first day, she was actually quite happy diving into them, starting with the inner workings of a demolition disc with an auto-adhering strip. She soon came to realize just how lucky she'd been. Once the disc she'd held in her hand on that fateful day had been set and the adhesive strip activated (presumably upon impact), it was impossible to break the bond. If Cody—Sally still couldn't think of him as "Daddy"—hadn't known the unlock sequence for her gauntlet, she'd be dead. But she'd be damned if she was going to owe that man a thing—that is, until boredom set in. Human beings of the twenty-fourth century were simply incapable of complacency. There were those, of course, who, with years of training and practice, could spend days or even weeks meditating with only their own thoughts for company. Sally was not one of them. By day four she was calling up specs for all the equipment she was likely to use. From battle armor, line guns, and even navy-issued toothpicks (which could be quite incapacitating when shot from an ARG). If Sally was going to be stuck in solitary confinement, she was going to make the best of it, even if the notion of doing so had come from her dad.

She was so engrossed in the assembly of a portable milspec drone sweeper that she hadn't noticed the intruder until he spoke.

"You'll need to tighten the guard plate on the intake port."

Without thinking, Sally shoved her elbow backwards, followed by a well-aimed round kick. But Thomas had anticipated the move and was nowhere near the point of impact.

"Hey, hey. Relax, Cookie," he said. "It's just me."

"Don't call me that!" she snarled, eyes narrowed into glints of rage. "You don't get to call me that *ever*."

Thomas sighed. "Fair enough. But in return, could you try not to beat me to death every time I want to talk to you?"

Sally considered the request. "Fine." Then she added, "As long as you don't sneak up on me."

Thomas nodded. "Excellent. Then I'll just stand here in silence and you can go back to practicing."

Sally looked confused and was about to ask a question but was curtailed by Thomas bringing his index finger up to his lips. He subsequently activated a small box on his belt. "Okay, we can talk. This," he said indicating the box, "will make it appear as if I'm observing you practice."

"How?"

"I accessed and recorded about three hours of your activities. Splicing myself in was easy. We have about three hours."

Sally turned her back. "You may as well turn it off. Your box has the right idea. I really have nothing to say to you."

Thomas sighed. "Well, can I at least get a 'Thank you'?"

Sally froze. She closed her eyes and tried to count to ten but only made it to three before spinning back around. "Thank you?! Thank you?!"

"You're welcome?" answered Thomas thinly.

"What do I have to say thank *you* for? Oh, that's right. Let's see." Sally started to count off on her fingers. "Should I thank you for abandoning us for your group marriage when I was five? Should I thank you for all the birthdays you weren't at?"

Thomas winced.

"How about for all the baseball games you missed? You know, the games where I kept stupidly looking for you in the bleachers? Guess how old I was when I finally stopped looking?"

Thomas shrugged his shoulders.

"Fourteen." A laugh escaped her lips that was an odd tincture of sadness and disbelief. "It took me nine years to finally realize, in my heart of hearts, that you weren't ever going to be there for me."

Thomas said nothing, head lowered.

"So," repeated Sally, "what do I need to thank you for?"

Thomas mumbled something.

"I'm sorry, Recruit Foster, I didn't quite get that."

"I did save your life," Thomas whispered.

Sally grabbed her father by his shirt and shoved him against the wall. "You do not get to claim credit for saving me from the live charge you left with me in a training exercise!" Then she noticed something strange about his face and, releasing his shirt, took a step back. "What the hell's wrong with your nose?"

"You like it?" Thomas's eyes lit up.

"No, it's crooked."

"It should be," he answered with his smile growing wider. "You broke it."

"That's stupid," she said, releasing him. "Why didn't they just fix it?"

"I didn't let 'em," he said, pride evident in his voice.

"It looks ugly."

"Does not," he countered, bringing his hand up to the appendage in question. "I think it gives me a bit of distinction. Besides, it's ..." he seemed to think better of it, and his voice trailed away.

"It's what?" demanded Sally.

"Well ... ," he fumbled. "It's just that ... it's the first thing you've given me in fifteen years."

Sally stared at her father, dumbfounded. "Fix it. I don't want to give you anything."

"Then let me at least pay you for it."

Sally's brow scrunched. "Pay *me* for breaking *your* nose?"

Thomas nodded. The stupid smile, noticed Sally, still hadn't left his face.

"I thought I'd made myself perfectly clear: I don't want or need anything from you."

"You got it, Cook ..." Thomas stopped himself when he saw her face tense up once more. "Sally."

"If you have to call me anything," she said, "it will be 'Recruit Meadows.' Is that understood?"

"Yes, Recruit Meadows, it is."

"Was there anything else, Recruit Foster?"

"Yes. I may have gotten us flunked out of basic training."

"May have?"

Thomas' mouth formed into a wan smile. "We're going to have to take it again … right here."

If Sally had a weapon, she may have been tempted to use it. Instead, she spent the next two hours and fifty-six minutes in abject silence—a far more effective means of hurting her father than any weapon she could have dreamed of.

* * *

Two days later, Sally had another visitor, one she welcomed with open arms.

"Gemmy!" she shouted and as soon as her friend crossed the threshold, almost tackling her in a bear hug.

"That's *Private* Suttikul to you, Recruit Meadows," answered Gem with mock severity.

Sally laughed, but there was little joy in it.

"Hey, it's okay," said Gem, giving her friend a gentle hug. "You can call me 'Gemmy' as much as you want."

"It's not that."

"Then what?"

"I was supposed to be with you," answered Sally. "I can kick myself for going through school and not having you as a friend."

"Me too," smiled Gem.

"But at least I was going to fight the war with you, and that would've made up for school."

Gem nodded. "A thousand times more."

"But now, thanks to my … to Cody, that's not going to happen!"

Gem sighed and touched a small box tucked within her belt.

Sally shot her a look. "You do realize he's the reason I'm still stuck here."

"And the reason you're still alive," answered Gem.

"He gave me a live charge!"

"Did *he* activate the adhesive?"

"I ... don't know," Sally began. "Maybe." Then honesty got the better of her. "No."

Gem took Sally's hand. "Correct. And when it happened, he ran straight towards you. No one else did."

"No one?" asked Sally, looking at Gem for salvation.

"No one," answered Gem in a voice thick with guilt. "I'm so sorry, Sal. I should have. I don't know why ... I just ... I didn't."

Sally grabbed her friend by the forearms. "Gemmy, don't you for a moment blame yourself."

"I do, and I always will." Gem then extricated herself from Sally's grip and took a half step back. "But I will *never* abandon you again."

"Stop it, Gem. You did nothing wrong. Anyone would have acted that way. It was a live demolition charge. *I* would have run the other way."

"Anyone but your father, Sal. He didn't hesitate for a second. He saw you were in danger, so that's where he went."

"Then why did he throw me a live charge?"

"You dope," said Gem with enough affection to soften the blow. "He tried to tell you, but you wouldn't listen."

"Listen to what?"

"He wanted you to blow up that building."

"Well, yes. That was the exercise."

"No, stupid. *Actually* blow it up. Not theoretically."

"Why the hell would he want that?"

"So you'd flunk out of basic training and have to do it all over again." Gem said this as if it were the most obvious thing in the worlds.

"What?" Sally's brain was suddenly feeling fuzzy.

"Honey," said Gem, "we're not ready for war. Eight weeks is just not enough time."

"But they said we'll get additional train—"

"Not enough," Gem interrupted. "Your father did this to increase your odds of surviving. At least listen to him."

"Why should I? He wasn't there when—"

"Oh, for Damsah's sake," shouted Gem, "he's here *now*. I don't know if you realize this, but your life is in danger *now*. He wasn't there when you were growing up, and yeah, that sucks. But the worst you really had to fear were spinal injuries and broken bones—big deal. In case you don't remember, my father chose to stay in the outer orbits and fight for the enemy. I may very well have to kill him and never know it. Or," Gem continued in a smaller voice, "he may have to kill me." She then comported herself. "Yours chose to change his face, risk death on occupied Mars, come back to Earth, and volunteer for a war we both know he doesn't really believe in and become an extraordinarily well-trained soldier. Why?"

Sally shrugged.

"To make you one too, dipshit. He's not perfect, but from my point of view, he's pretty damn good, and the least you can do is talk to him."

"Sure. Maybe. I don't know."

"Look, Sal. I gotta go. I've said my piece."

"Wait," said Sally, grabbing Gem's arm. "If I'm not ready for war, how can you be?"

"I'm not. Cody got me assigned to a lunar Repo/Depot unit and arranged for them to lose my paperwork. And I plan on taking advantage of that for however long it takes them to figure it out."

"Wait. How did he … ?"

"Sally, for Damsah's sake, talk to him!" And with a kiss to the air, Gem was gone.

* * *

Sally wasn't sure how to speak to her father but figured she'd use the forty-eight hours of leave they'd been given to figure it out. He had other plans, however, hardly saying a word to her on the trip away from their Siberian base. As they left the Moscow station, bundled up in thick overcoats and scarves with only the sound of snow crunching beneath their feet, he finally spoke.

"Thanks for waiting," he said. "Walking in the snow actually plays havoc with general listening devices, but this will take care of most anyone specifically listening in."

"This?" she asked in a frustration-tinged voice.

"Ah," he answered, realizing she couldn't see through his coat. "The box."

Sally shook her head. "You've got issues."

"More than you can imagine."

"Are you some sort of corporate spy? I used to imagine that you were and that's why you had to leave us." Sally realized that she was starting to sound very much like the five-year-old girl she'd spent so many years of her life being. She hated that girl.

"I was tempted to tell you exactly that when this moment arrived. It was going to be filled with all sorts of hazy yet convincing evidence to support the lie. But I can't lie to you anymore, Cookie." His face tensed slightly, waiting for the tongue-lashing that never arrived.

"Then if you're not a corporate spy, what are you?" The question was as plaintive as it was painful.

"A con man."

"A what?"

"I trick people into giving me their money."

"So you're a common thief?"

"No, Cookie. I'm an extraordinary one. And I can assure you I have never ever stolen anything from anyone who couldn't afford it."

"Uh-huh."

"Really," said Thomas. "It's also, by the way, how I met your mother."

Sally stopped walking and turned to face him, eyes piqued.

"Alright, alright," he answered, genuinely enjoying the moment. He indicated a bench in the distance. "Let's talk."

* * *

Two hours later, Sally sat quietly and digested the fact that, but for someone illegally having acquired an original printing of the Declaration of Independence and her father having stolen it from the thief, she would not be alive.

"So let me get this straight," she said. "You gave up an exciting life filled with danger and adventure to marry ... Mom?" Her confusion was complete.

"Yes, Cookie. Your mom's ability to find joy in the most ordinary things is what attracted me to her. In that respect, she opened up a world I'd long rejected."

"How long?"

Thomas laughed. "You get answers to many things, Cookie. More than most, actually. Just not that."

Sally allowed herself an uncharacteristic pout.

"However," offered Thomas, "that's not what caused me to stay. It was your sister, Emily, at first. Then you and your siblings. When I held each of you in my arms, so small and so amazingly perfect ..." He sighed, his mind wandering off for a moment. "I gave up nothing to be with all of you."

"Then why did you leave?"

* * *

By the time Thomas was finished his story, the sun had gone down and the weather had turned markedly colder. Had it not been for the internal nanites adjusting their metabolisms, the clothing they wore would not have sufficed.

"Then how come you never came back? How come you didn't give any of us the chance to go with you?"

"Cookie," answered Thomas, "I was not bragging when I said I was extraordinary. There are maybe fifty of us left in the entire solar system."

"Us?"

"Extraordinary thieves. And the Incorporated system does not take kindly to anyone threatening their monopoly on theft."

"You didn't think I could do it," she laughed. There was, however, an earnestness about the question that demanded an answer.

"Actually, of all my children," answered Thomas, "I'm pretty sure you're the only one who could've. I can tell you I had daydreams of coming back into your life and bringing you into mine. I would teach you all about the art of the con in the modern worlds. We would go all through the solar system and find the stupid and greedy and redistribute their wealth in our favor."

"So why didn't you?"

"Because I was happiest when I had you and the family. My life as a con man brought me a twisted sort of pride and no small amount of adventure, but not happiness. And above all else, I felt you should at least have that." Thomas shook his head. "And then you and your sister had to go and join the fucking marines?"

"You know why I joined."

"Yes, to avenge your sister. And I joined to protect you. I was too far away to help Ems. But not too far to help you—even if you didn't want it."

"I want it now, Daddy," she said softly.

Thomas smiled and gave his daughter a hug. "I can get us out of the marines and under new identities in less than a week. We can ride out this war in relative safety and impressive comfort." For the first time in a long time, Sally could discern real hope in his voice.

"No, Daddy." Sally put her hand gently on his shoulder. "That's not what I meant. You're a great soldier."

Thomas snorted.

"Don't do that, Daddy; you are. And if I'm going to be a great soldier, if I'm going to survive this war and keep Holly and Lee out of it, I'm going to need your help."

"Baby girl," he said, forgetting in his distress that it was her call sign and not his special nickname anymore, "please. This war is going to last a long time. I've lived as much of my life in the outer orbits as I have in the core worlds, and I can tell you the Outer Alliance will *never* surrender. We can blow them to pieces and take asteroid after asteroid and even some of their worlds, and they'll fight to the bitter end."

Sally's face went rigid, gripped in the throes of a barely controlled rage. "But they killed Emily."

"No, Cookie. The bastards who sent a teenage girl with eight weeks of training into combat against people who'd had a lifetime in space killed her. And those same bastards will do the same to you."

"Not if you keep on helping like you have. You can teach me enough to survive. Enough to make them pay."

Thomas Meadows sighed, realizing that his daughter's anger and rage could only be tempered by seeing things no human being ever should. You couldn't talk someone out of a fight if revenge was what drove them. Thomas knew that all too well. You could only hope they'd make it through with an expert hand to guide them. Sally was not going change her mind.

"Okay, Cookie. I got a contingency plan. Remember how I told you that there were fifty others like me, all of whom would love to see me fry?"

"Of course, Daddy."

"Well, the good news is that they were the ones I was most fearful of. The ones who could hurt our family had I stayed. Of the fifty, guess how many are in the Outer Alliance?"

Sally shrugged. "Twenty?"

Thomas shook his head.

"Twenty-five?" she guessed.

He shook his again, pointing his thumb upwards.

"For Damsah's sake, Daddy, how many?"

"Forty-nine."

"Why is that good news? Forty-nine 'yous' on the other side sounds like terrible news."

"It is for the war. I shudder to think how much of an advantage the Alliance will have if Kirk Olmstead can get even a quarter of them to sign up. But the good news is that since they're out there …"

"Thomas Meadows can come back here!" exclaimed Sally.

"Technically, he already has. A man matching my old description with my ident code has signed up and is about to start basic training. It's going to cost me almost all the funds I have access to and some favors I never thought I'd have to call in, but in eight weeks, he'll become Cody Foster and I'll become Thomas Meadows again. Hopefully for the last time. And Sally and Thomas Meadows will be posted to the same Marine combat unit."

Sally leaned across the bench and gave her father a hug that, judging by his reaction, was worth every credit he'd spent and was yet to spend. But then she stopped and leaned back, looking at him quizzically.

"What is it, Cookie?"

An uncomfortable silence hung between them. "What's my name?"

"It's Sally. Sally Meadows, Cookie."

"No, Daddy, it's not."

Sally knew she was asking him the one piece of information her father had never shared with anyone. The one secret he'd kept above all others.

"Your name is Ryan. Sally Ryan."

Sally digested that all-important piece of information, understanding the enormity of what had just been shared. "Thank you, Daddy."

"You're welcome, Cookie."

Year 3 of 7 of the Unincorporated War

Asteroid 17-43A7-9234 (aka Leary's Casino)

"Hey, Cookie."

Sally raised her eyebrow.

"Don't forget—we may come in upside down. Do you remember how to detach and flip?"

"Yes, Dad," she groaned. "You only made me practice it a dozen times … yesterday."

"That's 'Corporal Dad' to you, Private Daughter, and considering what happened at the last rock we took, you have no right to complain."

"So unfair," she muttered.

"How so?"

"I saved your life; that's how so!"

Thomas shook his head, mouth formed into a knowing grin. "Only after I did a *proper* flip from the harness in order to save yours."

"Not going to let me forget that, are you?"

Thomas pointed to the extra stripe on his armor. "Corporal."

"Fine, *Corporal* Daddy," she scoffed, using his call sign. "I know how to flip from the harness. I've practiced it so much I could do a double flip in armor and fire from a prone position. Hell, at this point I could probably do it in my sleep. I am so good at the flippin' flip!"

Thomas smiled, content. "That's all I wanted to know."

The transport shook violently.

The soldiers all glanced at their HUDs—not ordinance but debris. A second later, it was confirmed as pieces of a sister ship, meaning none of that ship's supremely trained marines would ever get a chance to fight for the UHF.

Sally went silent. On a look from Thomas, she gave him the reason: "This is how Ems died."

"I know, Cookie," he answered, "but it won't happen to us."

"How can you be so sure?"

He put his hand over hers and gave it a squeeze. "Because we're so much better trained than the marines were in the first battles. Because we have actual experience and none of those poor bastards thrown in back then did. And most importantly of all …" he paused until she looked up with a flash of annoyance.

"Most importantly of all what, Dad?"

"I'm your father, and I have not given you permission to die. You may think you're an adult and all grown up, but I'll find a way to ground you if you make me."

"Okay," she said, "and thank you, Dad."

"You're welcome, Cookie."

* * *

No comments had been directed to the father and daughter while they were having their heart-to-heart. But every marine knew that what they were seeing was rare—especially in the heat of battle. However the father and daughter had managed their improbable relationship, no one on that transport would dare interfere with it.

"Forty-five seconds to landing!" barked the COM.

"Alright, you lugs!" shouted the sergeant. "The navy's been kind enough to open the door, but we're damn well going to have to let ourselves in. Helmets sealed and safeties off!"

The transport was soon filled with the familiar hiss of faceplates sliding down and the thrum of weapons powering up. A few seconds later, the marines' faces lit up as the beautiful sound was heard of a harpoon being fired from the hull.

"Dad?"

"Yes, Cookie?"

"I don't want Holly or Lee to join the military."

"Don't worry, Cookie. Your mom and I may have had our differences, but I know this—she will not allow anything to happen to your sister and brother. Now look sharp, Private!"

His daughter's eyes went dark. "Yes, Corporal!" And then her faceplate sealed shut.

The second the marines' HOD's showed the harpoon as "Locked" into the rock, they released their harnesses as one, dropped to the floor, then flipped upside down to end up crouching the right way up … on the ceiling. The door burst open and the nearest marines fired their personal harpoons into the asteroid, which began pulling them even closer to the surface. As soon as the first marines got their footing, they covered the next group out. Everyone did their job and watched out for each other, but none so much as the father for his daughter and vice versa. Not that it helped.

* * *

"Get your asses down!" shouted Private First Class Thomas Meadows at what was left of his squad. The five marines, including Sally, were on the surface of an asteroid famous for having the only casino/whorehouse in an area known mainly for its religious adherents. If the local population had any say in the matter, they would have happily closed the place down and put up a seminary or hospital in its stead. Thomas amused himself with the fact that the locals had finally gotten their wish in that all the whoring had finally ceased on the Godforsaken rock. The gambling had continued, though, only this time they were playing for lives and the ante had been his daughter.

Thomas was pleased to see that Sally's practice had paid off. After reeling in the line and dragging herself to the surface, she'd made sure that her whole body hugged the rock and not just her arms and face. The first couple of times they'd practiced the maneuver she kept forgetting to pull in her legs and hips. So Thomas had programmed a shock droid to zap any part of her not hugging the ground. It worked.

But the other three members of Thomas's squad did what their terribly wrong, born-and-bred-at-the-bottom-of-a-gravity-well instincts told them to do—they *threw* themselves to the ground. The problem was that the slight forward leap, which made perfect sense in gravity, ended with them flying across the landscape like superheroes in the 0.03 gravity of the six-kilometer-long asteroid. Actually, Thomas saw that the recruit from Luna did manage to use her linegun after she'd leapt to ground, but since she hadn't attached it to her belt, she'd ended up with both legs dangling high above her head, making a perfect target for the Alliance bomblets dropped from on high. The munitions were primitive but smart enough, with rudimentary guidance and programming. If something were moving in their target area, they'd veer towards it. For instance, two UHF assault marines flying across the landscape like supermen. Thomas had to admit that UHF battle armor was impressively durable. He could testify as to how much damage it could take and still keep its occupant alive and fighting. The shielding could probably survive an attack by two, maybe even three of the Alliance bomblets. But by the time dozens of them had done their job, all that remained of the two marines were floating and expanding composites, liquid, gasses, and gnarled bits of frozen flesh. The marine from Luna had been smart enough to stop moving her legs, which had probably saved her, but her oddly prone status had managed to attract the attention of two bomblets, and as a result, the legs she'd stopped moving were now missing and all that was left of them were two bloody stumps. Her screams over the com were deafening.

Thomas checked to see that his daughter was okay and then he checked himself. Only then did he use his command overrides to take control of the injured marine's battle armor. It had already sealed the breaches where her legs had once been, but he ordered her Med-Kit to inject the max tranq dose—both for her comfort and the relief of his and Sally's eardrums. Once the immediate perimeter was clear, he dragged the comatose marine to the shallow depression he'd found for Sally and himself and then secured her to the ground.

"Something tells me," Sally said, looking over at the unconscious marine and then back to the barren landscape, "that we won't be linking up with Bravo squad."

"What?" said Thomas, absentmindedly trying to rub his long-healed broken nose. He then smiled awkwardly on Sally's you-can't-do-that-with-your-helmet-on look. Thomas moved his hand away and continued. "You're upset we won't be breaking the bank at the blackjack tables?"

"It's not that," said Sally, the corners of her mouth twisting downwards. "I was hoping to get to the whorehouse."

Thomas's eyes widened. "The what?"

"I heard the men were enhanced and genetically designed to be longer-lasting. Called 'em 'Eveready Bunnies' or something."

Thomas stared at his daughter, slack-jawed, until the corners of her mouth crept back upwards. He started to laugh, and then a moment later, they both were.

"We're the only ones left, aren't we?" his daughter asked suddenly.

Thomas pulled out his camo blanket and motioned for Sally to hand him hers. He then combined the two, and once beneath it, the three marines looked to all the worlds—and most Alliance sensors—like just another pile of rubble on giant rock filled with them.

"Yes," he finally said.

Grief, sobriety, and anger flickered across Sally's face like fire pit shadows on a moonless night. "But there were five thousand of us when we landed."

Thomas sighed heavily. "And now there are three. Well," he said looking over to the comatose marine with a lopsided grin, "maybe two and a half."

That elicited a brief smile from Sally.

Both their HODs flashed a perimeter breach warning. They went silent as Thomas activated the blanket's passive scanner. One second later, they had their answer.

Sally's eyes took in the Alliance frigate, then went as dull and unfeeling as the asteroid's surface. "We're going to get captured and spend the rest of the war as corpsicles orbiting Eris, aren't we?"

"We should be so lucky. Look again."

As Sally did, the ground began to rumble. The Alliance frigate was emptying a multitude of tiny objects from its bowels— a metal cloud unleashing a torrent of exploding rain.

"Oh, fuck me," she whispered. "They're sanitizing the whole Damsah-cursed rock."

"Guess we put up a better fight than we thought. I give us four minutes. Five tops."

"Fucking Alliance bastards,"

"It's not as if we haven't done the same to them." Thomas's words hung for a moment. "Or worse."

"You keep on defending them!"

"All things being equal, I think they're right." Sally knew this wasn't a death's door confession, just her father's forthrightness.

"But you've killed so many of them."

"Your point?"

"I dunno. In my book, that makes them wrong."

"Three minutes, ten seconds. Because they're trying to kill you, Cookie. Right or wrong has nothing to do with it. So, we going to stop this frigate or what?"

Sally's face betrayed her irritation. "How? By scolding it to death?"

Thomas smiled. "Me? I'm just going to provide the distraction. *You're* going to destroy it."

"With?" she asked.

He handed her a grenade. "This."

She looked at it and her father with incredulity.

"I agree," he said before should could speak. "But luckily, that is not an Alliance frigate. It's one of ours that they've captured. Two minutes, forty-seven seconds."

Sally looked at the image in the HOD and nodded. "So it is. And that matters how, exactly?"

Thomas sighed. "Too much time with Eveready Bunnymen, not enough time with manuals."

"Thomas Meadows Ryan!" She whispered, nostrils flared.

"Okay, Cookie. That's a Raider-class frigate. When it stops propulsion, it opens a small exhaust port on its lower section near the rear antimissile defense battery."

Sally's eyes narrowed. "Really."

"Yes," he said, sharing an image on her HOD. "It's open."

"And?" she asked through gritted teeth, "When we fire this thing, the defensive battery will get it way before it reaches the port, assuming it's even open."

"I said nothing about firing it."

"But ..."

"You're going to throw it. No weapons exhaust plus some clever programming means the grenade will look like just another piece of floating debris."

"I'm going to ..." Sally's face twisted further into confusion. "The second I stand up, they'll hone in on me!"

"Which is why I've slaved every one of our squad's weapons left on this Damsah-forsaken rock to mine. Right before you get up, they'll all start going off. The friendly fire mechanism will keep them from tracking on you and the grenade, but the melee should confuse the frigate's targeting scanners quite nicely, especially with all the debris floating up from the surface. That should give you time to make the throw. One minute fifty."

"That is a *two-kilometer* lob against a moving target not much bigger than the grenade I'll be throwing at it! It can't be done."

"Cookie, of course it can. You pitched baseball."

"I didn't have to throw the ball two kilometers!"

"Sally, there's no gravity here. Well, not much, anyways. You could throw that grenade a million kilometers."

"But I can't hit that target," she said, beginning to wilt.

Thomas took her gauntlet into his. "Cookie, I've seen you pitch no-hitters against schools with GEs," he said, using the nickname for the genetically enhanced.

"Wait a minute. You saw me? Holo-vid?"

Thomas shook his head.

"But I never once saw you there," she said, lost in memory.

"You were fourteen. You'd stopped looking by then."

"Daddy, I never stopped looking."

"You wouldn't have recognized me, Baby Girl. I wasn't even the right gender."

"But why ... the danger."

"Sixty seconds" flashed in their HODs. They both knew it was only an estimate, but that was of little comfort.

"Sally," Thomas said, "I came to every game I could—thirteen in all—and they were the best games I ever saw." He moved his hands up to the side of her helmet and stared deeply into her eyes. "You can do this."

The ground started shaking more violently as the frigate drew closer and its deadly cargo emptied onto the barren landscape.

"You son of a bitch," she said, her face lighting up. "You were at my games."

Thomas nodded with a shit-eating grin.

Sally looked down at the grenade in her hand and nodded back.

"Okay," said Thomas, steel in voice. "In three, two, and GO!"

All at once, every weapon on the rock still loaded and working started going off. Private Sally Meadows stood up, used her helmet's scanner to locate the target and, adjusting for the asteroid's movement against the ship's, made the second-best pitch of her life.

The grenade sailed into the exhaust port and detonated with two seconds left to spare.

UHF Capital of Burroughs
Mars

Father and daughter were walking away from an awards ceremony where they'd both been onstage almost as props. The story Thomas had convinced Sally to follow would have allowed for no other outcome.

"So the screaming amputee gets the UHF Order of Valor and all we get is a seven-day pass."

"Rather generous, if you ask me," answered Thomas dryly.

Sally shook her head. What seemed a convoluted mess of a story to her, the UHF High Command had bought lock, stock, and barrel: When the UHF had gotten to Leary's Casino, they found five thousand dead UHF marines, a crashed Alliance frigate with the crew safely evacuated and the ship stripped of almost all equipment that could be salvaged, one legless hero, and two unconscious dimwits who couldn't even hold on to their weapons. The badly degraded battle data did tell enough of the story for the Central Command to piece together what had happened. Apparently, when all seemed lost, Private Amy Santon had managed to throw a grenade into the exhaust valve of the enemy frigate. She then dragged the two surviving incapacitated

UHF marines to safety. Unfortunately, some falling debris had pinned Private Santon down, forcing the amputation of her legs. But she'd still been found with an asteroid-pellet-loaded ARG down to a 3 percent charge, her mutilated, unconscious body protecting her two perfectly healthy and utterly useless comrades.

The UHF had a hero whom they extolled to the heavens. They also had two at best incompetents or at worst cowards who they'd effectively pushed under the rug. If it weren't for the fact that every trained marine was needed and that cashiering the two out of the service would have proved too embarrassing, both Sally and Thomas would've been court-martialed and thrown out of the service.

Thomas had been hoping for that outcome, actually. But in the end, Sally agreed to go along with the story. If anyone looked too closely at Thomas's background, he would not have been able to answer questions that in normal times would have been asked. But the need for heroes was too great, and the need to ignore cowards was almost as strong. So when "Asteroid Amy's" story was told and told again, Thomas and Sally were either completely ignored or merely referred to as the two incapacitated marines. Thomas and Sally had each gotten a six-month reprieve from the war, and now that the publicity show of Private Santon's medal ceremony was over, they'd both been given a seven-day pass with one real order—"Do not draw attention to yourselves." Any reporters who did manage to track them down were to be directed to the hero. Although this suited Thomas just fine, his daughter was still smarting over it.

"Doesn't it bother you?" she asked as they walked down Sambianco Boulevard.

"The one-third gravity?" answered Thomas. "Not that much."

Sally's eyes flared. "I'm not asking about the gravity and you know it."

"You're not?" asked Thomas coyly.

"No one knows what we did or who we are. Worse, if they do know, they think we're cowards."

"Better that than a psyche audit, don't you think?"

"Yes, but …"

"But …" he coaxed.

"Dammit, I took out an Alliance frigate with a Damsah-forsaken grenade and a two-kilometer throw. And no one knows I did it!"

Thomas mouthed her exact words as she said them, causing Sally to gut him with her eyes.

"How could it not bother you?" she asked. "It's bugging the crap out of me!"

"Because," he answered calmly, "the only thing I care about is you. It makes my life much simpler and my ego much smaller. I don't need to be a hero. I need …"—Thomas's voice cracked—"I need to be a father."

Sally stopped walking, forcing Thomas to turn back towards her.

"I love you too, Dad."

"And I you, Cookie. Now, can I please arrange for us to disappear? Keeping you alive is getting harder all the time."

Sally didn't answer immediately. "But we're finally making a real difference in this war—even if no one notices."

"An unjust war."

"A war that cost Emily her life," Sally answered through thin, bloodless lips.

"It's not worth yours, Cookie."

"But what if that's what it takes?"

Thomas smiled sadly, and they walked on in silence, still not agreeing on the point—as always.

* * *

Coffee had become the main drink of the UHF, given that the best plantations were still on Earth. But tea had become the drink of the Outer Alliance as Saturn had developed dozens of asteroid farms dedicated to growing the plants. Cody Foster would have been more daring and ordered tea, but now that Thomas Meadows was back, new face and all, behavior had to change. He ordered a cup of patriot blend coffee just like a marine in dress uniform should. He and Sally were discussing their "exit" plan. Taking a boat cruise of the Thousand Canals, one of Mars's most spectacular sights, was one of them. Sally wanted to hit the clubs and go "flirting," as she referred to it, sparing her father's humorously prudish feelings. They were just starting to reach a point of compromise when someone tapped Sally on the shoulder.

"Gemmy!" she shouted and bounced up out of her chair to hug her friend, forgetting the one-third gravity. Gem had to grab Sally and bring her back to the ground.

Gem's face was pure marine. "That's Field Sergeant Suttikul to you, Private."

Sally looked at Gem in momentary confusion until Gem broke the spell with a radiant smile.

"Asshole!"

"Shitwipe!"

After the two hugged, Sally looked over to her dad. "Oh, uh, Gem, this is my father, Thomas."

"It's an honor to meet the man who's taking such good care of his daughter." With a knowing glance, Gem activated a switch on her belt. Then she reached across the table and slapped Thomas hard enough that the sound of her hand striking the back of his head echoed across the room.

Thomas laughed through his obvious pain.

"That," said Gem, "is for being stupid enough to keep the broken nose. And this," she said as she hit him harder, "is for keeping the call sign! They're both a direct link to Cody!"

"Who's Cody?" asked Thomas innocently.

Gem raised her hand for another blow.

"I had to keep them."

"What on Mars for?"

"They're both from my daughter," he answered softly. "Besides, 2,749 marines already share the 'Daddy' call sign."

"Of all the stupid, sentimental, pointless, dangerous ..."

Gem's use of adjectives was inventive and seemingly inexhaustible, but Sally noticed her best friend's hand was now lowered.

* * *

"I can't believe High Command bought it," Gem said, relaxing on the luxury deck of the Edgar Rice Burroughs. Sally and Thomas had parked themselves in deck chairs next to her. The cruise ship was filled with soldiers on leave, most with their "special" friends. There was also a leavening of corporate executives. "I mean, we are supposed to have an Intelligence Department in the military, aren't we?"

"We're a lazy species by nature," answered Thomas. "It's one of the traits I relied on in my old profession."

Sally looked over at her father and raised her brow slightly. He never hinted to anyone about his past—ever. Sally figured he'd either had too much to drink—doubtful—or perhaps Gem had managed to fuck her way into family status—probable. Gem and her dad had been spending a fair amount of time together. Sally should've been upset that it wasn't with her mom, but that quickly passed. Sally no longer thought of her father as the man Augustine Cooper had married. He was in a totally different class now: Thomas Meadows—dad, warrior, conman.

"Give 'em an easy enough script," continued Thomas, "and they'll follow it."

"And now," grumbled Sally, "no self-respecting unit will have me."

"More time away from the war," Thomas said, contentment evident in every line of his face.

"It should bug you, T.M.," said Gem, using the new nickname she'd given Thomas. "The war needs bodies. Which means no matter what, you'll eventually end up right back in it. Only this time with some idiot no one else wants to work with who'll get you and Sally killed."

"I've got my connections," answered Thomas.

Gem was unimpressed. "That'll only take you so far. What's your plan after that?"

Thomas raised his drink. "We're supposed to be relaxing, right? I'll think of something, I'm sure."

Gem's eyes were fixed and determined. "Why don't you join my unit?"

"Uh," began Thomas, "given our activities over the past couple of days, I may have a tough time separating the private from the professional."

"Don't worry, T.M.; you may, but I won't." And for a brief moment, the tiny, bikini-clad woman relaxing on the deck chair with the sugary sweet drink had all the menace of the trained killer who'd left countless bodies in her Valkyrian wake.

Thomas twitched a nervous smile. "I guess not."

"Besides, it won't be permanent," continued Gem. "Once you both get a few missions under your belt, I'll have no problem transferring you to another unit in my fleet."

"*Your* fleet?" asked Sally.

"Okay, Admiral Trang's fleet. But it's the best in the UHF. He wouldn't have left five thousand marines to die on a rock like that idiot Tully. If he couldn't have supported the landing, he wouldn't have done it."

"I hear Tully's taking credit for the successful conquest of Leary's Casino," said Sally. "Like he planned it that way!"

Thomas raised his glass. "Damsah help the poor souls who end up in that idiot's fleet."

Gem nodded. "Which'll be you if you don't take me up on my offer." Then she used the one argument she knew was going to work on the man who was currently Thomas Meadows. Looking over to Sally, she said, "And that will be her."

It took Thomas and Sally a moment to realize they'd been had. That Gem had arranged everything—the "chance" meeting, the cruise, the lovemaking, the evening's deck soiree—all in order to make her irrefutable point. The father and daughter smiled knowingly.

"What are your orders?" asked Thomas.

"Why don't you carry me back to the cabin," answered Gem mischievously, "and we'll figure something out?"

And that is exactly what he did.

Year 4 of 7 of the Unincorporated War

Fourth Battle of Anderson's Farm

Sally and Thomas were on the rock for three hours—a record for a UHF force on Anderson's Farm—when Sally's world came crashing down. She'd entered a warren and had managed to clear it using her grenade-shaped charges. It was at the moment of feeling good about another job well done when she saw the body. She could tell by the blood-damaged eyes that the brain was beyond repair—a permanent death. It was a boy who could not have been more than sixteen and, even more horrific, looked eerily like her younger brother, Lee. It was not an exact likeness, but it was close enough, especially the way the kid had worn his hair—grown long, set in place with a saucer-like depression at the top; like having a bowl permanently balanced on your head. It was such a stupid look that Sally was convinced that Lee had gotten it just to bug her. It had never occurred to her that the Alliance could have stupid, annoying teenagers too.

"Dad," she called out over their private com.

Thomas was over in an instant.

She pointed at the body. "I killed a kid."

Thomas nodded serenely, then pointed to another one further down—a girl, not more than twelve—clearly the sibling. Sally threw up in her helmet. The suit cleared the mess in seconds.

"Sergeant," barked Thomas over the com, "the tunnel's clear, front and back about fifty yards. Private Meadows got her head rattled by the blast. I'm taking her back twenty meters till she settles."

"Understood, Corporal," came Gem's crisp reply. "Good job. Take all the time you need. Just so long as it's not more than ten minutes."

"Yes, Sergeant," said Thomas, gently moving Sally back down the tunnel. He toggled them back to private communications. "Cookie, you had no choice. They would've killed you."

"Why does the Alliance recruit and send children to fight us? What's wrong with them?"

"I don't think they recruited anyone," he said gently. "I saw the names on the suits—Anderson."

Sally stopped looking down at her feet and looked up at her dad.

"Baby Girl, they weren't sent here. They never left."

"Home," whispered Sally, trying to understand and desperately wanting not to.

"The home we came to … and attacked."

"We came to their … home," repeated Sally, "and … and I killed them. I murdered that little girl. Oh, God." Tears pricked at the corners of her eyes. "She … she didn't even get to be as old as Emily."

Thomas waited patiently for the tears to stop flowing before he continued. "Sally, my dear, darling girl, yes, you killed them. But if you hadn't, I would've. Them and everyone else on this cursed rock. I don't care about the UHF or the Alliance. I'll kill everyone I must to get you out of this war alive. As long as you have to fight this war, I will fight it with you."

A heavy sigh escaped from Sally's downturned mouth. "I don't have to … I don't even want to … fight this war anymore, Daddy."

Thomas Ryan closed his eyes and nodded, a barely perceptible smile could be discerned through the battle-scarred helmet. "Once this skirmish is over, Honey, you won't have to. We're going to go back to Mars, and Thomas and Sally Ryan will disappear."

Sally nodded. "We have to talk to Holly and Lee. I have to let them know. They can't join up."

Thomas patted Sally on the shoulder. "We'll send them a coded communication. You can tell them what they need to hear. Maybe they'll even hear it if it comes from you."

* * *

Neither of them saw the boy. He was as silent and undetectable as only a lifetime spent on a rock he called home could make him, and he was going to avenge his brother and sister even if he died trying. The boy dropped behind Thomas and Sally, charge in hand. The father and daughter's HOD's instantly made them aware of the intruder. They both spun to face him, ARGs at the ready, but Sally knocked Thomas's ARG aside as the boy's charge landed at their feet.

* * *

The emergency cryo units were prepped and ready by the time Gem cleared the tunnel. The Medic leapt to the prone forms.

"Sell me for a penny stock," he said, relief evident in his tone. "They're alive."

Gem closed her eyes and thanked an uncaring universe. She supervised the placing of her two most important humans in the universe, making sure they were safe and secure.

"You're safe now," Gem whispered over Sally's body. "I told you I wouldn't abandon you again." She kissed her fingers and touched it to the top of Sally and Thomas's helmeted foreheads and ordered the units sealed. She then made sure that the units were taken to the secure triage area.

Gem had been tempted to go with them just to make 100 percent sure that nothing went wrong. But at the end of the day, she was still a sergeant in the UHF Marine Corps, and she had a job to do.

* * *

One hour, fourteen minutes later, Sergeant Suttikul's job was over. She'd missed the signs, missed the telltale signature of nanite subterfuge, and so had missed the Alliance assault miners waiting in ambush. She remained alive long enough to watch her unit slaughtered before her eyes. Even as one of the attackers plunged a mining laser through her back and out her chest.

"Die, you child-murdering piece of shit," snarled the attacker. He expertly flipped her body over in order to shove the drill into Sergeant Suttikul's brain, making the death permanent. But as the drill was poised over Gem's helmet, the attacker suddenly stopped, his face paling to a shade of gray almost as deathly as the landscape he'd suddenly sprung from.

"Oh, dear God, no," he whispered, as the drill floated down to the ground. "MEDIC!" he screamed.

The medic was at his side in moments, surprised to see his commander cradling a fallen UHF marine in his arms. "Sir?" he asked in confusion.

"Save her."

"But Captain, we may not have enough cryo units for our own wounded. Why waste it on a fucking ..." then the medic saw the name stenciled on the marine's armor and realized at once what was going on. "Jesus."

"Save her," pleaded the officer once again.

"You got it, Captain." And he bent down and activated the suit's protocols to oxygenate the brain and reduce its temperature. A cryo unit was rushed up.

As the body was placed inside, the captain put his hand on the woman's helmet. "You'll be safe now, little one. You'll be healed and put in secure storage far, far away from this war. When you wake up again, it will be over and you'll be safe."

He stifled his tears. His greatest nightmare had happened, and it was over. Exactly one hour and fourteen minutes later, a thermite charge exploded, vaporizing Captain Tam Suttikul and most of his unit. His daughter would never know the man who'd both killed and saved her.

Year 7 of 7 of the Unincorporated War

Ceres: Capital of the Outer Alliance

Sally remembered the explosion, remembered killing her father, or at least allowing him to be killed. But she couldn't allow the boy to be hurt. She'd killed far too many innocent people. She'd chosen to be killed rather than kill again. It had brought her such peace, that decision.

But Sally Meadows Ryan had not expected to wake up—and certainly not in pain. *This doesn't happen*, she thought to herself.

"I'm sorry about this." The voice was strangely mellifluous—almost in direct contrast to the extraordinary amount of pain she was feeling. "You will not be awake long, but I needed to talk with you."

"It … it burns!"

"You and your father have been purposely infected with nanites by an entity that had planned to use you both to horrible ends, a side effect of which has been to make your nervous system even more efficient."

"Side effect?!" screamed Sally as sweat began pouring off her body.

229

"I have managed to limit your suffering quite a bit, but any more intervention and you will not be cogent enough to make the decision."

"Who … did—" She let out a scream as the pain of what felt like a thousand needles exploded through every one of her joints.

"His name was Al," the voice answered. "He was killed by my"—there was a slight pause as the voice seemed to search for the proper word—"father. That may be the closest analogy you would understand."

"Questions …" uttered Sally through her clenched teeth. It was the only word she could manage.

"You can call me Pam," said the decidedly masculine voice. "You're here because in trying to undo the horrors committed by Al., I discovered you and your father."

"But … we were killed … Anderson's Farm."

"Not killed, I can assure you. I have the records from your sergeant." Pam brought them up on a holodisplay. Sally watched Gem's efforts to find and secure them. Even though the blaze of pain, Sally was touched by Gem's parting kiss and parting words.

"You survived," continued Pam, "but I must ask you to decide for you and your father if you wish to continue to survive."

"What?"

"Sally Ryan, you and your father were diverted and the records changed. As far as the human race is concerned, you died on Anderson's Farm."

"But … Gem … she saw."

"Everyone was either killed or suspended. Sergeant Suttikul is frozen in a prison cryo center in orbit around Eris."

Safe, thought Sally. A smile appeared momentarily through her clenched jaw.

"Please, this is taking too long, and I can't keep up the pain abatement for long. Listen and answer. I can save you and your father, but it will take time."

"How much time?"

"Long enough that history will have moved on. I can give you no specific answer, but your time and place will be long gone. Do I have your permission to suspend you and begin the healing process?"

"Gem," said Sally.

"Your sergeant is fine," said Pam. "She is due to be awakened soon."

"She'll … know we didn't die. She'll … search." Sally then let out a scream as the shockwave of pain hit her once more.

"She won't find you. You're going far away. Farther than you can know."

"Won't stop. You … don't know her … can't stop."

"I can't tell Sergeant Suttikul where you are. I have another I must protect," Pam answered. It was evident in his voice that he was not sure what to do with the unanticipated complication.

"Let us die … leave … bodies where they'll be found," answered Sally. "Gem deserves … life."

The voice of Pam sighed. "I cannot take that risk. I'm sorry. I can grant you your death, but I cannot let you be found—at least not right now."

"Not … location. Hope," Sally said to the surrounding shadows.

Pam chuckled. "Humans," he said with obvious affection. "Very well, Sally Ryan. I promise that your Gem Suttikul will have 'hope' concerning you and your father."

Sally nodded her assent and collapsed, a weak smile forming at the edge of her lips.

It was the last sentence she heard before fading into blessed, if somewhat temporary oblivion.

The End

Epilogue

Archeologist First Class Katherine Black had returned after far more years than she would've thought possible. It was like wandering through the halls of a legendary castle. But she remembered these halls, and it wasn't legend, it was home—one she hadn't visited since childhood.

It had taken Katherine and her companion the better part of a week to find the chamber. There'd been rumors of its existence, but she wasn't foolish enough to believe in them. No, what Katherine chased were leads, leads that had led them to this one spot, on this one asteroid—the most famous in human history. They could have spent a thousand years looking and not found it. But technology had gotten better in the time since the room went dark, and find it they had, guarded by an avatar no less, one as much out of legend as the place itself. But unlike the legends of old, this guardian was friendly. Indeed, it seemed he'd been waiting for them for quite some time.

Katherine turned to her companion. "Well?"

Her friend nodded nervously. There was a strange calm about her that Katherine had never seen in their centuries-long friendship.

"So what are you waiting for, the Blessed One to come back to life and give you an invitation?" Katherine looked over to the suspension chamber. "Wake her up!"

* * *

Sally's eyes flittered open. Her last memory rose up like driftwood from the depths of a sea. It was of a voice talking to her, but how long ago? Her vision was blurred, and now there was a new voice, one more gentle and familiar. Then her vision cleared.

"Gemmy!" she said as loud as her unused vocal chords could muster. She tried to raise herself out of the suspension unit but could not. Her body was still unwilling. Gem, tears now flowing freely, reached in and with the delicacy of a mother cradling her infant for the very first time, pulled Sally up into her arms and didn't let go for a very long time.

"I told you I wouldn't abandon you," Gem whispered softly, and then with her achingly familiar mock stern voice, said, "and by the way, it's Archeologist Second Class Suttikul to you."

"My dad ..."

"In the chamber behind this one."

Sally's eyes widened. "Nanites ... infected—"

Gem gave her friend's shoulders a reassuring squeeze. "He's fine. Pam told us everything. The only nanites left are the good ones. We'll wake your dad next."

Sally nodded gratefully. She was able to slowly move her head. "Where … are we?"

"Ceres," answered Katherine. Sally looked over her.

"That's my friend, Katy," said Gem. "You can thank her later."

Sally thanked the stranger with her eyes and looked back to Gem. "Ceres." Then the rest of her conversation with Pam returned. "I … thought Pam said we were going far away."

"Oh, we are; you have no idea."

"Not near Mars?"

"Not even close."

"And the Outer Alliance?"

Both Katherine and Gem giggled. "Well, let's just say it hasn't been a factor in galactic affairs for a long, long time."

"Galactic affairs?" Sally repeated in confusion. "How long have I been down?"

"Discounting relativity," Gem said as if discussing the weather, "10,826 years."

Sally desperately tried to wrap her mind around the number. "Impossible."

Gem's lips drew back impishly. "You think that's impossible?" she asked, turning her back to indicate the far wall. "Just wait till I tell you who's in *that* chamber."

ABOUT THE AUTHORS

Author siblings Dani and Eytan Kollin's debut novel, *The Unincorporated Man*, was designated a SyFy Essential and went on to win the 2010 Prometheus Award for Best Science Fiction Novel of the year. Their second, third, and fourth novels, *The Unincorporated War*, *The Unincorporated Woman*, and *The Unincorporated Future*, were also nominated for the same award, with the fourth becoming a finalist.

IF YOU LIKED ...

If you liked *Grim Tales of the Brothers Kollin,* you might also enjoy:

Five by Five 3

Escape Plans
by David Sakmyster

Time's Mistress
by Steven Saville

OTHER WORDFIRE PRESS TITLES BY DANI & EYTAN KOLLIN

Five by Five 3

Our list of other WordFire Press authors and titles is always growing. To find out more and to see our selection of titles, visit us at:

wordfirepress.com

Eytan Kollin
230 S. Pierce Str.
El Cajon, CA.
92020

Made in the USA
Middletown, DE
20 October 2016

35947025R00147